THE AUSTRALIAN CLASSICS LIBRARY

Oh Lucky Country

Rosa Cappiello

Introduction by Nicole Moore

Translator's Introduction by Gaetano Rando

General editors

Bruce Bennett, University of New South Wales

Robert Dixon, University of Sydney

SYDNEY UNIVERSITY PRESS

Published 2009 by Sydney University Press

SYDNEY UNIVERSITY PRESS

Fisher Library, University of Sydney

www.sup.usyd.edu.au

First published in 1981 under the title *Paese fortunato* by Giangiacomo Feltrinelli Editore, Milano. English translation published in 1984 by University of Queensland Press, St Lucia. Translation by Gaetano Rando

This, the Australian Classics Library text of *Oh Lucky Country*, is a repaging of text files on SETIS, themselves input from the 1984 translation published by University of Queensland Press

The publication of this book is part of the University of Sydney Library's Australian Studies electronic texts initiative. Further details are available at:

www.sup.usyd.edu.au/oztexts/

Front cover image: portrait of Rosa Cappiello (c.1984), courtesy of Arcangelo Cappiello

ISBN   978-1-920898-97-7

Contents

Introduction

Oh Lucky Country should not be thought of as a marginal novel. In the title's use of Donald Horne's name for a migrant haven, Cappiello sought to thrust her bitterly parodic, lushly obscene, eloquent, grotesque, snide, plangent, heartbreaking construct of Italian migrant experience right under the nose of white Australian complacency. Adding 'Oh', the sign of the vocative, the translated title renders this lucky country chimerical, invoking its (non)existence with a sarcastic portentousness that is also a demanding address.

Paese fortunato was first published in Italy to a warmly receptive Italian readership. Released by the Italian publisher Feltrinelli in 1981, it was awarded the prestigious Premio Calabria prize for that year. Rosa Cappiello arrived in Australia from Naples in 1971, an economic migrant, looking for opportunity and a new home. *Paese fortunato* was her second novel written in Italian, begun in 1978 when a car accident meant a fruitful stay in hospital.

Italian papers in Australia reprinted an appreciative review from the Neapolitan daily, *Il Mattino*. But when actual copies of the novel arrived, according to its translator Gaetano Rando, 'it was greeted with cries of horror and vilification' from some parts of the Italian community, especially the more affluent (v–vi). Cappiello was working in clothing factories and facing regular unemployment. Rando was a lecturer in Italian at the University of Wollongong and Cappiello was a writer-in-residence there in 1983. As part of its then strong list of Australian literary fiction, the University of Queensland Press released Rando's English translation in 1984.

Australian reviewers welcomed it as something of a sociological curiosity. Here was a highly individual novel in the first person by a working-class Italian woman, writing back to her own troubled country in damnation of the migrant's paradise. In the early 1980s, Italy was rocked by a major political scandal that saw the corrupt government collapse and the stock exchange closed, while leftist groups kidnapped major figures, the Pope was shot and an earthquake in Southern Italy killed 3000 people. By contrast Australia was at the beginning of what now seems a period in which public embrace of national 'multiculturalism' was at its most rhetorical. The policies of the Hawke Labor government in 1983 were registering the demands of postwar European and more recent Asian migrant communities for greater access and recognition. Public debate was questioning the singular priority given to white Australian British heritage and looking to cultural expressions of ethnic 'difference' as a register of national maturity, aiming instead for postcolonial, 'tolerant' diversity. *Oh Lucky Country* vituperatively refused the standard story of grateful migrant made good.

Andrea Stretton in the *Sydney Morning Herald* welcomed *Oh Lucky Country*'s 'fast, intense and chaotic language', while in the feminist magazine *Womanspeak*, poet Carolyn Gerrish praised its 'relentless energy'. The *Australian*'s reviewer, however, patronisingly recognised 'Rosa's feeling of alienation', confusing narrator and author, but recommended that Cappiello 'learn something—anything would do—of the novelist's craft'. Even Rando felt compelled to note that the novel's style and language displayed a 'lack of competence', in its excessive heterogeneity, mixing Neapolitan syntax, oral traditions, slang and Italo-Australian elements, an apparent lapse that he excused because of Cappiello's background.

In 1985, in an article that remains the most significant study of the novel, Sneja Gunew identified this response as typical. As in so many works by writers from non-English-speaking backgrounds, as well as by women and historically by working-class writers, a first-person narrative is heard only as confessional by the established literary culture. The text's difference is received as an often inexpert and transparent reflection of this (unknown) experience. What struck Gunew about the novel, instead, was its self-consciousness, its complex textuality and intertextuality manifesting what she identified as a 'continual parody of high or received culture of any kind'.

Oh Lucky Country is most extraordinary in its voice and textuality. Rosa's narrative is explosively, angrily digressive, both hyperbolic and excessively frank. The focus in this 'basically plotless' novel is not on events or history, but on the central character's often amused and tender, often perplexed and alienated, responses to people and place. The parade of caricatured characters—Rando notes that in the Neapolitan tradition, Rosa names one the Calabrian Dwarf and another the Lebanese Poofter— speaks volubly and excessively, in a dialogic structure (even Socratic), as their monstrous self-obsessions and self-pity bleed into Rosa's own voice. Their voices and points of view slide into her monologues and vice versa, and 'you' and 'I' become confused, as Rosa is cast as the observant, disengaged (importantly virginal) writer. Yugoslavian Helen accuses Rosa, but this could easily be Rosa accusing us,

> Through the screen of the abstract you observe me as I shamefully drink, eat and copulate. Yet you don't know about the invisible backdrop to the absurd anxiety of wanting to keep an even keel amidst all this shit.

As the novel progresses, Rosa herself begins to lose her bearings. Living with the melodrama and desperation of Sofia and Beniamina, fending off Zio, facing relentless poverty, boredom and alienation, in a brutal sexual economy in which young migrant women must sell themselves, Rosa loses her voice:

> They have gagged me. I have lost myself. I don't even know who I am, the she-devil, the adventuress, the borrower of others' mannerisms, is drifting, shattered into a thousand pieces, every piece pregnant with things unsaid.

Her experience of the lucky country proves incommensurable with her self-understanding. The novel evidences this gap between reality and subjectivity in the breakdown of her capacity to distinguish her anger and grief from that of others.

Cappiello is often grouped with other writers of the 1980s of European heritage, such as Ania Walwicz, Anna Couani, ΠΟ, and Thalia, and like them Cappiello combines an anti-realist experimentalism with a feminist take on sexual politics, and an aesthetic deeply informed both by gendered structures and a European imaginary. Her novel is more hardheaded in its Marxist links between economics, experience and understanding, however, while Rosa's frustrations at her inability to write because of factory work are inflected by a feminist questioning about the sources of a woman's imaginary. Cappiello's intertextual referents are the obscene and tragic books of Jean Genet, banned in Australia until the early 1970s, the films of Pier Paolo Pasolini, Dante's *Commedia*, and Rabelais; as Gunew notes, she employs 'the rhetoric of the outcast and the powerless'(518).

In its portrait of working-class, migrant Sydney, with its evocative summoning of crowded rental housing in Newtown, the welcoming, sordid exchanges of Kings Cross, Glebe boarding houses, and the pleasures of sea and sky on the edges of the harbour, *Oh Lucky Country* offers an outsider's view of white Australia that is unforgiving as well as envious. For contemporary readers, the novel offers an exciting ride into the possibilities of a moment when a working-class migrant woman could win prizes with an experimental, provocative, allusive, sexually explicit and pointedly angry novel about the failures of white Australia. To relaunch it for today's readers is to wonder how far that country has come.

Nicole Moore
Macquarie University

References

Rando, Gaetano. 'Introduction.' In Cappiello, Rosa. *Oh Lucky Country*. St Lucia, Queensland: University of Queensland Press, 1984.

Gunew, Sneja. 'Rosa Cappiello's *Oh Lucky Country*: Multicultural Reading Strategies.' *Meanjin*, 44.4 (1985): 518.

Translator's Introduction: *Oh Lucky Country* and Italian Australian Literature

This new edition of *Oh Lucky Country* makes Rosa Cappiello's novel the second most published work by a first generation Italian Australian writer after Raffaello Carboni's *Eureka Stockade*. Like Carboni's chronicle Cappiello's narrative promotes at one level a critique of certain aspects of Australian society—for example, both bitingly remark at length on Australians' propensity for drink. And despite ongoing controversy both works have achieved a measure of institutional recognition.

Oh Lucky Country proposes a powerful counter-discursive view of Australia and Australian society from the periphery. It may be taken as an emblematic example of Homi Bhabha's claims that minority discourse as a subaltern voice of the people can transcend time and space and that the possibility of cultural contestation posited by cultural difference has the ability to shift the ground of knowledges. Written at a time when the Fraser government was redefining multiculturalism in cultural pluralist terms, *Oh Lucky Country* highlighted the structural marginalisation of migrant workers and a perceived ghettoisation of ethnic communities. In this respect the novel, rather than give lip service to a conceptual multicultural ideal, engages with a continuing undercurrent of latent racism that every so often comes to the surface in instances like Pauline Hansen's One Nation party and the treatment of boat people by the Howard government.

Despite the different perceptions offered, some 75 per cent of narrative produced by first generation Italian Australian writers is written in Italian and is thus unavailable to Anglo-Australian readers. This includes Pino

Bosi's seminal novel *Australia Cane* which has some interesting contrasts and parallels with *They're a Weird Mob* but, despite interest expressed by Angus & Robertson, was never published in English translation due to a series of unusual circumstances (Pino Bosi, '*Australia Cane*—Fifty Years Later'). Rosa Cappiello's *Paese fortunato* was to encounter a much more fortunate outcome with the commissioning of the translation by University of Queensland Press. Work on the translation was undertaken during and in the months immediately following Cappiello's nine weeks as writer-in-residence at Wollongong University in 1983 and proved to be a fruitful collaborative effort between author and translator.

This collaboration was an important part of the translation process since Rosa Cappiello proved a constant and constructive critic of the first draft, thus leading to the elimination of errors and misinterpretations which may otherwise have occurred because of the highly individual nature of the language. In undertaking the translation, a decision had to be made whether to give a relatively close rendering of the original or to engage in re-writing in order to make the text read like an 'English' novel. The Italian original is written in a language that is both precise and explicit yet metaphorically complex and which sometimes reflects the influence of Neapolitan syntax and lexemes, popular oral tradition and some elements of the Australian variety of Italian. This somewhat heterogeneous mixture makes language a powerful element in the novel, a force which would have been radically underplayed in a free translation. Thus in producing the English version an attempt was made to follow the language of the original as closely as possible, perhaps sometimes at the expense of what may be considered 'good English'.

Despite, or perhaps because of, a marked controversial reception by reviewers, *Oh Lucky Country* was awarded the Ethnic Book Award (one of the NSW Premier's Literary Awards) in September 1985 and was listed in the 28 July 1986 issue of *Time Australia* as Editor's Choice for fiction. There was also a proposal to turn the novel into a film which did not come to fruition because Rosa Cappiello and the producer could not reach agreement. The mix of success and notoriety led to Cappiello gaining some acceptance in avant-garde Sydney literary circles, invitations to lecture at universities, attend seminars, workshops and writers' festivals as well as to publish poems and short stories in translation. While her poetry was to a large extent closely correlated to her novel in that it dealt with similar migrant-related and feminist themes and presented similar stylistic and linguistic elements, excerpts of her third novel in progress (begun during her Wollongong residency), whose intertextual references combine the raunchy sexuality of Boccaccio's *Decameron* and the existential alienation of Franz Kafka, as well as short stories such as '10/20 Dogs Under the Bed' (in *Beyond the Echo: Multicultural Women's Writing*) indicated that Cappiello could get away from autobiographical migrant themes and capture something of an 'Australian' quality while at the same time retaining an Italian cultural and linguistic base. '10/20 Dogs Under the Bed' is a whimsical, spirited, punchy, paradoxical story told in the first person by an old man obsessed by sex and death whose existence is plagued by his mate Josse's obsession with greyhounds in yet another vacuous get-rich-quick scheme. Ultimately, however, the language barrier and other factors were to prove a difficult hurdle and in 1993 Rosa Cappiello decided to return to her 'dusty and provincial' Viale Agrelli on the outskirts of Naples. She died in Italy on 4 September 2008.

Her novel *Oh Lucky Country* remains a classic text of Australian literature and an emblematic example of a corpus of Italian Australian writing that is only occasionally available to the Anglo-Australian reader. It will be interesting to witness the reception afforded to the next translation off the rank, Emilio Gabbrielli's novel *Polenta and Goanna* which presents a postmodern interpretation of a previously unknown aspect of Western Australia's colonial history: the outback meeting and intermarriage in the early twentieth century between traditional Western Desert Aboriginal women and Italian migrants in the state's remote and inhospitable Northwest Goldfields region. Gabbrielli's novel is the latest in a series of texts written by Italian Australian authors from the mid-nineteenth century that present positive and non-racist perceptions of Australia's indigenous peoples, thus countering colonial notions of social Darwinism and the supremacy of the white Anglo-Saxon race.

There are currently about 100 active writers of Italian background in Australia. These writers, along with other ethnic minority authors, propose a return to questions of both origins and belonging and have changed our national literature into a pluralistic one. Through perceptions emerging from both local Culturally and Linguistically Diverse (CALD) communities and global diasporas, their work functions to interrogate and destabilise hegemonic views of nation and identity, as well as the temporal and spatial dislocations resulting from the mapping of two overlapping cultural contexts. Rosa Cappiello has been a significant part of this transformation and *Oh Lucky Country* remains as an important cultural legacy left to us by its author. This novel, together with the work of other first generation CALD writers, gives a distinctive profile to Australian literary culture which, like any great cultural force, is never complacent and always in a state of transformation and self-interrogation. In some respects it might be possible to define Australia, through the work of writers like Cappiello, also as an *Italian* space, very much inscribed and described by the many voices that characterise it.

Gaetano Rando

University of Wollongong

References

Bhabha, Homi. 'DissemiNation: Time, Narrative and the Margins of the Modern Nation.' In Bhabha, Homi, ed. *Nation and Narration*. London: Routledge, 1990.

Bosi, Pino. *Australia Cane*. Sydney: Kurunda, 1971. [The novel was originally published in serial form in the Sydney Italian language newspaper *La Fiamma* over 1955–57, before the publication of *They're a Weird Mob*.]

Bosi, Pino. 'Australia Cane—Fifty Years Later.' In Rando, Gaetano and Turcotte, Gerry, eds. *Literary and Social Diasporas: an Italian Australian Perspective.* Brussels: Peter Lang, 2007.

Gabbrielli, Emilio. *Polenta and Goanna.* Milan: IpocPress, 2008. English Translation by Barbara McGilvray. Gabbrielli's original Italian text was published in Florence in 2000.

Gunew, Sneja and Mahyuddin, Jan, eds. *Beyond the Echo: Multicultural Women's Writing.* St Lucia, Queensland: University of Queensland Press, 1988. English translation by Gaetano Rando and Tony Mitchell. [An interesting feature of this anthology is that the original versions of all translated texts were also included.]

Rando, Gaetano. *Emigrazione e letteratura: il caso italo-australiano* [Migration and Literature: the Italian Australian Case]. Cosenza: Luigi Pellegrini Editore, 2004.

Oh Lucky Country

Rosa R. Cappiello

Translated with an introduction by Gaetano Rando

University of Queensland Press

ST LUCIA • LONDON • NEW YORK

[Facsimile of first edition titlepage]

THE sky here compensates for solitude. Blue-clouded. Cloudy blue. Intensely blue. It's not the promised land. Maybe in the distant future it'll be the last one on earth—the basis is here for the much-vaunted lucky country—but for the moment it's neither the realisation of one's dreams nor the land of milk and honey. It's a kaleidoscope of dances: gigs, gavottes, minuets, boogiewoogies, twists, madisons, rhumbas, often of burps and farts which catch you full in the face at the pictures or at a party.

Over-exasperated thoughts. Not produced by a rigorous process of logic but by the rhythm of personal and impersonal emotions. Well-sifted on the migrant bus and then refined at the hostel or in the streets. Right at the start I felt like saying to hell with it all and commented ironically on, of all things, the subject of public toilets! This land we had to conquer did not seem to stimulate our sense of the ridiculous or the poetic but rather our hope, the unforeseen and the unforeseeable. What struck me was the unforeseeable. Oh, to discern a time-worn grey-stone urinal in some corner of a public square! What sort of people were these Australians? Where did they answer the call of nature? In the little square asymmetric red brick houses as arid and depersonalised as their souls. In my most intimate being a stone urinal in the shade of a gum tree was all I wanted as a background monument to my long-awaited celebration-initiation. It was a decidedly negative impact. How could I be so hard-boiled at the very moment that the city was welcoming me with open arms? Where I longed for the human touch expressed in the architectural lines of a public toilet, the other girls missed their mothers, a terminated love affair, the national anthem, the promenades in the main street, the display of elegance, human understanding. My travelling companions were better than I, more sensitive, more refined. They took in their surroundings by degrees, reaching ill-defined conclusions which, later on, they would have to take back with a curse. It would come to them while they were awake. Mysteriously and inhumanly wronged, they would lower their heads and cry. For years they felt shattered because they had got all mixed up about brotherhood, manners and togetherness. They had a very high price to pay.

In the space of a few hours I took in so many strange things that the brain could hardly register them. The novelty of Christmas in summer held me spellbound. We got off the boat at Sydney on 24 December, an iridescent sun-soaked day which abruptly separated me from another time, another culture, another life, and projected me towards a dualistic conception. Discontinuous eurhythmy, I think it was, because excitement, fear, and the remains of the euphoria which were stuck on me like a label on boarding ship combined to strangle my adenoids.

When we arrived at the hostel a few witless old women took us in charge. We soon got the hang of the inhabitants of this particular zoo: lesbians, expectant mothers, delirious old women, dole bludgers, drug addicts, sluts, misfits, divorcees. The stench of the poorhouse, cockroaches, worn carpets, cats, orders in an incomprehensible language. Then the first, second and third floors, dark and damned with the sleeping cells all boxed in one inside the other. A prison. You go to prison to be punished. We must have made some mistake. Maybe in our choosing.

The doghouse assigned to me didn't have windows. A bed, a bedside table, a chair, a small wardrobe, a dresser with a mirror. The wooden partitions were raised some twenty centimetres from the floor and by standing on a chair you could spy on your neighbours in their most intimate moments. Draughts all over the place. I caught cold, dyspepsia, constipation, found it difficult to breathe in bed, had diphtheria, nausea. I attributed my cretinous behaviour to the food and to disappointment. I raved. I had to give vent to the raging frenzy churning inside me. I begged for strength. Only the walls heard me. I felt so empty and disgusted I took to having temper tantrums. I was falling ill because of emigration rejection. I plugged the gaps in the floor and the keyhole with crumpled up newspaper. I bought fresh fruit and vegetables which the cockroaches ended up eating. I developed a terror of finding myself atrophied in bed with no one to look after me. Then, very gradually, I returned to normal. I began to appreciate the good side of the situation and to evaluate the results. Nearly all the factories were closed for the Christmas holidays. It was a bit hard to find work. They told us to be patient. I bided my time. In any case I didn't want to take up anything without first settling down. I discovered the marvellous beaches. Young people barefoot in various states of casual undress. Men in shorts and long socks walking in a grotesque and tired sort of way as if they'd had a little too much to drink. I couldn't think of a funnier sight than this latest male fashion juxtaposed with the women's long gaudy dresses. Then there was the plain ordinary Australian housewife, condor profile and sun-dried skin, driving her car or doing the shopping with curlers in her hair. I discovered the huge parks, cream laden milk, indifference, the diverse nationalities of my fellow lodgers, the same defeated melancholy. I found out there were different hells: one for single girls, one for single guys, one for married women, one for children. Together they added up to a single prefabricated hell—the migrant's inferno.

The atrophied breath of the ethnic communities was wafted to me on the wind. As a new member I adamantly refused to have anything to do with it. I spat on it since, rather than being a cohesive basis for race or tradition, it served as a pretext for the creation of separate, mutually inimical little universes. I would not, must not, sacrifice my individuality.

During the day we sunbaked on the balcony. From there I could take in the view of the narrow streets and the houses, the filthy little yards, the washing hanging on the umbrella of the clothes-hoist. Through an open blind you could see what sort of life they led. Like the sounds of a muted struggle filtered through the screens. In one corner a knitting machine, a sewing machine. Europeans or South Americans for sure. People who'd come long ago knowing absolutely nothing. Primitive people who just wanted the bare essentials: a hearty appetite, good health, a steady income. I wanted more than a full belly. Maybe I was shooting for the impossible. Not to be like a quarter of beef or mutton thrown casually onto the butcher's hook. I was waiting. Waiting for a god without wings who would set free my fantasy. A solidified ocean I could cross on the tip of my tongue. Consolation not through sex or religion but wafted from out of the mist, soundless and without abstruse words. Meanwhile I took everything in on the run, careful to notice even a sigh tinged with affliction, a raw-pained thud on the wood ... there wasn't time to note things down. I would have gone over the notes later, stale and undigested.

Things changed at a dizzy pace, like a centrifuge cracking and turning the surface of the fresco. Pictures of delicate doves and sparrows whose only mark of delicacy was confusion and agonised screams. The malaise, the hullabaloo, increased. Who wasn't crying? Most people enjoyed themselves, their eyes damp with complaints. In the evening everyone was in a tremendous rush to get all dolled up and slip out onto the footpath, the steps, in front of the hostel, where pretty young lads, satraps, bedouins, canecutters, layabouts, lay in constant wait to grab the first tart who came out to take a breath of air. Christ, who wasn't crying? Stunted, broken-down penises floated in the air. On the faces of those licentious, sex-starved men the tension of weeks, months, of abstinence. They would strike at once, anxious lest they should lose that piece of juicy meat flaunted in all the newspapers. They would surround, pester, molest those women who, by their demeanour, accepted or encouraged their advances. No, males didn't represent the ideal. Nor did work, nor did hope, to cut a long story short. Once we had arrived here the past was all played out, aimless, senseless. Memories were quickly sucked up by the present and withered, drained away through the torn pages of the calendar. Days on end piled up invisibly one after the other. When dwelling on the past, memories of December 24 were never present because with the act of migration we had ordered ourselves a fine funeral for our identities, to be reincarnated in sewers, as factory workers, in machinery, in knots, as tender morsels for despotic men. When the Greek girls came in at night there would always be a ruckus. They looked like a herd of unleashed fillies. Ignorant and very young, they kept close together as though they were relatives or friends of long standing, thus forming a basis for group solidarity. They were cruel towards people they didn't like. The discovery of the lesbians was the final straw. Those lousy Greek cows, extremely excitable sexually, wouldn't let an evening go by without climbing on the dressing table or on the backs of chairs to spy on the Yugoslavs in the middle cubicle or on the French and Danish women. To spy on the Danes they had to take the chairs into the corridor, an operation always accompanied by grunts and giggles. As long as the Greeks stayed at the hostel we had music and folk dances on the landings and fights and quarrels in the bathrooms. Then one Saturday they all disappeared together. They were quick to get their bearings and to find a male companion to share their new life.

One night about eleven—this was before the Greeks left—I'd stayed up late to watch a film on television downstairs. Tired, I went back to my room. All I wanted was to go to sleep. On opening the door I heard whispers and, raising my head, was thoroughly astonished at what I saw. There, in a row, along the top of the Yugoslavs' partition, were eight faces, looking as if butter wouldn't melt in their mouths, engaged in a jaw-breaking exercise to maintain their precarious balance. Winking and grinning, they invited me to join them so I hoisted myself up on the dresser. Despite the fact that they had become the targets of such intense curiosity the two women, maybe because they didn't give a damn or because they'd got used to these voyeurs, pretended not to notice their presence and kept on caressing each other, whispering phrases which, as far as I could judge from my vantage point, were full of heart-rending passion. One of the Greek girls was inciting everyone to look while chewing on a lock of her own hair. I really couldn't understand why the Greeks were pestering the couple in this way as the two women were among the few who never caused anyone any trouble. I was already beginning to feel sorry that I was hanging about up there like a monkey when, suddenly, the youngest girl winked and gave out a tremendous spit which hit Irene in the ribs. All hell broke loose. The Yugoslavs rushed out in their pyjamas and, since they couldn't get into the Greeks' room, climbed up the partitions throwing punches and shouting threats. The Greeks jumped down and cowered round the bed, pale and astonished. They had really done it this time! One of them held a chair by the legs like a lion tamer in a circus. The uproar didn't impress me in the least. Without thinking I took the side of the lesbians and collected a punch on the nose for my trouble. It was always like this until the Greeks went.

The funny thing was that from that time on Helen, Irene and I, although only for a short while and in an odd sort of way, became inseparable. We used to get together in one of our cubicles and, while Irene played her mouth organ softly or whistled through her teeth, Helen nostalgically reminisced about Rome by night. She spoke Italian well. For three years she had managed to eke out a living and to study in Italy. In the end she had decided to emigrate to Australia thinking that there she would find the golden land. She was very small, like a rag doll with all its joints out of place. She was disjointed in speech, too. She hated Greek and South American women. Uncultured oysters, she called them, slobberers hunting after husbands. Irene, on the other hand, didn't make much of an impression at first sight. Shy, placid, and fat in all the wrong places, she always wore the same pair of slacks with humps at the knees and a check shirt. A lazy voice. Eyes like a meek ox. The least communicative of our trio. I didn't know whether to be sorry for her or to be envious of her. Always silent and stand-offish, like a goddess who from her pedestal observes the fallen and wicked women left to their own devices in the slime. She didn't desire a better world, didn't want to change her ways, didn't give a damn about it all. She found a sort of relief in lowering herself to cleaning out toilets and wash-basins in office blocks. She wasn't a woman in the normal sense of the word nor was she, metaphorically speaking, a man. She was neither here nor there, refuted any sort of diplomacy or comparison. She considered my friendship an intrusion. Her impressionable twisted thoughts jumped about on a tight-rope, whirlpools of obsessive ecstasy directed towards Helen's microscopic genitals. She identified herself in Helen—divine breath, virility and fantasy—thereby transforming herself into a man. She'd get mad if you called her Irene. Remo was her name, a change of identity which had nothing to do with what was written on her birth certificate. She had assumed it at the same moment that she had deserted her husband and son. She had become so used to thinking of herself as the male of our threesome that when we went for walks with little Helen in the middle she would strike a solemn posture, hands behind her back, head held upright, hard suspicion on her face. She obviously enjoyed protecting us and derived a great deal of personal satisfaction in walking beside us with her chest thrust out. I concluded she was a little bit crazy. Merry-cunt Irene was the nickname I'd bestowed on her since the evening I had seen her from the partition. I was able to observe her at leisure while, bare-bottomed, she chanted songs in Helen's ear. Irene's cunt menstruates for seven days a month. It's a bother which doesn't purify her, doesn't lift her up. It embarrasses her. A not very virile burden which brings in its wake back-aches, stomach-aches, migraines. A trap in which she struggled and still continues to struggle in an attempt to escape from a name and a body. Rebaptised, she glanced round like a migratory bird and took flight towards the unknown. She gave up the whole intestinal package, forsaking progeny, kidneys, ovaries and vagina. But she's got a vagina all right. I've seen it, correctly placed at the centre, where it ought to be. An enormous jellyfish strangled by a bush of curly hair. A dark wood which has to be explored with a torch, examined, studied. Irene upside down is a paragon of generosity. Irene loves.

During our walks we would talk of many things, each one more incoherent than the other. Did we have to be coherent? Helen would have bouts of hysteria and pedantry. She taught me about poisonous sea-snakes, sharks, the Chinese, the Japanese. She was terrified by rumours of an imminent invasion by the yellow peril. Actually, everything on the earth's crust seemed to terrify her: dark skin, languid eyes, the unknown. Of course we would talk about men too. The first obstacle to our dreams, our wild impossible schemes, invariably had its origin in the opposite sex—the lure flaunted in the publicity pamphlets for migrants: the future husbands, the lifelong mates, the paradise for women, the land populated mainly by males. The male—we gradually got to know him prick in hand. He belongs to all races, bearer of diverse customs and cultures, speaks the international idiom of fucking but not fluent English. Jokes there were aplenty about the Australian variety: spineless, drunkard, not much interested in females. Faced with choosing between a glass of beer or a woman, he opts for the beer. From what we've heard he derives the same sexual enjoyment from it. What was it to us? Irene would have a good laugh over it. But it was no laughing matter when we sat in the Rumanian milk bar in Oxford Street nibbling pastries and sipping Turkish coffee. Helen would read the future in the grounds left in the cups. She didn't believe in it but she liked to tell us stories. What we were experiencing was nothing but a desperate illusion. Hers was a desperation different from mine, a repudiation of hope. All I learnt was how difficult it was to have patience and fortitude. Why did she turn to me with that strained grin after asking about Italy? Why haven't I managed to understand after so many years? What was there to note in her hysteria that would protect me from the bitterness and the horrors of loneliness? In moments like these Helen would seem just as crazy as Irene-Remo, an impression reinforced by that dried-up doll-like face of hers which resembled a worn-out broom. She wasn't pretty. In any case, what did being attractive mean to her? Nothing, given her strange ideas. She didn't love Irene. She could barely manage to put up with herself. Sometimes they'd beat each other up and in the morning you'd see them with black eyes.

While making love her partner might as well be fancying she was skating on the moon and Helen wouldn't even have noticed. She would follow her own fixations, giving the unhappy impression that she was a pain in the arse, an out-and-out egoist ready to swear at the drop of a hat and to exploit those who were weaker than she was. You would often find her waxing philosophical, a cup of coffee in one hand, tugging at the curls on her forehead with the other, making fun of the city, its people, work, love. 'The development of this country is connected to us and those who came before us with blinkers, shit, refuse, there's your squalor.' She used to repeat it like a ditty. She wasn't tactful in handing down judgments. Nothing would make her shut her face once she'd got going. One afternoon a man at the next table was having a go at us. He was acting tough, shirt open on his chest, showing off his gnarled muscular neck like a braggart. His better half, an Aboriginal woman wider than she was tall, with bleached hair, collected one on the mouth when she tried to shut him up. The cafe proprietor threw us out without beating round the bush. He'd got brassed off with Helen's routine. What's more, he told us never to show our faces there again. Those evenings we spent wandering the streets, specially on Sundays, in an absolute emptiness, looking for something, maybe a miracle that would make reality bearable for us.

A bus-load of South American and Greek women arrived. Some went to the YWCA hostel in Oxford Street. The South Americans wear expressions of fulsome surprise and contentment. The Greeks you can tell by their basket-shaped bums which droop down to their heels, their thick ankles, the glances they give without even a hint of naivety. Many of us were lined up to witness the arrival. Rumours were rife about the imminent landing of a thousand or so Cypriot virgins complete with medical certification in their suitcases, irrefutable proof of their purity and sentimental sincerity. It seems that the Southern European men had been complaining about not being able to find a virgin bride. The stupid men had rushed en masse to telephone, make arrangements with the newspapers, consulates, committees, priests. A tidal wave which stunned everyone. Ah, women, little did you know the value of an intact womb here in Australia as we approach the twenty-first century. Many of the women were kicking themselves because they hadn't had their virginity surgically restored. When that black hole was being discussed, that sacred hole put up for auction, a wave of homicidal rage would sweep over me. Guys on the short side, queers who can't get it up if it's not guaranteed pure and immaculate like the Virgin Mary's, rejoiced and heaved huge sighs of relief over the genial solution proposed by some Australian public health welfare organisation. The bomb burst at Easter time creating a stupefying shock wave. I read in an Italian newspaper that even the local press gave out the news in highly shocked tones. Amen, we would say. The lucky bride, as well as being strong, a good worker, an impeccable housekeeper, an angel and other bullshit is also envisaged as a bearer of pay-packets as well as the odd child, but first she must provide documentary evidence that her sex has been sealed from birth.

This does not mean the end of all I had promised myself I would seek, demand. No, I will not leave, I won't. I love what I find here, the sun, tropical flowers, parks, the sea, and the knowledge that tomorrow I won't go hungry. I'll be the one to adapt. That's the right thing to do even if it's hard to swallow. Yesterday I was propositioned by someone who wanted to squeeze my bellybutton, original surely, but not all that original. On the hostel steps. The other women, about ten of them, were chatting away quite clearly, formulating their plans. Each one had before her a glowing vision of Australia the beautiful about which they had read back home and they still took delight in fanciful, mysterious adventures, courtly love and the encounter with Mr Right. Here he is, there are thousands just like him, Puerto Rican, black, crisp curly hair, habitué of cut-price brothels. Master of five thousand dollars which he displays one after the other, small change included, in his Wales passbook. 'Five thousand. Not a penny less,' he says passionately. That nest-egg mirage was an incentive for accepting cohabitation. He then says that he's married … and hastily: 'Don't let's talk of the wife. I've decided to separate.' Maybe the whole thing wouldn't have seemed so trivial if together with his rattled-off riches he hadn't sprayed me with tobacco-stained saliva. I should at least have pretended to piss myself in gratitude or winked simperingly in the direction of all those zeros. Instead I was shuffling from one foot to the other, impatient and disgusted.

My job? What could I do other than blow up. At the A. & D. factory where I'd been working for a week or so, the women workers were blessed with worn-out arses and addled brains. During menopause, widows, sluts, old maids in search of husbands, were capable of having plastic surgery just to convince the marriage brokers that they were born again. The manager—a short stocky Friulano, unhappily married to a wrinkled asexual Australian woman some fifteen centimetres taller than he was. The supervisor—an extremely thin Calabrian dwarf madly infatuated with the ever-lustful short guy. The manager assigned me twenty-nine as my payroll number. He bestowed it upon me as though it were an order of merit, accompanying it with a wink and a pinch on my arm. Then, standing at the far end of the row of sewing machines, he kept miming the number with his fingers, two four five, two nine, two nine, twenty-nine, twenty-nine. In Naples said number is synonymous for prick. The short stocky guy mimed it to me continuously with his lips, with his outstretched hands. For a while it was great fun. The dwarf, fearful that I might reciprocate the manager's advances, was very kind to me. It was the first time in my life that a woman paid me court so I wouldn't steal that half man of hers complete with his tooth decay. The dwarf would look at me from afar, a thoughtful glance, then she would come forward, with a waddling walk like that of a pregnant duck, the packet of material for sewing in her arms, and she would almost bow, almost kiss my backside—with us being *paesane* because pride and dignity dictated that we should help each other. I let her carry on. It was to my advantage. I was philosophical and pliable.

The married workers were not well-disposed towards the single ones. The superiority of having a pair of pants for company, even if the pants were empty; even if you saw those women at dawn running like hell with sleepy toddlers hung about their necks, whining, so that you'd really feel sorry for them. Children looking more like bags of rubbish than fruits of love. This is the female factory worker, wife of the modern coolie and coolie herself, who has got down to a fine art the act of tying her baby to the bed or to the downpipe of the kitchen sink so as not to forego the happy hour on Friday which is pay day. Slave of the dollar, she sends her newly-born babe to relatives in Egypt, Yugoslavia, Spain, Greece, and after a few years back it comes like a postal package by sea or by air. That little boy, that little girl, sometimes two, deprived of their weaning, guaranteed the deposit for buying a house or a re-entry visa to the home country with riches without regrets. Bitter details. Structure of modern society. You have to adapt. Go along with it. Those who have no possessions aren't worth anything. The only thing modern about it was that women worked just as hard as men, but for the rest they were still in the middle ages, with their minds fixed on virginity, on the washing of their consort's socks and on cooking. They all boasted that on their wedding night they had laid a spotted sheet on the bed so they would bear female children.

Since I was on my own, orphan and of no fixed abode, the matrons were plotting to marry me off. I don't know how, but the rumour started doing the rounds that both my parents were dead, buried in the lava of Vesuvius. I, the only survivor, without a shirt to my back, in a strange land, was pointed out as a sort of comic-strip heroine. There were two Calabrian sisters they worked on the irons—who took pity on my misfortune. Having scrutinised me from head to foot for days and weeks on end, they finally pulled out of its envelope the photograph of the betrothed. He looked like a curly hedgehog, fat cigar in his mouth to symbolise his acquired wealth, hat hanging on his knee. No objections, so far. It was his eyes which frightened me. They didn't display a spark of intelligence.

'Do you like him? If you marry him you won't have to work. You'll be a lady of leisure,' said the sister who wore her hair in a bun.

'We'll write if you say yes ... he'll come at once by air ... first class,' added the other. 'Provided that ...'

Provided that I was whole. Their brother-in-law considered this important. Just like my mother made me.

Of course, I replied, I'm the spitting image of my mother. We look like twins. I explained that since birth I hadn't had a nose job, hadn't had my breasts filled out or lifted, hadn't had my buttocks raised. My teeth are white and all my own, ankles like a filly's, childbearing hips, clear skin, the odd little pimple, shiny hair, tanned all year round, healthy ... but, as you already know, orphan and without a penny to my name … As for my vagina, don't ask embarrassing questions. I carry my vagina between my legs, all light and motion (poor pussy). It belongs to me, only to me, I screamed, just like a hernia, an ulcer or a haematoma.

Mad fantasy always strikes my fancy, even when it's not generated by a fit of friendship, a burst of sincerity. It's an attempt to spy out, conceptualise, the secret processes of the paradoxical. The insensitivity of a rattlesnake. When they realised that I wouldn't take any notice and that I despised them, the women took to baiting me in cowardly fashion, inventing all sorts of horrifying genealogies about me. It made me froth at the mouth but I still had to eat. I suddenly found myself with three husbands on my back. I was a nymphomaniac, then a lesbian, then a murderess. My third husband, such a disgusting woman was I, I'd buried because of an overdose of lovemaking, having sucked out the marrow from his bones through his penis. What was happening didn't make sense. It was fever, delirium, spittle, phantoms created by frustrated women who kept trying to dazzle and astonish themselves. Reality and unreality became superimposed, presenting me with slices of a life which, in my greatest desire to explore the superfluous, I would never have dreamt of living. I often asked myself how long a sane person would have held out. My question was answered with the arrival of Lella the Greek Cypriot girl. She turned up one Wednesday, worked quietly at the finishing table cutting cotton for a couple of hours. During the coffee break, when she went past, she left a piece of paper on my machine and disappeared. The note contained her address. She had picked up my SOS. I should add that I already knew her, having been introduced to her briefly at the Apia Club.

A new chapter opens up for me. Lella is slipshod, out to enjoy herself. She takes easily to any aspect of Australian life. Sometimes I think that she came into the world martyred to bootmakers, butchers, bricklayers, blacksmiths, painters, the puppets she goes round with. Partly through desperation, she says, partly because that's what the marketplace provides.

In Newtown, where she rents a wretched little room, she has been branded a prostitute, wrongly, I must state. For a month she hasn't earned a cent by the sweat of her brow and she's changed jobs at least four times. She happened to come to the A. & D. factory by mistake. Sent by Beniamina who had worked there before. It was an intolerable place. The women at the work-table stank of sweat, had bad breath, venomous tongues. She isn't convinced by the fact that I always turn up for work on time, am around when there's work to be done, and, if it's available, do the odd hour of overtime. She invariably compromises her job from the start. She does the same thing everywhere. Rebellious to orders, she wants to manage the whole show as soon as she's hired. There's no servility or tendency to follow the leader about her. She grates on the nerves of both workers and customers in the firm where she's employed. They don't understand her. She's an artist. Instead of working hard she plays up by drawing real-life sketches of the workers. Beniamina, Susanetta and Claudia are sure she's downright dangerous. To her credit, she does make people react. The truth is that I like her. She's the only one for whom I have any respect. She is without malice and pure inside. A great talker, she can spend a whole night telling tall stories about her degrees, about her education, wasted in this lousy country. Right away I catch on that she's an incorrigible liar. Proud of having obtained various degrees, of impressing me. Bullshit. It doesn't take long for her to break down and, in the end, she too rubs salt into her wounds. She's not even twenty and has never received a degree. A captivating smile. A face like a beardless urchin and a surprising aptitude for languages. She speaks Italian, English and French as well as Greek. Lately she has enrolled in a Japanese course. She loves marvels and mysteries, the glances of hate and suspicion from those who have been Australianised for more than a generation. Blind imbeciles who kill themselves through their idiocy and immaturity. Imbeciles, too, are the police, men with beer guts, the stupid little man who laughs and makes a face when he hears a foreign tongue and looks at you as if you were a Martian because the world ferments and dies within the confines of Sydney.

The Newtown Greeks are stupid, foul people who point the finger at her like straw inquisitors. They are imbeciles because of that florid look they have from gorging themselves to bursting point as if they feared a famine. She can hardly stand the landlady who guards the fridge as though it were an idol and has a thing about decorating the living-room with paper flowers, convinced that it's fashionable. Utter imbeciles her friends, Beniamina, Sofia, etc., who dig an abyss in a gratuitous hell just to drain off a few dollars, and fuck in the hope of getting married.

Yes, our friends work at and exploit many trades, midwives, prostitutes, saints, pizza cooks, messenger girls, bankers, con-artists, greengrocers. Let each one play her part without inhibitions. Very chic, cunt cleaned with a wet rag, a touch of lipstick. Well-mannered in public, they buy their clothes at Merivale's, eat their fish with a knife. Those born here even cut their spaghetti with a knife. They go to the hairdressers twice a month, pedicure, manicure, body hair removed, blackheads squeezed, hair tinted a lighter colour. They spend a fortune on themselves, especially the younger ones. Saunas, massages, exercises, diets. Plastic surgery to recast bum, nose and breasts. Their intellect still in an embryonic state they emulate their male companions in stupidity.

Sofia is their founder. A sow in heat. She lets out her ample breath, attracting to her lap the Opera House, Ayers Rock, the Kwinana Freeway, Koala, Kangaroo, Emu, the Three Sisters, the Great Barrier Reef and fourteen million Australians. A superhuman task for anyone but not for her. In fact her intuition and often her ingenuity allow her to make up for the boredom of everyday living. She possesses a belly capable of doing in a whole regiment. A frothy blond, malicious, affected by acute infantilism, she suffers from obscure unfulfilled desires. A candle which splutters continuous spectres of depression. A boiling pot giving off useless steam. Weeping she curses her ill fortune. She never completes a thought, an act, a deed. She is stupid too. As soon as she latches onto some fool of a man, she reveals her weakness. Her cunt, which, when all's said and done, she cannot manage with cunning, boils and sparks within highly restricted horizons. Although she longs to hold court, surrounded by vassals lavish in munificence and favours, honours and gifts, she barely manages to keep body and soul together. A reflection of the munificent generosity of the nineteenth-century cocottes. This is just the right country for a bloodsucker like her.

Zio Lino—Uncle Lino. A family relationship conceived in bed. He swears he's thirty-eight. It's not true. He's pushing fifty and he shows it. He has tremendous sexual drive, or maybe he's sick. Just someone obsessed with cunts. Moved by the tears and problems of his 'nieces'. Beniamina and Sofia often cry and ask for help. They telephone him all over the place when they can't find him at the Consulate, to tell him about suicides and the imminent birth of babies, with the superficial ease of a Neapolitan scenario. It seems the only way to make him part with his money. He becomes soft and tender as putty in hastening to put things right. A sentimental bloke of few scruples, no better than his business associate Peter.

Peter is crassly ignorant nouveau riche. When he utters ten words in Italian five are in dialect. Five out of ten English words come out distorted beyond recognition. We get a lot of laughs out of him. It's a huge joke. He's always after new girls to fuck while waiting for the right mother for his two little children. He buys, sells and refurbishes houses. Distributes visiting cards all over the place: Engineer, Architect, Sir Peter C. To look at him he's very like a shepherd or a rubbish man. Neanderthal man discovering thunder from heaven.

Giacomo D. is a pimp by profession, as far as the law allows. Cleaning, medical consultations, income tax returns. He heads the aphrodisiac industry, a venture on which he embarked after certain society games in which he exchanged his wife with his friends and finished up by throwing her out in the street. At the moment he manages two blocks of flats in Brisbane which allow him an expensive lifestyle. He's rarely seen in Sydney and he usually comes when he's after new flesh. I remember he was keen on Beniamina and courted her quite assiduously, to the point of proposing marriage. He had recognised in her all the necessary skills for a perfect brothel manager. He said he did not trust Sofia and Claudia. Too independent and sentimental. And, as everyone knows, sentiment, in that line of work, ruins the product.

Fabia emerged with an air of incredulity about her. Pity that she dragged behind her a bum open to all sea winds (this is the exact definition given by our group) and a belly stretched by several interrupted pregnancies (another collective observation). A horrible sight in a bathing suit. She was the last niece presented to us by Zio Lino. Just arrived from Northern Italy. Once she came into the group she brought with her upsets, quarrels, jealousy, spite, discord. We began to fight among ourselves, couldn't meet each other's eyes, something which had never happened before. Poor girl, she was so shattered by that avalanche of nieces that later she tried to kill herself. She claimed right of family relationship since puberty and unwillingly accepted the role of second fiddle. There were Antonietta, Victoria, the rabbit-faced Dutch girl, Susanetta, Claudia, Lella, myself, Mary and a couple of Greeks. But it was Beniamina and Sofia who kept their claws firmly fixed on Zio's heart and wallet. Two tough women who wouldn't have let go all that easily.

I often shut my eyes and, slowly and deliberately, try to recall Helen, Irene and the others of those very early times. If I could only manage to dissociate them from that mass of values which I hoped to find. All I did was take flight. A flight towards light, dignity, respect. A flight from myself and the toad which was eating me alive. I thought I had suffered. I still firmly believe this. I am suffering. Suffering is incorporated throughout my 1.6 metre frame. Wherever I go my suffering is already installed to clear the way. I'd recognise it anywhere, even if it were to transform itself into a peaceful butterfly, because it always comes towards me with clenched fists and knocks me down.

There are people who make disastrous decisions and play the part of hysterical women. I, Lella, Sofia, the other girls, at the end of every show even expected applause. In this open pit, all sorts of tricks, all sorts of blows below the belt were tried. A wearying war to the point of annihilation. Friendship was a pretext to defame, to give credence to our shame, to our solitude. The amphitheatre was full of flying splinters and bubbling tonic. Nothing gave strength. Nothing at all. Casual giddiness and outbursts. Restlessness imposed by the circumstances. To get rich. Emerge from this heap of shit. Because inside that's all they were, shit. I was on the way to becoming worse than them. We despised each other to the point of folly, to the point of wishing to die and then live again. Suicides weren't always faked. One of the girls would try to jump off the bridge or would swallow a bottle of barbiturates, first, however, having the sense to show signs that she was going off the deep end in advance so we would watch over her, spoil her, sometimes threaten to slap her and kick her in the shins. Our understanding was a mutual self-help, a mutual exchange of courage, of morale boosting.

The help we gave each other often took a violent form, overshadowed by the exuberant nature of the girls, nearly all hot-blooded southerners. Hysterical fits, accompanied by the breaking of furniture, rending of sheets and pillowcases, and, now and again, by getting drunk. The girls were funny when they got drunk. Couldn't take their liquor. They would break out into incoherent mystical death-laden ramblings. Crying, they would invoke their dead mother, grandmother, stepmother, an abortion.

Lella was part of my metamorphosis. The decisive encounter which profoundly changed my soapy rage-prone personality, my counterfeit provinciality. Instead of avoiding disaster she would very carefully court it. At first I would follow her like a puppy on a lead, docile and thirsty for knowledge. I needed her just as I needed food and sleep. She had a penchant for merry self-destruction which, later, I was to note only in Sofia. They were both mad probably. Why such a waste of energy? To what end? If not for the certainty of taking a leap into the unknown. To go to sleep in the evening anticipating the end tomorrow and not have the strength to change.

With Lella, hamburger for breakfast, watered-down cappuccino, tinned spaghetti, sitting on a bench in the sun twiddling our thumbs, joining that group of crazy people in the street who had shaved heads and pigtails and who senselessly sang, danced and aped the glory of their gods. Then there was the alcoholic old woman who touched Lella's Samaritan soul. As soon as she saw us she would snarl and Lella, passing by her, would give a tug at her knapsack to take a look at the booty assembled from the rubbish bins, tipping out, together with the rancid smells, chicken bones, vermicelli rolled up in balls, bits of bread, lettuce leaves, pizza crusts, which the old woman would then devour after making her bed for the night in the shelter of the toilet wall in the park. She would lay her black waterproof jacket on the grass, spread out her long skirt, pull up her web stockings, one pink, one blue, draped around her emaciated ankles, pull out the fodder from her knapsack and slowly begin the banquet. A mouthful of food followed by a mouthful of spirits. I would never have believed that old people could be so totally neglected anywhere. Then there were the regular customers of the fish and chips shops. Drunks who would come from the pub, always at the same time, men of no fixed abode, down-at-heel guys and girls, all with dried-up faces deprived of vitaminic splendour. Pupils which could compete with a fried potato, flattened rough lips shaped like a stinking battered sole, nose like a hot dog, drooping cheeks complexioned like butter or margarine.

The young men went round barefoot summer and winter, faded jeans, shapeless cotton T-shirt, an indolent stance and a total lack of pretension, brashness, arrogance, masculinity. These things appeared beyond their reach, beyond their comprehension, or perhaps they did not need them. They were not continually preoccupied with, harassed, obsessed by sex to the point of making it a life and death issue, of becoming completely maniacal about it. Between the two sexes there was no barbed wire, there were no barriers, no courtships. There was a pure and simple giving and taking as among equals. I think that for European men this was the most difficult thing to come to terms with. A shoddy demonstration of virility. A devaluation of masculine supremacy. If a couple hugged and kissed each other in public, the practised eye of the little European male would run over the Australian male's groin and he would then exclaim cockily: 'Some men! They paw and grope all over the woman and they don't even get it up.'

For some time we had been doing the rounds looking for a room to rent near the hostel. For one reason or another, the few we inspected, after critical examination of the people with whom we'd have to live, finished up being unsuitable. I would have taken a small room in Nobbs Street, with a long, narrow window like a guillotine which gave a view of the yard and a lemon tree whose branches you could touch by reaching out with your arm. Seven dollars a week. Use of kitchen. The only flaw was that the landlords, two dotard Italians who lived as voluntary recluses guarded by an Alsatian who never let them out of its sight, locked all doors and openings at nine, nine-thirty at the latest. If by ill luck I'd have been late, I would have risked spending the night on the doorstep, because after locking up they wouldn't have opened even if God himself had come knocking. And that wasn't all. The ground floor windows were all wired up for an electric discharge strong enough to fell an ox. For intruders, they explained.

At lunch time we're still going around. Wet because it's been raining all morning. We've just come out of the house of a Greek woman in mourning. We took off without even stopping to barter. The rooms were decorated with photos and portraits of the deceased with little lamps. The thought of living, maybe watching television, reading and laughing in that catacomb seemed to us sacrilegious. Helen suggests we drop in on some Yugoslav acquaintances who'll likely insist, given the time, that we stay for lunch. In the taxi she brings me up to date on the couple's situation. For fifteen years they've been vegetating and spitting in a side street adjacent to Redfern Station, in a single room with the verandah converted to a kitchen with shared bath. Ernest, Rachele's husband, has never had a steady job, a secure income. His latest work is with the dogs: at dawn and at dusk he takes the greyhounds for their walk. The rest of the day he loafs at the pub. Once we get out of the taxi I look around. Under the rain the houses are all the same, more like funeral parlours and, inside, a pervasive smell of dead cats.

Redfern, like Paddington, Surry Hills, Chippendale, Haymarket, Darlinghurst and lots of other suburbs, seems designed like a cemetery. They remind me of the grey avenues of the Poggioreale cemetery, but without the addition of well-kept flower beds. The fossils which live there begin to fatten, their stomachs swell, like satisfied worms. In each of these hovels at least a dozen bodies are crammed and kicking, tenants and children, owners and children, singles. A Tower of Babel.

Ernest greets us, his face reddened by lord knows how much drink. Rachele isn't there. Going up the stairs we have to support the drunk by keeping our hands taut against his back. A soul-destroying task. He goes up with his head hanging transversely, violently invective towards Rachele, at every step on the verge of falling on top of us. Upstairs we help him to lie down on the settee.

'Sit down,' he burps loudly. 'You get on my nerves standing there.'

Helen pulls up broken-down armchairs. We've just sat down and Ernest mumbles that he feels like vomiting and starts to make a dash for the kitchen sink, but his legs won't support him and he falls back. Helen quickly rushes to the sideboard and brings him the crystal soup tureen. A few spasms of vomit. I swallow hard, feel like throwing up myself. I won't look at him. I shift my gaze to the furnishings, the bed covered with a cream knitted bedspread, a wooden trunk standing on termite-ridden lion's paws, the settee and the two armchairs. Flaking plaster, the rain entering through the broken panes and forming a small puddle under the table on the verandah. On the fridge a few plastic bowls full of biscuits for the dogs. The thunder and the noise of the rain cover up the gurgling noises made by the suffering man.

'That's better,' he says, tapping his stomach which is taut and tight as a drum. 'I need a beer to get this bitter taste out of my mouth.'

He puts the tureen on the floor and gets up, staggers back violently and falls all in a heap like an octopus. We laugh while he coughs and spits out a bit more bile. Our laughter, rather than offending him, seems to cheer him up.

'Gees, what a pair of gawkers you are. No respect for the sick,' he exclaims, a grimace of good-hearted disgust twisting his face. 'I'm too weak. I don't eat enough,' he moans. 'I hate my wife. She keeps me short. Doles out the drink. The dole isn't enough. But now, that's it,' he says resolutely. 'Rachele has hidden her savings in the sugar bowl in the kitchen. Do me a favour and get it. We'll go and drink it all to spite my wife.'

'Be quiet and don't get worked up or you'll throw up again,' says Helen, going pale.

She bends over Ernest and keeps him down on the settee. He grabs her hands and puts them on his brow.

'I'm hot, I've got a fever,' he whimpers.

'Come on. Let's go,' I burst out, annoyed, shaking Helen as hard as I can.

'What's she saying? What language is she speaking?' shouts Ernest, who hasn't understood because I've spoken in Italian.

'My friend has to go to the toilet,' Helen whispers confidentially in his ear.

'Oh, tell her to do it in the rubbish bin. Tell her to make herself at home.' And then, turning to me with a rotten smile. 'It's raining cats and dogs. You'll get wet. The wind has opened up the toilet roof. At night Rachele and I use a pot so's not to go down into the yard. Go on, use the rubbish bin and then throw the piss out the window.' He finishes up by bestowing upon me a drunken cackle.

When we say goodbye there's no way of persuading Ernest not to go to the pub. He cleans the bowl, puts a waistcoat on back to front over his shirt still wet from vomit and leans on us, staggering. Once out in the street he slips on an orange peel.

'Great,' Helen eggs him on and, throwing me a meaningful look, takes off with all the speed her short, stumpy legs can muster. We run all the way to the hostel, hoping to get there in time to eat a plate of slop.

Monday, this time with Lella, hunting after the room. I'm sick of having pigeon eggs at the back of my spine. Even just a hole where I can stay on my own and cook some decent food. Eat and work. A Greek or Italian film and, if there was money to burn, a pizza and a chinotto. What a bore. At the factory demoralisation and various headaches. Shorty has resigned. His successor is a Jew of German origin. The owners are fourth-generation Australian Jews, a fact they are proud of, although they are a little less proud of their religion, it seems, because we're not allowed to mention it openly. The dwarf supervisor has gone utterly mad. She forbids me to laugh, joke, even breathe. The dirty old crone is dying and I should die too. Wash away your sins. No matter how much I slave doing my work swiftly and conscientiously, she sends it back with ever-growing obstinacy and malice. Here the collar is crooked, there the edge has come unstuck, the sleeves don't fit, the thread breaks. You've used the wrong number on the jersey, undo it and sew the whole batch all over again. God, it makes me sick just to think of it. What'll you do if they give you the sack, and you can barely manage to say a few words of English? the workers ask in pitying tones. Well, I won't die, that's for sure. I'm not a Neapolitan for nothing. I'll exploit my talent for versatility. Meanwhile, I sharpen my teeth while waiting for things to come to a head. I know very well that it won't be long before I'll have to pack up and go.

After all, what's it like to find yourself unemployed and in a strange land to boot. I didn't know. Like I didn't know that there was the NSW family assistance, unemployment benefit, sickness benefit, special benefit, which allowed extra earnings for the enterprising types. All I knew then was that there wouldn't be any bread, or security, or fun. Sure I was a stranger and then I hated those beasts who collapsed around me exhausted. Well, then, I say to myself, say you get your marching orders from the dwarf. How will you make out? Easy, I'll copy to the letter the stunt pulled by that shoddy tailor from Avellino. The cunning fellow, inspired by a Jew who traded in cloth, converted to Judaism and, what's more, invented a grandfather killed by the Nazis. Now he manages a shop with lots of windows at Double Bay, wears a skull-cap and on the counter he's put a card which reads 'Wherever thou shalt go so shall I, and wherever thou shalt live so shall I. Your people shall be my people and your God my God'. A conversion to the god money. Your god and my god have made a pact. I get convulsions when I think that people should be so lucky. No more poverty but riches and honey tarts, duck liver, caviar and stuffed snails. Ha, ha, ha, the women in the factory make malicious jokes.

After all they are just idiots without any imagination. After finishing work for the day they beg for sewing to do at home. Most of them deny themselves the satisfaction of bearing a child and living a quiet life just to procreate dollars. Children ruin the budget. At lunch a couple of mothers-in-waiting sit together at the table. I don't look at them. If I do I lose my appetite. They're having a lively discussion about the cost of foetuses. The woman in an advanced state of pregnancy is downcast and depressed, she says that an abortion would only have cost her three hundred dollars and that it was a big mistake not to have got rid of the child. Adding it all up, the birth and the new child will cost fifty times three hundred dollars.

If you think of the months needed for weaning, children's ailments, fevers, diarrhoea, colds, teething, which will force her to stay away from the factory, and then paying someone to look after them, the bother of bringing them up, school, the energy for work which they suck from her. The youngest of her unfortunate children is losing clumps of hair, the eldest wets his bed. The family doctor has diagnosed a substantial lack of affection. The good mother understands and is sorry about it, but she won't leave the sweat-shop until her belly bursts like a ripe melon.

One by one we're leaving the hostel. This morning, on my way to the bathroom, I noticed the windows wide open and the mattresses folded over in the cubicles occupied by the French lesbians. I'm going on Saturday, Helen's off this evening. She's organised the removal of her effects like an escape. Most of her things have already reached their destination by means of a series of short sporadic journeys. About eleven, when the front door is shut and the old women go to bed, Irene and I will help her to carry the remaining odds and ends.

When the time comes Irene, who is quite strong, balances the suitcase on her head so it won't knock against the iron railing. Helen follows with a pile of dresses on their hangers. I bring up the rear with the crockery box. We advance with caution. Silently. I'm so scared that I nearly shit myself. And all this just so as not to pay the final week's bill. She runs off, guest without farewell, scorning the behaviour dictated by good manners and the trust placed in her. Full of hatred towards the maids, the cooks, the supervisors who in turn guarded the milk jug, careful that we wouldn't take a drop more than necessary for our coffee or tea at dinner or breakfast. This disjointed little Helen doll was a punctilious type. I wouldn't have dreamt of brooding for months over an affront of this nature.

We reach our destination after jogging through an obstacle course, puffed-out, but with a great desire to laugh. In fact we are laughing and our laughter echoes round the deserted corridor lighted by a swaying lamp hanging from the ceiling. No light over the stairs. You can't see a thing. A door opens at the far end, and three devastated faces, as if emerging from sleep, filled with beer up to the gills, glare at us with expressions of hostility. Irene swears. When she put the cases down she didn't notice a certain slimy patch on the floor and, bending over, she looks at it by the light of her cigarette lighter. Helen huffs nervously, incapable of bidding the tenants goodnight, then with a turn worthy of a flamingo she begins to climb the stairs with cautious little steps.

As soon as we're in the room, simultaneously with the click of the lock, a hellish noise overwhelms us, tipped-over chairs, bottles and glasses smashed, neighs and barks of horses and dogs. The fans in the flat downstairs are barracking at the races on TV. Irene does her block, she begins to jump up and down, dance in a zigzag fashion, stamp her feet. She goes to the window and tears the bright red rag off the curtain rail, tears the poster of the naked girl off the wall, throws the cushions up in the air, tramples Helen's dresses, throws about belts, shoes, zips, magazines, pears, bananas and, to top it all, still unsatisfied, grabs the keys and throws them on top of the wardrobe. I'm so taken aback by the outburst that I stand there gaping. Helen, with a graceless smile like someone who has been stabbed in the back, begins to warble in a thin, high-pitched falsetto di, di, da, da, bo, bo. Irene stands stock still in the middle of the room, torn newspaper in her hand. I get the idea that she's paying very little attention to her friend's disjointed warbling. I am struck by Helen's tired defeated look and even more by the ridiculous, tragically indifferent tone she adopts when withdrawing into herself.

'What do you think?' she begins. 'She's got another lover.'

I have to make an enormous effort to stop myself from sniggering.

'And she's acting all crazy over her.'

'Don't listen to her,' interrupts Irene. 'She's delirious. Just pretend you're deaf.'

'Yes,' Helen admits in a humble tone of voice. 'I'm delirious. But you understand. You're a wide-awake girl,' she says, turning to me. 'And do you know who she's going with? She's taken up with a stinking Polish woman. A woman who's over forty and has a young daughter. This way she kills two birds with the one proverbial stone, seeing as they all sleep in the same bed.'

'That's enough. Stop it. You're getting on my goat. I don't want to see you again,' screams Irene. 'I don't care a bugger if you're from the same country as I am and if you're suffering. Suffer, go on. I've been through a lot.' She stops talking and heads towards the door.

'Sure, go away. You're still in time to take her out to a restaurant. Send her flowers, first, and don't forget to kiss the lady's hand,' Helen shouts after her.

Irene turns and gives her an intense look.

'It's undignified the way you're behaving,' she says, shaking her head. 'But I'm not sorry about it.'

'What, you sorry? Poor Remo-Irene. I'm the one who saved you from the madhouse, anguish, failure, and this shithouse of solitude. Don't you remember that you wanted to slash your wrists, run away, have an operation, revolt?'

'You're mad. Go see a shrink,' Irene says coldly. 'The Pole is a grateful sort of woman. I would change her for a hundred like you ... Goodbye forever ... and don't try and find me ...' And touching her lips with two fingers she flings her a farewell kiss.

Helen is shaking with rage. She retrieves an embroidered tablecloth from the garbage on the floor and hangs it over the window.

'Bye. See you tomorrow,' I say, embarrassed.

'No.' She draws near to me, frightened, perhaps distressed at the thought of being left on her own. 'Listen, don't start up again about you losing sleep. You sleep and dream. What sort of world do you live in? I know, I know, you're one of a kind ... sorry.' She smiles, feigning a reluctant thought. 'I'm always saying embarrassing things ... I'd like to put an end to all this one of these days. I'm so tired. Doesn't it ever happen to you? That you feel like leaping out of this web of incongruity, I mean, and yelling I'm the one who's dying? Through the screen of the abstract you observe me as I shamefully drink, eat and copulate. Yet you don't know about the invisible backdrop to the absurd anxiety of wanting to keep an even keel amidst all this shit. You don't see my bloodshot eyes. Because the oasis of our former world has disintegrated. I am alone in my anxiety-ridden struggle in the midst of phantoms ... That bitch,' she says, after a pause for dramatic effect, obviously referring to Irene. 'It was impossible to carry on. She would tell me everything down to the smallest detail. White shoulders, firm breasts, no bra in summer. Tender and sweet, maternal and available. A burning ember, and those thighs, you could almost touch them, absolutely perfect in their alabaster whiteness, framing the pit of that fucking Polish woman. As soon as I got up this morning I looked at myself in the mirror. I've got short legs.' She pulls up her skirt to show them to me. 'So what? Was I her confidant, her psychiatrist? ... and ... and supposing I'd fallen in love. It could have happened. I'd have ended up with a broken heart by now.'

'Go on, you're joking. A smart girl like you.'

'Bullshit, you're having me on.'

'No, not at all. Go ahead and get it off your chest.' But I'd rather she stopped it. She is right on the edge of collapse and I wouldn't have a clue what to do if she had a turn. I don't feel any sympathy for her at all. I don't belong to their clique, I assure myself, so as to stay calm. As usual I have my own nightmares at night, that constant falling, and if she lives with her head upside down, has a sobbing heart, insomnia, if she drowns in her own spit, I don't exactly enjoy it. I don't understand why she opens her heart without restraint. What the hell does she expect? That I should take her in my arms? I return her sad smile. I seem to magnify her faults two or three times. There isn't a square inch of skin which strikes an aesthetic note, a finger nail, a well-shaped arm, teeth. Hard work for one's poetic inclinations.

'The Polish woman waits for her outside the factory. Would you ever have imagined it?' she says, pointing her index finger at my breast. 'You can never guess what these old wrecks of divorcees get up to. They throw a scene, let fly the fireworks, just so they have someone to console them when they remember what they've lost. They have no consideration, no pity, no spice. They are happy to accept a substitute and even farts with blinkers in the hope of making the embers glow again.'

I would like to admonish her that she is in the same boat but luckily I hold back.

'Do you find that proper human behaviour?' she says.

I blush as though she'd found me in a compromising situation.

'Go on, say exactly what you think. I won't be offended. Give me your advice. What sort of life do I have?'

'It could be better,' I answer, but I haven't the strength to look at her.

'Well, these setbacks don't stop me from hoping for the future … but what will it be like? You think I'm obsessed. I can see it on your face. You're like an open book.' She says it mincingly, quite firm in her belief. 'Have you ever asked yourself where you'll be, what you'll want in ten years' time? I have. I don't sleep at night. Ten, fifty years from now I'll be undergoing exactly the same torment, the same frustrating attempt to get an honest meal for this cunt of mine.'

I'm quite certain that in mentioning it she does so with reverence. But for me her thing conjures up sticky visions of snail shells emptied of their contents and full to the brim with snaily slime. And if I didn't know her with that screw-loose wildly promiscuous channel of hers, I'd be convinced. Yes, I'd say. Yes, you've got it in technicolour with a luminous tail which can be seen hundreds of kilometres away. Yes, the whole galaxy and hundreds of billions of stars are packed in there. Yes, your uterine length possesses the clairvoyance of a telescope. Allow me to take a look at those far-away planets where the perfect man lives. I won't steal your flock. Your flock of real men, warriors, war chiefs, patriarchs, philosophers, scholars, lesbians, fingerstalls, knuckles, papyri, blocked tunnels and plots out of novels. Because you believe yourself to be untouchable, unsurrenderable, incorruptible, just like the martyrs and like them you want us to adore your stinking carcass. Your sermons are millions of light years out of date. You make me laugh. You almost make me die laughing. What is it that you're after? The writhings of innocent little virgins raped on their chamber pots as they clean their bums? The bawls of sparrows in agony on the surface of the water and of roses with their petals torn off. You draw the balance of flattery, laughter, forgiveness, the coming together of different races. Ah, these shitheads from all over the world gathered here together to breathe your air and pollute your oxygen. You always sum everything up with the word 'shit'. Shitheads in heaven and shitheads in hell. You complain that necessity and not choice has forced you to function as a cage for wing-clipped penises ... what's that you say? There's a mirage here for women whose ovaries have rotted. I admit that if I were a lesbian I'd willingly have my toes scratched and I'd be proud of it. I'm not. Don't give me any grief. Put a padlock on it, a chastity belt, and don't weigh me down with your opinions they would have to pass through my hysterical impulses, which are becoming increasingly bloody. What do you want? I try in vain to pull myself together … I try in vain to pull you together. If you looked less like a toad, if you were taller … if your cheeks had more colour in them … if, if, if … if I were a man I wouldn't have it off with you. There.

'It's late, I'll be on my way,' I say.

A shadow of disappointment flits across her face, enough to nail me to the spot. Hell, she doesn't pay me to stand here nice and passive listening to her. Damn them all, lesbians, homosexuals, sick, wise and normal people, what do they live for anyway?

'No, no …' she pleads. 'Sleep here, don't go. Let's talk some more. You probably think I'm crazy … and maybe I am. You know, it's tremendous playing with an experienced lesbian every night. You should try it. A thousand times more pleasant than being with a man. The fact is that in the beginning I let her fondle me because I took pity on her. I felt sorry for her and didn't understand that her need to communicate was my need for affection … Well, why are you gaping at me in such astonishment?' she yells all of a sudden. 'I offer you the benefit of my experience and you don't appreciate it …' And she piles on the detail. She opens up completely.

I don't know what to say to her. I get the nagging thought that perhaps she really wants to seduce me.

'Maybe you'd rather listen to Lella, the conceited little bitch. Watch out because that little number is dangerous. When you least expect it you'll find yourself up to your neck in trouble, drugs and stuff like that, you know.'

'Where did you meet her?' I asked, surprised.

'At the hostel. She was there for a couple of weeks, a few months before you came. The old women were always busy croaking out her name over the intercom.'

This serves as further confirmation of my theory. Migrants live in a huge village square, or rather an immense rubbish heap, no matter what nationality they are, trapped into mouthing false repelling words which they then set free to wander from one lewd mouth to the other. A big happy family. Just like those universal preachers dream about. All joined together as though by an umbilical cord in a brotherhood of wheeling and dealing, trampling and dishonour. Maybe it's because they lack specific interests. Who knows.

'Hey, did you notice the gents on the ground floor?' she asks point blank. 'Jesus, they'll make my stay here difficult.' As if right on cue we hear a faint scratching at the door. One of the drunks pokes his head in and politely asks permission to go through the kitchen in order to reach the toilet out on the balcony.

'So what's all this about?' Helen launches into a verbal assault, face bright red, hair over her nose. 'The agency assured me that the toilet is mine. This floor is exclusively mine. Don't you layabouts have any toilets? Am I a servant to the whole building? Sure, sure, what do you take me for? What right have you lot to intrude into my shithouse?'

And she would have gone on spitting out these graceful phrases, if the drunk hadn't interrupted, timidly but decisively, explaining that theirs was being repaired and it was only a matter of days before they would have a modern comfortable toilet.

'OK,' she agrees, calming down just a little bit. 'You can go through.' We follow him in case he should pilfer some wrapped-up knick-knack. 'I'll raise hell. It won't finish here,' she promises. 'With the quantities of liquid they're used to swallowing they'll be up for a piss every other second. There'll be a veritable procession through here. Shit. I detest them,' she bursts out and, unable to contain her pent-up rage, she trots back and forth over the humped floor in her stiletto heels. 'What people,' she suddenly stops walking and starts talking again. 'They measure everything with the standards of beasts. But I've travelled. I know the world. Ask me about art, music, literature, politics and remove from my sight these bastards who trot around pulled by dogs and horses and who drown in beer ... I'm neither a quadruped nor a trained seal ... Did you notice how he looked at me?'

In the meantime I go out on the balcony. Opposite there is another balcony just like ours. A beam of light is shining through a coloured glass door striking the freshly-painted toilet which shines as bright as snow. An old woman and a young man so thin that he seems to dance in his pyjamas come out through the door. The man holds a stuffed eagle in his arms. He gives me a vacant look, probably does not see me. The old woman at his heels holding on to his pyjama cord for support. Neither utters a sound. The lad stands motionless at the railing gazing at me and Helen.

'Poor wretch, he's blind,' says Helen.

When the woman prods him he flings the bird out into the void and they balance precariously in order to follow its flight all the way down to the heap of rubbish piled up in the deserted yard.

'No, he's not blind,' she exclaims, taken aback. 'God, it's worse than being in a madhouse. What sort of place have I ended up in?'

After the Sunday afternoon nap, rested, washed and deodorised, I sit on the pile of bricks in the Portuguese family's yard, anxiously awaiting Lella, so we can go and have our usual cappuccino at Maman's cafe-brothel in Newtown. Record players blare maddeningly nearby offering me music and sound at full blast for free. A small group of people, gathered together in the open air, drink straight from the can and nibble on potato crisps. The men sport long hair and reddish beards, the women have a slovenly look about them, the consequence of a low degree of self-confidence. Some of the group are painting à naif the front of the house where they live all together. Violent colours which hit out at the anonymity of the lane like a punch in the eye. The Turk's child is squatting naked against the wall, shitting. On the corner the pub reigns supreme. Young fellows in shorts and white singlets, brimful glasses in their hands, restore the energy expended in training in the park, cracking jokes and laughing loudly. There's the newsagent, the takeaway, the stench of fried fish and rancid potatoes, the laundromat, the delicatessen which sells continental delicacies. This is my kingdom and I fit in like a gardenia in a dandy's buttonhole. I'm sorry I'm not a painter. If I were I'd express through my painting the trust this street inspires in me and the privilege of being able to live here. I'd paint the wretched gutter where the cat slakes its thirst, the unkempt woman who in the morning, already drunk, pops out in her filthy dressing gown to collect her bottle of milk. I'd paint the pretty Lebanese poofter with the misty eyes and the sincere smile on his lips when he says 'hello' to me. I'd paint the mothers with their little children dangling from their breasts who, without having brushed their teeth, run still sleepy to their work, the sound and the fury of that precise moment when they rush out into the street, spurred on by the chaotic hurry to free themselves of their offspring, blood polluted by cents when boiling over with pride and boasting, guts tangled in the machinery, tears without salt, faeces constipated because of a sedentary life, hands which give bitter caresses, the absurd words which they exchange when they gather together for their meal. I'd paint the feverish race for gain. The impulse which turns simple people into their own executioners. I would generate the song of songs in paint. The Apocalypse with an alarm clock in its hands. There would be no other canvas, pictures or displays at my passing. I'd mutate the flesh of workers into paper money for bank reserves, their sweat into the ribbon which ties it, their feverish eyes into diamonds and gold nuggets as big as pin heads. With their fatigue and their suffering I'd paint the side dish to accompany their plate of minestrone, on a yellow canvas two metres by three point four.

If only it could last forever, my unconscious state. To feel satisfied with my work. To dream in all innocence and not to die of hunger or of idiocy as I chirp about these horrors, this rot which springs from the roots, as though it were innocuous entertainment which is not in the least innocuous, because I am too tender-hearted, I suffer and get all concerned about even the least important things. My interest-disinterest in the love-thy-neighbour routine is poised on the outer fringes of my awareness. I never remember, to begin with, the place where visions run ceaselessly, frozen and mediocre. From the depths it is easy for me to reach into my irascible fantasy, to give it free rein and, if necessary, to isolate myself within it. Isolated. Pushed into a cage by a tide of sound, bristly voices, insatiable laughter, house numbers, street names committed to memory, bus routes travelled thousands of times, newspapers read upside down, the sound of running on rooftops and under houses. All this hurts me, makes me angry, makes me lazy. I've got to the point where raising my head to look at someone passing by costs me a tremendous effort. Nasty little worms with a vanished destiny linked to me only by thought, continuous round-the-clock thought. In the evening I dismiss these reflections, tied together by a band of pain, in the same instant that I lock the door behind me. Safe and sound in the shadowy stuffiness of my minute room, far away from the vampires, the stifling smell of armpits, the stench of piss and farts delivered in the spasmodic expectation of Friday. Far away from swallowing the dust from the cloth which gets into your hair, nose, ears, from the compromises you have to make, from the last word. In solitude I contemplated the process of my poisoning. And the indisputable fact was that there was no stopping it. I would cry in private. I changed radically in the space of a month. To think, even from a distance, of my workmates did not free me from immersing myself in the chamber-pot of their eyes. I would have strangled them one by one, because in their present state they degraded both the role of motherhood and the struggle for women's rights, and in this I saw my own future to a large extent destroyed and unacceptable. My own reality, my rage, my savage animal nature rebelled at an exploitation of this magnitude of human identity. During my nocturnal soliloquies I would ask myself if these sow-slaves possessed a soul and I would come to the conclusion that the chimpanzee, the tapeworm, the hyena, the jackal, the vulture, the sea-scorpion, the giant octopus could all concede points to them. But perhaps it was I who was different, even if condemned to be part of this pack.

The insistent soaring exploration of this marvellous future has encircled my head in a band of pain. My ears are ringing because I've stored in my head too many twisted things. Away with worry and grief, I conclude, as soon as Lella turns up in a rust-bucket car driven by an ugly bedouin-like guy, a type common enough in this neighbourhood.

'Jump in,' she orders me peremptorily. 'Angelos is taking us for a ride and then to dinner.'

To tell the truth I'd rather have gone to Maman's in Newtown. Going to her cafe for a cappuccino or a drink is like going to Tahiti, Hawaii or Honolulu. She serves them under plastic coconut trees, decorated with little lights, and you can dance the hula if the fancy strikes you, complete with grass skirt lent to you by the establishment. The old crow, really old, has developed a maternal concern for Lella and myself. She dresses in mourning clothes like Greeks and Italians do when their relatives die. The brothel business is dead, she complains. There's no more respect. Too much freedom. Shoddy quality. Indiscriminate fucking. They give it away for a feed or a drink. Bad times. There are no ladies or gentlemen around any more. So business stagnates, but you wouldn't think so judging by the customers who have a quick word with Maman and then disappear through a side door. Lella consoles her by immortalising her beauty in the damask room upstairs. Naked, wearing only a ringlet wig, just like a courtesan of times gone by. Sometimes she shows me the album with the photographs of flabby unswathed Maman languidly leaning against curtains, lying on the sofa, crouched down on kangaroo skins for an exotic touch, straddled across a chair, or taken from behind bare bottom in full view as she sweeps or dusts.

My friend Lella considers herself an artist. Ambiguous, against the mainstream, defeatist of the most rarefied imagination. Indispensable qualities to keep one from perishing on the rusty disused railway tracks of Art. Onward she forges, head held high, photographing the genital organs of stallions, bulls, cows, ewes, cats, female tramps and male drunkards with their pants down. She expects to publish her collection 'as soon as possible', probably in Europe—here they don't understand a thing—a masterpiece of three hundred horror photographs. I wish her the best of luck. To my mind she's a creature with few troubles. She adapts birds, insects, mammals, vegetables, minerals to everlasting exaltation. When the film is developed it gives her a thrill more intense than an erect penis slowly thrusting through the folds of skin. She firmly believes this and I agree. What's the use of cultivating some stupid dull-witted man if in the morning it's always the same worn-out creature who drags himself along to the bathroom, places the hair-plastered soap on the tub, a lit cigarette on the sink, and whistles while shaving thus giving you a start and making you run the risk of cutting yourself because you're sure to be shaving your legs. And then the bother of hunting for a louse dancing about in your pubic hair. You think, dismayed, today he's given me lice, tomorrow clap, syphilis, scabies and other such things and you die, and for thousands, millions, of years the same parasites, carried about by a lunatic, jump from one sexual organ to the other, their environmental condition unchanged, while my ashes have been scattered centuries long past. No thanks. If lice last infinitely, now, while they are enjoying themselves at my expense, I'll frame them and thus show the natives that there is no difference whatsoever between local and immigrant lice. They're not more intelligent, enterprising, introverted, capable, adventurous, white, rosy, they're only worn-out lice resting in cotton wool. Heaven knows which filthy fly-by-night made Lella fertile in insects. She gave up ablutions and spoke electrified of her infested pubis. When you got near her she gave out a smell of camphor and medicine like a hospital emergency ward. But on thinking it over, I feel certain she was telling me a lot of bull. I wouldn't know. It's difficult to evaluate properly what she says. While she's thinking of one thing she's inventing a hundred others.

In the car I'm surprised to note her silence. Her face, turned towards the window, has a faraway gloomy look. Could be that the conquest at her side doesn't satisfy her. Any attempt to get some sort of conversation under way is unsuccessful. The driver bites his nails at every intersection. I observe him with indifference, athlete's body, muscular, a painter by trade.

After a longish ride, with the car parked near Kings Cross, we go off in search of the cheapest possible place where we can eat and admire the occasional tit. The main street—the only one in the whole city which is crowded day and night, noisy, lively, with that sensual atmosphere which makes you nostalgic for the disruptive Neapolitan way of life. Pale but dignified whores leaning against the walls of cabarets, queers and homosexuals walking along arm-in-arm, female drug addicts and pimp-faced Yugoslavs, Italians, Greeks. A veritable leap from suburban vacuousness to the altar of pleasure. It is the meaning-laden night which brings a solution to all things in its purple train. Kept constantly under pressure by the screams and the imagination of Gorgon-like women tirelessly jerking up and down as if jumping on well-oiled mechanical bums tuned up for the occasion. A source of ecstasy and delight for the new arrivals, who find love and homeland there and all that really counts by buying the warmth of a whore for even just a few seconds, thus multiplying their moans a hundredfold and snuffing out the legitimate thirst for affection generated in the inimical dismal and damned darkness of rented rooms. The night drags on enormously in Sydney. Nights without end. The sun which rises over this splendid city is for many people almost a mortal struggle. They look upon it with hate and malice. They look upon it with malignant hunger as an expiation for uncommitted sins. So it comes as no surprise if the fellow who has asked us out heads inevitably for the Cross. It's an obligatory stopover, a genuflection to the life which escapes us, to sex which overwhelms by its reflection the stunted prick who is our escort. Rough, rude people who, having become emancipated late in life, render rich and incandescent this little dot in a huge, inexpressive, boring metropolis. Sleep, city, sleep, over your inept little men who, trapped in your golden womb, see nothing, know nothing. Don't wake up. You'll do me as you are, tremulous confusion which estranges us one from the other.

In the place where we end up there are ten times more male than female spectators. Bodies exhausted by overheated skins and the music sends you off your brain while everyone accompanies the beat with knives and forks. On stage a rather statuesque brunette is performing, two pasties covering her nipples and a chequered apron tied to her waist which she lifts, swinging childishly, to expose her neatly combed thing. Not a hair out of place. The poster at the box office advertised for the benefit of the starving an 'Avant-garde Continental Show' in the same way as one would advertise salami, bread, macaroni. A handsome young man is seated next to me, nicely dressed in a chalk-grey double-breasted suit, newspaper opened out on his knees, quietly pulling himself. Further along a mature-age couple in full expansionist crisis. Men staring wild-eyed, sweaty brows sparkling under the spotlights. A carousel of beauties who bring on stage snakes, ostrich feathers, trestles, whips, leather boots, cigars they blow the smoke out through their legs. Everyone is masturbating in a million epileptic contortions. When the show is over Lella turns to our escort and says: 'I know an intimate little classical theatre where Asian beauties play with a donkey. Shall we go?'

If there's one thing I like about Lella it's her frank manner and anyway from what I've gathered there's no need to be all that subtle with our painter friend. Having agreed on our second itinerary we dash off in the direction of donkeys, chickens and other animals—and guess who we run into while crossing the street, Giacomo D., white as flour, all swollen by venereal disease, a strumpet dressed in panther stripes hanging on his arm. Having exchanged the conventional niceties—how are you? What are you doing? Where are you off to in such a rush?—G.D. suggests that we should immediately join him in enlivening an intimate little party in his apartment.

'Do you give away your wife's favours at your parties, or has she lost her shine?' Lella replies brazenly, not even pretending to appreciate the invitation extended with such friendliness.

Taken by surprise, Giacomo blushes. Having earned a reputation, a certain notoriety as an industrious pimp, the reference to his wife—rumour has it that she's in hospital at death's door—moves him to tears.

'I've heard she's sick, dying,' Lella goes on. She's enjoying this.

'You've heard wrong,' Giacomo corrects her in an icy tone.

'No fear. Beniamina told me.'

'Beniamina is a piece of shit,' retorts G.D., livid and very offended.

And, in an effort to restore his tarnished honour, his dignity as a male married with all the sacramental rites, he hastily covers up by speaking in a disparaging tone, almost choking himself: 'I was joking about the party. A man in my position doesn't mix with the likes of you.'

'And for that we're grateful to you. Keep your worm-eaten whores to yourself and the next time you see us look the other way.'

At this the panther immediately arches her back, shows her teeth in a snarl. I expect a battle royal to break out right in the middle of the street. Giacomo unexpectedly makes her abort it by roughly shoving her to one side and, having cancelled our presence before his eyes, respected and established businessman that he is, he busily engages himself in attempting to hail a taxi by making exaggerated vulgar gestures but, to his misfortune, the taxis speed by uncaring and engaged.

'Rotten egg,' says Lella, spitting on the footpath.

But it doesn't look like the end of the altercation. The painter senses he's been cheated of something. Having set eyes on the panther it's difficult for him to understand how the matter ended and he candidly expresses his personal disapproval.

'It's unheard of,' he starts up, scratching his chin. 'Far better a whore dressed as a panther than to pay out money to see chickens and donkeys Anyway ... You could have asked what I thought about it, couldn't you? Gees, you always do just what you like. You're deaf and blind to a man's needs.'

'Go on, run after her. You can still catch her up,' Lella eggs him on, laughing.

'How? You haven't introduced me to her ...'

'And since when did you need an introduction? Run after her with your fly undone. It's the best type of introduction for that sort.'

The painter stops to ponder this piece of genuine impartial advice, weighing up the pros and cons. To choose Lella's uncertain and self-interested friendship—because she considers herself educated and up-to-date Lella flaunts her right to have you pay for her dinner and then, the

41

day after, she could make out she doesn't even know you—or Giacomo's red-hot handmaidens. He wavers, undecided, turns to look back at the point of encounter, and establishes to his relief that the twosome has by now disappeared, swallowed up by the crowd.

I often read over these passages, animated and unanimated notes on unfamiliar past experiences. For me, an Italian woman, or rather Neapolitan, which is tantamount to saying Sicilian, Sardinian or Calabrese, who drags along with her that touch of the unusual, of ill luck, but who nevertheless is not without a savage perspicacity, the arrangement was a colossal melodrama. No need to invent things in order to have a good laugh. Just a touch of imagination and you could liven up your destiny and your boredom. At the Portuguese couple's place where I was staying, an insipid Rumanian used to live, a fat and stupid man who hanged himself from the bathroom ceiling after filling himself with wine. He preached my salvation in deadly earnest. Seeing I was from the South, and going on all those worn-out idiotic commonplaces put about by people who had reached the apex of slovenliness, I needed to blend with his noble blood in order to raise myself up the social ladder. Yuck. A good job he didn't survive. It was a pain in the bum to listen to him. And it was a pity I didn't get the chance to tell him exactly what I thought of people who were so fair, so beautiful, so intelligent, so charitable …

I would lightly bend till my breath gave out but I wouldn't break. The sweet apathetic muttering which I would build up round my person like an iron fence was enough to raise me above it all, make me indifferent. Weigh me down with your excreta, your hates, your fights, your wretched little quarrels, and I shall take them all in and make them bear fruit. Everything that lies buried in the depths of your stinking carcasses, sex, murder, song and gangrene, that travels in the hinterland and the wide-open universes, I take it all in. And now, Rosa, that you are saturated with chatter and logic, go to Helen's and eat some cabbage and baked tomatoes. You haven't seen her for a long time. But remember to give three long rings on the bell. She warned you about it a while back. Irene's new flame has sent her a fully-fledged written declaration of war. She'd better be on her guard.

As I go down Bourke Street, I smile to myself. I find Helen's fears absurd, the precautions she's taken, not going out, locking herself in her flat, so as to avoid the confrontation which would put an end to the stream of chatter and threats put about by the fiery Polish woman. I can't work out who set the fuse. All of a sudden Helen has become discreet and secretive, withered up, virtually evaporated. Avoids making drastic decisions. Avoids doing her duty. Actually I'm dying to see two lesbians fight it out. When I've nothing to do, I keep walking to and fro under her window in the secret hope that I'll be in the right spot at the right time, at that fortunate instant when the Polish woman will charge in, scissors in hand, to cut off all her hair, as written in the letter. Instead the window is forever shut in the rays of the setting sun, decorated by the pigeons on the sill and the embroidered tablecloth.

When I get there I wait for a few minutes on the footpath opposite. I see the old Italian barber sweep away the last locks of hair, the tailor turning his dummies with their display of clothes towards the window, a thin wisp of smoke rising from the ironing board. The office girl at the travel agency changing the water in the flower vases. The monotonous repetitive actions which mark closing time. The day is coming to an end. The old men on the benches in that green rectangle of grass called Taylor Square, their veins glowing through after sitting in the sun all day, leave their seats and wend their unsteady way towards the pub. They file across the pedestrian crossing like blindfolded bulls charging towards the smell of the byre. They use their sense of smell to guide them. They sense the sharp crackling of foamy beer. There's always a crowd at the bar. It'll never go bust. Everyone stops off there, some thirsty, some not, but all, without exception, to forget the terror of living. The walk signal goes on. I go across. I ring out the coded message on the bell and thank my lucky stars that I'm still young, still sharp. Inside a clucking hen-like voice cries out in astonishment.

'Who is it?'

'It's me,' I reply, jumping up so she can see me through the little opening set high up in the door.

Helen opens, stick in hand.

'Better not to trust anyone,' she says, glaring at me crossly. 'Anybody could disguise themselves.'

She shows me in, leading the way, muttering something about the light not working and to feel my way against the wall. I notice that she walks like an old woman full of aches and pains.

'I just came out of hospital the other day,' she confides.

The news startles me. I didn't know anything about it. I scrutinise her from head to toe in the dark, looking for sticking plaster and bandages.

'No,' she immediately catches my unspoken query. 'My womb kept giving me trouble so I had it scraped. You know about these things … By the way, you're covered. I put in a word for you with my gynaecologist. Good man. Very understanding. Abortion's illegal in this country. If you get into trouble you'll know who to turn to,' she says.

'I haven't had time, and, anyway, I don't need him just now,' I reply.

'Sure, you're not a woman,' she throws out angrily. 'You've either got it plugged up or it doesn't work. You should know that three-quarters of the inmates at Parramatta are migrants. You could point out that they're already sick when they get here, fine, but the climate and the social structure do the rest of the job. There's too much loneliness, and those who don't fuck and let off steam end up in the madhouse. Would you like to end up like that? I wouldn't.' She concludes on a note of satisfaction.

Deep within myself I look upon her as a formidable misfit and if I take the trouble to visit her it's because she always presses me to stay to dinner. Also because at the Portuguese's I can't cook, damn it, and with all that fish and chip rubbish the pigeon's eggs in the small of my back are getting so big that it's agony to sit down. I nibble on a boiled cabbage leaf and casually pop a morsel of mince in my mouth, so she gets the message that I'm hungry. An almost carnal odour wafts out of the hot oven, quite a different matter from gynaecologists, scrapings and orgasms. At least she's not forever talking about money. It looks as though she's got insurmountable spiritual problems to grapple with.

'I'd like to help you so you don't make any mistakes,' she says, dragging it out as though taking a load off her mind and at the same time placing her stick well in view on the mantelpiece.

I don't know why but that stick makes me angry, an anger connected to that thin stridulant voice which lists one difficulty after another at breakneck speed.

'You're concerning yourself with things which aren't your business,' I say.

'Sure, maybe so. But you'll see, you'll see, even though you think you're above us all. You'll go through the mill same as everyone else and there's no amount of self-preservation instinct or skill which is going to spare you that experience. You've got everything going against you. The language, your own *paesani*, and if you say mamma in that English of yours they'll all understand prick and if you say pap they'll understand something entirely different. That's what will happen. I'd like to disappear. No, I'd like to stick a bomb up Australia's arsehole and then go sell papers among the ruins. You're laughing, are you? Well, go ahead and laugh. You adapt yourself. You get by on dry fucks by reading books. You stuff yourself with dumb words. I can't take it. I can't bear this wasteland. I'm going to pieces.'

'Jesus, why don't you migrate to another country?' I burst out, exasperated.

'Where to? The world's got its balls cut off. It's at death's door. Crumbs and ashes everywhere. There's nothing, a void, I'm a figment of the imagination. Someone says that the being comes into existence by its name becoming matter. Helen, Helen, millions of Helens exist, but the best was Helen of Troy, the one who gave her name to all the whores whose name is not Helen. Funny, isn't it? Let's say my name's not Helen but Fiorella, tender-stalked Fiorella, who, in her imaginary life has taken flight beyond money and has crashed into the forger's mint of a forged country ... Where do you expect Helen of the fable to go?' she says and starts whistling bitterly.

This woman, me, this imaginary Helen, has scared the shit out of my morale, still, there must be one woman born who, while striving to get the most out of life, doesn't swear like Beniamina and Co. against inflation, taxes, inadequate wages, animosity, cons, solitude, hardship, the collapse of civilization, while all the time hoarding away cents and stale crumbs in the expectation of spending her old age in her native village. Nor does she impose upon herself continuous sacrifices, privation, self-denial, belt-tightening such as not buying a juicy steak, a fresh chicken, offering a cigarette to someone who doesn't have one, or a free fuck. Subtle niceties which bring relief to the grim existence of the exile. No, Helen shops regularly at the supermarket, stocks up on both the necessities and the not-so-necessary. Great hostess, she offers her guests coffee, a drink, without regretting the waste and expense.

'Rosaaaaaaa!' She suddenly screams as though the kitchen were going up in flames. The fright makes me jump. I had gone out on the balcony, keeping myself to myself and looking at the view. 'What are you doing? Playing in the moonlight? What are you gawking at? Can't you see the floor is giving way? Do you want to fall through ... Who'll pay you compensation?' She goes on yelling, keeping out of the line of sight of the door, eyes flashing like a maniac's, desperately ordering me to come back in.

'What a way to call me! You gave me such a shock, damn you,' I stammer, green in the face.

'Sorry,' her apology is sweetened by the hint of a smile. 'I'm like a prisoner in here, I don't even allow myself to indulge in a breath of fresh air. See over there?' She points to the flat opposite. 'A dancing teacher lives there. She's got a hairy wart in the middle of her forehead and because of that Indian shit she's convinced that she's descended from an ancient Hindu religious sect. She threatens to turn me into a scorpion and other nasty things and she doesn't spare me insults, dirges and incense. Did they see you?' she asks, clumsily losing her balance.

'No. All shut up. No lights,' I reassure her.

'Thank God,' she sighs painfully. 'They give me the creeps … the teacher and that TB case. That rare creature who composes sonatas in his sleep, dreaming that he's better than Tchaikovsky, Schubert, Beethoven, etc. etc. …'

Now I remember the old woman and the young man, the stuffed eagle which they threw out onto the rubbish heap.

'It's really strange what's been happening to me lately,' she explains, finding the strength to come out with it. 'It all happens to me. I don't have a moment's peace. Really. You wouldn't read about it … When they called out to me from their balcony to come and have a cup of tea I gratefully accepted. I didn't feel like staying all on my lonesome at night, especially after the row with Irene. I wanted to communicate, talk, I was going off my head. Loneliness gets me down the same way as stupid people do. The teacher seemed just the right type for an exchange of views, for establishing a rapport of peaceful cohabitation … She's got a cultured way of speaking, you know … you wouldn't think so to see her all wrapped up in that dirty cloak. She's travelled a lot. She would tell all those interesting stories of her youthful tours in the best theatres of Europe as if it were all true. Little white lies, they were. What do you expect? Everyone's got a right to a glorious past. And, anyway, here you cultivate friendships and get on with your neighbours by listening to that sort of rubbish. I used to congratulate her in a most warm and understanding manner. The good neighbour caper was getting along like a house on fire. She offered to teach me to play the piano, and to give me dancing and English lessons But, now that I think about it, I'm sure she wanted to start me off doing it from behind in seven languages. The musician queer, absorbed in his creative hallucinations, seemed to reject me. He rarely joined in the discussions. You didn't even notice he was there … and then, just listen to this … this is the best part. The teacher and I were trying out a dance step, he was whistling the tune, baton in hand. Really … I swear I can't explain to you what the hell came over him, all of a sudden he drags me out of the woman's arms and, all choked up, implores me to favour him with inspiration and sex.'

'He's probably suffering from amnesia. Must have mistaken you for the muse.'

'I'll introduce him to you, if you like,' she says, noting my sarcasm. 'But let's go back in now because if they see me they'll probably throw stones and lumps of wood.' Having lowered the blinds over the windows she continues. 'He's a type worth considering. He's got a romantic air about him. You should adopt them and see to their nourishment: raw sugar, semolina, cereals—and they must be unrefined—they don't eat much but only natural foods ...'

'What sort of connection do they have? Mother and son or what?'

'Lovers. That's why that piece of gallantry didn't impress me much. A guy who lets himself be seduced by an old crow like that must have a screw loose somewhere ... have some excuse,' she says, maybe to excuse his behaviour, maybe to get me interested. 'The old woman weaned him away from the bottle, gave him mother's milk ... maybe he got to like the taste. I think the boy was placed in her care by another dancing teacher or maybe it was a ballerina, I'm not sure. One day she disappeared, ran off with a Neapolitan travelling salesman, a small-time con man who manages to keep body and soul together by flogging gold-plated copper objects, dud watches and bolts of worm-eaten cloth. So now he calls the old hag mummy, dear heart, little sister, rosebud, little flower. He's not pretending. Wouldn't be capable of it. He's a retarded cretin who creates in his sleep ... and maybe one fine morning he'll wake up and accomplish the miracle ... tip over the musical golden egg ... and you would find yourself married to a genius, to God praised on earth. You'd get to be counted amongst the gods. What do you say?'

Say? You're crazy, Helen. You're becoming an idiot, if you weren't one already. This is a *terra incognita* which has never existed before. On our planet, old women with warts, TB cases, broken-down pianos, throwing tomatoes and apple cores, curses, cons, the self-interested morbid curiosity of those who pass themselves off as friends, we used to put up with as external factors, not as an active vital force necessary for our salvation. People were elegant, refined, wanted to live. And there was more, more than a guaranteed wage, more than the chance to latch onto three jobs a day, more than cows, sausages and tripe at export prices, there was that little bit extra. Stupidity and lack of imagination were the gravest of sins. Ours was the planet where you found that something extra. Genius and the restless urge to search sprang from our cultural origins. Those were my people, in my likeness, no matter what you say.

'I'm dying of misery,' Helen confesses. 'This house makes me sick to my soul.'

Poor Helen. She shells out fifteen dollars a week. The room upstairs is occupied by a young, neat, rose-complexioned Australian girl. On the stairs a continual stream of dirty-minded men who go up for a fix and a fuck and drip blood all over the stairs when they fight amongst each other.

'Oh,' she exclaims, a bright flush on her cheeks, 'I almost forgot. I've got a man to dinner tonight. Move over so's I can set the table.'

I take my elbows off the edge. She puts on two tablemats, two pumpkin-coloured straw coasters at the head of the table. She blows on and wipes a couple of long glasses for the pre-dinner drinks. An intimate candlelit setting. My face puts on a display of interrogative expressions, making her wrinkle her nose in indecision, scratch herself, then confess.

'Ah, life,' raising her eyes to the ceiling as if asking for enlightenment on the great truths she is about to reveal. 'Funny how I met the fellow … by tripping over a coffin … empty it was … but the fact remains that he's an undertaker, well, actually, he works at the funeral parlour, which is the same thing. I can't remember the name of the firm where Jack works … but if you want to satisfy your curiosity look out the window and you'll see the large neon sign and the black windows on the corner of Campbell Street. I don't mind at all if he handles dead people, he's a man after all, better than cracking up playing solitaire, and then in some fields technical progress here is very advanced, maybe they handle the dead with gloves and tongs … when he comes remind me to ask him if he has a suitable friend for you.'

I don't have the strength to protest. I don't want the undertaker. I wouldn't be able to sleep. She's started singing and turns her back to me. Then one, two, three long rings on the bell. Helen rushes to open. None of the tenants bother if they don't recognise their code. I'm convinced that everyone who lives in this building has some skeleton or other in the cupboard. The girl upstairs is a minor, a drug-addict and has run away from home. The police and the Salvation Army are looking for her. One morning two parasol-armed little old women stopped Helen at the front door of the building, thinking she was the other girl, even though Helen looks like my rachitic old grandmother, but let's get back to us. More than anyone else she has to guard herself against enemies, the Polish woman, Irene, the dancing teacher and the composer. I'll bet my bottom dollar that this affair with an Australian man will end up affecting her brain in some way and that she won't recover easily from the experience. They come up the stairs chatting. They come into the flat. Helen's knees are shaking. I shake hands. Jack puts the carton of beer on the table. Just the type I'd imagined, loose-fitting short trousers, short, shiny jacket out of fashion by at least a generation. Helen makes the aperitifs, with jerky nervous motions. Ice cubes, lemon rind, hands the drink to yours truly with the look of someone who is being given offence. She'd like me to get lost. While she hands me the glass she lightly touches my fingers, throws me a pleading glance. I pretend not to notice.

'Jack's Australian,' she says with a touch of pride.

'For a hundred and fifty years,' he adds, looking at the still-intact carton of beer and, with a grimace, at the red liquid of the aperitif.

'Well then, you must be as old as Methuselah,' I joke.

'Pardon?'

'Oh, nothing really.' I wouldn't want to start an argument or offend Helen who's unusually excited and wrapped up in herself. But I didn't like Jack all that much. He's responsible for the final indignities carried out on the frozen bodies of the dead. As he brings the glass disdainfully to his lips I ask, 'Do you wash, tidy-up, paint the corpses? Do you embalm them?'

'What an idea!' he says, spluttering politely. The Rosso Antico didn't go down too well. 'We put the bodies in refrigerated cells and ...'

'Right, you're a pertica of progress,' I retort instinctively, happy that I'd managed to make an original remark.

'Pardon?' he repeats.

'Rosa doesn't speak English all that well,' Helen throws out fiercely.

'Yes,' I insist stubbornly. 'Those dishevelled women who used to wail and rend their hair. Pertiche, that's what they were called, pertiche.' I immediately get the impression that I've made a mistake. What a fool I've made of myself! I don't remember if they were called pertiche, pertugi or befane.

'You're referring to those women in ancient Rome ... prefiche, prefiche ... hired mourners ... Jesus, we're in Australia, a young country, virginal, functional. We look to the future not to the past ... Is it true that you don't have electric lifts in Italy?' he says. The question takes me completely by surprise.

'And what do we have then?'

'Lifts run by water,' is his ready reply.

'Maybe so, but I've never seen lift attendants pump water for Italian lifts.'

'See, there's a lot of things you don't know,' he says, giving me a magnanimous pat on the cheek.

Helen is fuming. She throws me threatening looks. She'd drag me out by the hair if she could. I'm cruelling her pitch. She mutters on about the oven which keeps breaking down and about the dinner that'll be served in a couple of hours—that's if it'll be served at all—they might have to end up going to a restaurant. What she means is that I should get out of there. Oh, well, maybe it's best to go without this evening. Start the diet because I'm getting fat on butter, milk and fried food. I get to my feet uneasily. It's an odd feeling that your friend should find your presence burdensome. I open the curtain and begin smiling in the general direction of the projectile-launching dancing teacher and musician. Wouldn't it be funny if they appeared attired in their battle regalia. I smile but the smile freezes inside me. I see Helen's reflection in the glass as she surreptitiously hands the undertaker a second aperitif.

'It's quite late. Aren't you frightened of walking through the streets? Someone could rape you,' she says.

'Shit, you really are tactless,' I reply.

'Oh, don't get excited. I'll invite you to lunch next time,' she promises pleadingly.

'Let's arrange to meet tomorrow, I'll come with you to the gynaecologist … we can go to the pictures …'

I grab my bag and go.

Five days sick leave a year are not enough but they are better than nothing. After the first three months' service, which is the qualifying period for sick leave entitlement, I ring the factory and tell them I'm sick. I want to enjoy them all at once, as compensation owing to me for years. It wouldn't matter if they fired me afterwards. I go to English classes two nights a week. Please speak English. Won't take notice of you if you don't. Not going this week. There's an Italian ship in port. Lella and I have taken on the task of acting as guides for two kitchen hands. Streets, buildings, restaurants, the bridge, monuments, the unfinished Opera House, museums, cathedrals—preferably with alcoves at the entrance. The odd present. I get a Japanese cigarette lighter. The other one doesn't smoke so we hurry to Circular Quay, to the ship. The second fellow dashes up to ask for a carton of cigarettes and a bottle of liqueur. Ten minutes later we see him walk down the gangplank as if he had a hernia. He rubs his hand together and asks where the toilet is so he can go and take the loot from out of his trousers. We steer him towards the toilets under the station. He comes out with a bottle of Ferro-China, a carton of Muratti cigarettes and a bundle of pornographic comic books which he waves from a distance. Lella makes a face. I don't drink much. The tonic will probably be useful for treating my ulcer. We finish up the evening drinking Ferro-China mixed with coke. In any case I was afraid it would end up like this. She asks if she can stay and sleep on the floor. Her landlords are bastards and make life difficult for her, she can't have men in. But I like to sleep in comfort. I need a big bed all to myself which is impossible when you rent a room with a family. They scarcely give you the bare essentials: a chair, sometimes a small table, a single bed with a mattress full of stains which look like blood or urine, and, if you strike it lucky, a wardrobe and a sink in your room. But I didn't have one and I couldn't let her use my bed. As I was saying, I like to be comfortable when I sleep. Lella says it's all right if she can sleep on the floor. I don't argue with her. She turns off the light.

Towards dawn, I still can't manage to get to sleep. My bedfellow has spread himself out like Christ on the cross, legs wide open, arms flung out, and he snores. Rage rises within me. I'd be capable of committing murder. To calm myself down I breathe deeply, one, two, a hundred breaths, then I start counting sheep. And by the thousandth I'm perched on the edge of the mattress, a foot and a hand on the floor to keep myself from falling. It is an impossible situation. I'm precariously balanced on a bed which is mine, the room is mine, the things around us are mine, just like the glasses and the ashtrays that they used so why the hell do I have to forfeit my well-earned rest? I'm so furious that I bite the pillow. At midday the two men go back to the ship. Lella has a quick snack and says she has to rush off home to prepare her equipment. She's begun to make good money out of her hobby and is augmenting her income by taking photographs at Greek and Cypriot weddings—like the Italians they hire receptions halls, orchestras, singers and masters of ceremony when they marry. She's often the animator, the life of the party, the court jester. She's very much in demand. Writes poems on request for the couple. And strange as it may seem, the verses give rise to admiration and debate among the guests, dull-witted and full after four, five courses irrigated with generous quantities of ethnic wine and local beer. She's the most satisfied person I've met since I emigrated. She'd rise to any occasion. A glib talker and a cynical look in her eyes which stops her from getting involved. 'Want to come?' she asks. No thanks. They pay you to put up with them. Me they don't pay. You scrounge a free meal, hors d'oeuvres and all. But do keep me in mind for the next wedding.

Towards dusk I pass by Helen's place. An unplanned visit but one I felt I had to make since I'm still smarting from the affront in the undertaker's presence. Fancy, giving him the aperitif on the sly. What a turncoat, to treat me so meanly at the smell of a male. I'm not taking this lying down. She must say it openly. I prefer to state things clearly. At least she could have put a notice on the door 'Come back later. I'm busy screwing.' And she's the one who talks about a world with its balls cut off.

I get to the front door at the same time as the girl upstairs and worm my way in like a thief. On the landing there is a cat meowing sadly. The girl pats it, says it belongs to Helen and that it's probably hungry. I'm not interested in the cat. I put my ear to the door and hear muttering. I knock in code. Silence and the angry meowing of the cat reply. I knock again. Nothing. She's in there all right. I try pushing with my shoulder.

Her timid voice asks, 'That you Rosa?'

'Who do you think it is?'

'Would you mind ringing me at the factory tomorrow at one … one o'clock, don't forget …'

In the street I bitterly regret not having gone to the Greek wedding. I don't know where to go. Downtown to look at the shops maybe. At the bus stop I change my mind. Why not visit Sofia on the North Shore? That is if I find her at the same address. She's like the wandering Jew. Persecuted by her jealous boyfriend who comes after her with a knife, she's forced to move from one end of the city to the other. It's because of her I know my way round so well. I snigger. Boyfriend isn't quite the right term. Obsessed by the concept of virginity, even though he's so young. A year younger than Sofia. He invariably brings up the subject of her defloration during copulation and only then, demanding the name and a detailed description of the vandal. For Sofia, although she would gladly tell him all, it is impossible to do so because mother nature gave her that imperfection at birth, rudely deflowering her even before she opened her eyes. And while Nicola beats her she swears again and again that he's been the only one. There's just no way to make him understand the medical explanation. There must be proof and there's no proof of virginal scent. The rose-red pigeon's blood was missing.

I go back on my tracks, hands deep in my pockets. Virile thoughts whirl round in my head. Masculine thoughts also. Since I've started reading in English with the help of a dictionary a beautiful poem has struck me to the marrow of my bones. I almost seem to have become fond of that man Hope who wrote 'The Arabian Desert of the Human Mind'. I associate with the human mind of youth, the one buried in the sand, and I've never seen a nightingale in a tree. Where have all the nightingales gone? They expect to have nightingales just as pigs expect to have their pigsty decorated with roses. They wouldn't even see a nightingale carved in wood. Yes, I confess that I'm guilty of glossing over curses and lies in my frenzy. Lies. Lies. But are they lies? Wait another day before you penetrate this mess, before you prick yourself with the splinters that are there outside. Wait another day before you become shrivelled like the fly in the stiffened cobweb. Wait, wait, before you spit out your livid breath onto the perfumeless flowers, onto the tasteless fruit …

When I'm on the northbound train and after two stops the train comes out of the tunnel and clatters over the bridge suspended over an infinite expanse of transparent green water—the ferries full of people passing underneath, the lit-up Luna Park which comes towards us, the islands which seem to float in the distance, the lights in the windows which reflect the waves caught up in the foliage of the trees—it's as if friendly arms open out to welcome me. To take me in, and my hopes as well. As soon as things are fixed up again, that is, as soon as I manage to receive a weekly bonus, if the dwarf allows it, I'll look for a place to hole up in over here.

I get off at Milson's Point, ask the man at the newsstand where I can find the Miami Private Hotel. Ten minutes, climbing up and on the edge of the bay. I immediately get my bearings from the description Sofia has given me. And there it is, rising like a green and white mastodon to dominate the bay, an enormous beehive which stretches beyond the shore and stands directly on the sea. Other spurs stop at the cement wall which acts as a safeguard for the windows virtually on the water's surface. Sofia has found refuge in one of those windows and like a bobbing cork spies out the arrival of Nicola, an event both terrifying and desired. Judging by the name I had pictured something gay, touristic, possibly luxurious. Instead, starting right from the decrepit lobby—without even a coat of paint to alleviate its atmosphere reminiscent of a prison or a witches' cavern—I ask myself what sort of place this idiot has got into. The receptionist seated in her cage behind the round window favours me with a fresh angelic smile. Along the corridor, turn left, and take the stairs. I thank her. I walk along the canyon-like corridor which seems to split the huge building in two, the ceiling is so high. I get the impression of venturing out on the back of a caterpillar with its legs spread out. All the doors are wide open because it's terribly hot and the tenants in shirt sleeves enjoy the ventilation. Neon lights on the damp walls. A sanatorium would have a healthier look about it. Sofia's flat is in the depths of the basement. The spiral staircase is swallowed up in pitch darkness. Two men are climbing up, a woman and a little girl too. I climb down grasping the railing, my eyes wide open, without making way for anyone at all until I can see the bottom. The stairs are steeper at the bottom and finish up in a sort of cave, different from your usual run of the mill cave because it has three doors with rust-encrusted enamel numbers, a sign in the shape of a white hand pointing to the right and a small notice which requests that record-players should not be played too loudly. There is the sound of the sea. From number 103 come bursts of laughter, Sofia's infantile bleating, a snigger which I swear is that bitch Beniamina who with her harsh voice goes on about the faults and sexual activities of people she knows. I'm uncertain whether I should go in or not. Still, since you've come so far, take a chance. Don't tremble with apprehension for the unexpected encounter.

She opens, letting out a little cry of surprise and immediately disappears with a waddling kind of walk. She goes through the first room which is the bedroom, old broken-down furniture which a second-hand dealer wouldn't touch. In the second room the attention of Sofia and Beniamina is centred on two bowls full of rice bubbles and milk and some slices of cheese. They whirl about like a broken grandfather clock numbing the palate in this puppet-like, frothful sharing of their meal when both are short of funds. A pastoral picture, filial, maternal, paternal, biblical, consanguineous, with cheap overtones it'll give you an idea of the harmony which true friendship still manages to generate in our time.

'Next time, come straight across the park, there's a path. You'll save yourself that horror … terrible, isn't it? But why don't you rent a room here, you'd be near to Sofia,' Beniamina advises me.

'Big deal. I don't want to give offence but what sort of million dollar view do you have from this flea-pit?'

'How much will you give me for the lease of the flat? You could even move in tonight,' says Sofia, rubbing her beautiful hands together.

'You're on the run again.'

'See,' she screams pointing the spoon at Beniamina. 'I told you so. She thinks she knows everything. Becomes suspicious straight off. Look at her, like a bloodhound at sniffing out trouble. I earn my daily bread honestly …'

Beniamina sounds off at this outburst on the subject of honesty. Honesty, a word lent to a wide and disparate variety of situations, otherwise you wouldn't be able to explain why it crops up so many times when we thrash out the differences between me and them. Them, uninterrupted seasons, wheelchairs, deposits of slime, vagrants, bottled-up feelings, thrills blended and mixed in with almonds, nutmeg, cloves, chopped garlic, pure olive oil, random flights that last for ever. But I am a cagey kind of beast, contempt is in my blood, my eyes are shut in solitude.

'I don't understand these hick provincial women,' she says. 'They keep their minds in a muff. Patched-up yokels they are, I avoid them like the plague.' She uses sophisticated phrases taken from *Epoca, Storia, L'Europeo, Look, Live,* and she repeats herself like a broken record. 'Same thing if you meet a man.' Here I've got you. 'They meddle in your affairs and in your vagina. A girl who's got an ounce of sensitivity suffers, is tormented, what an obsession! I've saved up my money, why should I share it with the first con-man to come along, the result of my labours, my sweat? Ah, bugger it, I don't go for the sluttish behaviour of these pricks, they can't fool me. I know what it means to pedal an industrial sewing machine while you're having your period and the heat's at a tropical thirty-six degrees. If I subjugate my soul to the service of a man, in exchange I want at least that he remain European, that he use that finesse to which we have been accustomed for centuries, but they don't even give you your due because by dint of killing themselves with work they've become impotent, and a man incapable of satisfying his girl might just as well go and cut his balls off because he's an enemy of the human race.'

'Good God, in that case ninety-nine per cent would go round without ...' says Sofia, with a pout.

'Shut up, you put up with these types. Are we like the Australian women that we should give payment in kind for the privilege of having a little prick next to us? Remember Paolo? Sure you remember him, that bludger who always looked out the window when the conductor came round in the bus and at the pictures always shut up and made like he didn't know what was going on ...'

The look on Sofia's face showed she did. 'So? You still going out with him?'

'I've dumped him. A liberated woman, available every night wasn't enough for him. He also wanted her to cook, keep his clothes in order and share the expenses. And for what? For a minute prick and a jet of tepid piss which just tickled.'

'I don't have any problems,' says Sofia.

'Me neither, since I've been going with Carmelo,' says Beniamina, and she gives a list of his sexual abilities just as she would give a list of gastronomic delights. She mutters that his favourite position is an upside down one. And he's Sicilian so he knows all about it. A master of dribbling, feint, defence and attack. He's not mean … that's real nice.

Sofia tells about her experiences. She lists all her exploits on a sheet of paper. They're both with their heads over the table, almost touching. Now and then they whisper and laugh. When she laughs Sofia puts her hand over her mouth. She's beautiful. Men turn to look at her in the street. She should have more luck but she's so stupid and such a stinker. Dangerous. A stupid, jealous and malicious woman who frightens all her friends except Beniamina whom she twists around her little finger and dominates with her cunning.

Get rich. Get rich or, if not rich, well-off. That's the goal set by the migrants, if not all, most and then some. That's why they call us wog and we call them addlebrained drunks. Oh, if it wasn't for the sea and the sky … get rich. With the Italian newspaper spread out in her lap Lellina is on the track of the easiest way to get rich. I've taken a room in Redfern in the house of a jaded Greek spinster. The room is very small but furnished with a hotplate and running water, toilet in the yard. I've made my first housekeeping purchases. I'm taking root. The coffee pot, a couple of terracotta cups. Glasses, utensils, salt and pepper shakers, oil decanter, filched from clubs or restaurants.

Start up as a fortune-teller. There's reason to believe that it's the best business. Fortune-tellers are proliferating at such a rate that soon Australia will be bursting with them. There's the Wizard of Rome, Bari, Milan, Avellino; Turks, Arabs, Egyptians, sorceresses expert in herbs and with degrees in epitaphs, their photos in the newspapers, wide menacing eyes at the click of the shutter. Being Neapolitan I'll play the part of the Sibyl or a descendant of the Sibyl which is the same thing.

'Right, but what'll they consult us about?'

'Oh, we'll help them by making them bust laughing. Don't you worry, we'll hire Maman as a receptionist—with that witch's face she'll be just right, okay? You'll be the Sibyl and I'll be the Greek shaman ... what do you say? Shaman is Aboriginal ... okay, I'll blacken my face, no, that's no good you say, better to be related to Venus, it'll draw more people. All right, let's have Venus and the Sibyl, I've got some old odds and ends to wear and a hernia truss ... I had a hernia then I had an operation, so we'll show the truss and say it belonged to Venus. Why not say it's an heirloom? Those stupid women believe that donkeys fly and spend thousands of dollars. We'll get them to put on the rare old truss and look them straight in the eye giving them the psychomagnetic routine. And so housewives in harness, frustrated married women, oppressed women workers are transformed into enchantresses. We'll become famous. What do you think Rosa? We've got a head for investments—oil, diamonds, silver ... my head is a mine of ideas. We'll predict typhoid, paratyphoid, plague, dysentery, epidemics, lightning bolts, floods, evil eye, spells for their friends' enemies ... happy marriages, love affairs, wins on dogs horses bed-bugs frogs lotteries, fertility (sterility and impotence for rivals), love, joy, remedies and we'll give ointments ...'

'It's an interesting proposition,' I say.

'I'll have to curl my hair though.'

'So curl it and tint it a vivid red so it'll look like tiny snakes.'

'Right. Now about the dress. I'd like to wear a brocade dressing gown, slippers with a tassel ... I've always dreamed of having beautiful clothes, you know.'

'How does a live snake coiled round my head like a laurel crown grab you?' I'm leading her on a bit.

'You never stop clowning,' she huffs impatiently.

'But you know these people, eternally quarrelling with neighbours and relatives whom they would like to see down-and-out or dead. It makes me hopping mad to think about it. I break out in a sweat when I think of those cunning little pricks showing off. I've decided that we'll start off somewhere in Leichhardt or Marrickville, where there's lots of Greeks and Italians. Lots of potential, guaranteed takings and later we can open up a chain of offices with machines which spew out coupons for programmed happiness. Your people, like mine, deserve to be conned. And we'll give them their money's worth. They've found the right types in us. Blah, blah, blah. And don't breathe a word of this to anyone.'

For the last few evenings Lella has been sticking to me like a shadow. She eats at my place, arriving with a bag of boiled prawns, lemons, buttered buns and a pile of books on magic borrowed from the council library. She reads my palm. She's identified perfectly with her role, lit cigarillo hanging from her lips, eyes wide open. Interested in sex. A peculiar type of sex, a bit mixed up with God, zombies, demons, floods, earthquakes, the moon falling on the earth, solar eclipses, horns, horseshoes, monkeys' tails, hairs of a woman who has menstruated to pass off as those of a stone-age woman, the crystal ball, the star-tipped wand, flags of various countries at the entrance, various signs in different languages which say not to spit on the floor, not to flick cigarette ash on the pot plants, not to stick chewing gum under the seats of the chairs. We burn the midnight oil leafing through anthroposophic erudition, weather reports, highbrow stuff by philosophers Catholics psychologists heads of state followers of Christ swastikas rubberbands buttocks, going over the cheque account, just like a properly accredited business, business is business, after all.

When we've got it all together my friend Lella adds the final touch. An appointment with a super seer, a real one, not a fake. One who can die, rise again, levitate, perform miracles, just like in the movies. We go to the station to take the train to Wynyard, then the bus to Crows Nest. As we go Lella assumes the determined stance of a special correspondent, pen, notebook, cigars sticking out of her back trouser pocket. She would have been really sorry not to have her ever-present camera with her. She's now decided that I should levitate. A matter of habit, she asserts, like not eating. The proposal doesn't appeal to me. It doesn't even occur to her that she should try out the experiment herself and go without eating. No, she's above the rat-race, she's director, producer, electrician, cameraman, multilingual secretary.

At the seer's place we announce our arrival over the intercom. A modern luxury apartment block with lots of glass and gold-coloured carpet, fountain with a pissing cherub, goldfish and climbing plants. On the eighth floor the seer answers the door as naked as a maggot coming out of its cocoon. Lella nearly has a fit, turns white, then livid, then gets jumpy. The wizard smiles, shaking his balding braided head and moves aside to let us in. As if hypnotised I look at his withered testicles and the little penis which bobs up and down.

'I've never seen such a repulsive penis,' Lella whispers.

The wizard walks in front of us, erect, buttocks sticking to his pelvis. Naked the old man is a nauseating sight. A withered fruit not even good for the worms.

As if he had read our thoughts he says in a clear voice: 'Nakedness is freedom. Nude is beautiful. Man is born naked. The soul is naked. Sex is nakedness, away with frills. Animals go round naked and we've got a lot to learn from them. God is a naked word. Clothes weren't invented in his time.'

He invites us to sit down. As he sits he adjusts his penis. Lella and I lean against the backrest of the sofa for support, fearful that we will receive sermons and platitudes on heaven and hell, useless and dangerous as a first lesson on the activity we are about to commence. The wise man goes on regardless, eyes fixed on a painting of the inquisition, witches dancing their saraband round a fire. He complains that he is not allowed to take a walk in his birthday suit with only the addition of a fig leaf and a walking stick. He does everything naked, everything, absorbing wisdom through his bared pores, assimilating vitamins directly from the air around him. We ask if we can smoke but he won't allow it. Smoke obscures his visions of the hereafter.

Lellina yawns. She's put away pen and notebook. I'm sitting there thinking that the old man should be hauled off to a home for slobbery pant-wetters, when he suddenly turns, raising himself ever so slightly on his buttocks, and eyes me suspiciously. There's a shifty look about me and he doesn't trust me, he says. An evil fluid filters through my subconscious, have I ever been in a lunatic asylum? I'll die young, same as my mother, so there's nothing more to say other than that I do not have the three circles, the ones in the fold of the wrist, magic signs which are like a window opened out on the future. My window is non-existent and I almost feel like crying over my skinny, skeleton-like wrist, about to break.

'I feel you want to steal something from me ... what?' he asks. Beads of sweat, large ones, shine at the roots of his braids.

'The skin off your skull, the sacred bone,' Lella suggests. Her sarcasm is getting the better of her.

'No, no.' The seer waves his hand as if to drive away bad breath. 'She won't collaborate. She's against me ... schizophrenic ... a bundle of nerves.'

'Oh, come on,' I protest. 'You're joking. I'm as sound as a bell.'

'What nationality are you?' he asks all of a sudden.

'Italian, half Greek, half Cypriot,' Lella replies.

'You Italians have perfect teeth,' he says with a strange demented smile.

Lella and I look at each other. He's finished with me and now he turns on her. He observes her battered face, the rings under her eyes, the red pimples, the copper pendant over the sloppy T-shirt, the hard nipples, no bra under. The examination disgusts him and he turns his head against the backrest as if going into a trance. There are a few minutes of religious meditation. The wizard appears to have fainted but he really hasn't. He mutters and mumbles meaningless phrases, mouthing like goldfish do.

'It's his age catching up on him,' Lella mutters. 'Let's sneak off while he's got his eyes shut, the son of a bitch doesn't deserve twenty dollars.'

Cautiously we slide towards the end of the sofa nearest to the door, ready to take off.

'Stay where you are,' orders the wizard in a deep hollow voice without moving his lips.

Embarrassed, we fall back onto the sofa, our fists bunched in our laps. He carries on whingeing to himself. All the while he's muttering away I hear the buzz of my ten dollars lost and all those dollars to come which won't come now, now or never, because we apprentice con-women hadn't counted on ventriloquism. If it is a duty to get rich, sacrosanct, and for some a creed, it rarely happens with the wholehearted collaboration and consent of a mind entirely subject to the senses. But neither Lella nor I had an ounce of determination. Her ideas went off like firecrackers on a string, the latest one overtaking the others and driving them away. In this manner she spun futilely and desperately in an eternal search for stability. And it would have seemed strange to me, if not downright abnormal, to learn what a font of knowledge she was in the art of conning the populace. Pity, though, because, of the many ways you could con them, it was the best one, like walking on clover. But any activity, big or small, requires patience, perseverance, a continuous twenty-four hour debate between you and your ego, your ego and yourself, a debate not to be interrupted even when you're on the dunny, even when you're welded to a well-hung penis, a penis which is not just strong but is backed up with a bit of intelligence.

We pay the man. There is no way out of it. He threatened to have us arrested. You should have seen the way he carried on. It seems that in a civilised country it's bad taste to protest when it's time to pay. You pay up and say 'thank you' even if you're given shoddy service by incompetents or charlatans. He yelled that he was the Master of the Masters of the occult. People of all races and classes came to consult him. Those who found it hard to defecate should take a laxative to get rid of the abnormality—perhaps this was an indirect reference to us. If we had known we would have taken a laxative the night before so he could have clearly read our washed-out guts.

In the lift Lella starts laughing, she laughs in the gold-carpeted lobby, strokes the leaves of the plants, spits in the fountain, pulls an azalea out of its pot, empties the pot and puts it like a hat over the jet of water in the fountain. With a discerning eye she chooses the most expensive plant, beautiful tendrils and fleshy leaves, costs 24.90.

'Grab as many as you want,' says the wretched woman. 'We'll get our money back.'

'I wouldn't know where to put them,' I say.

'Gees, you're stupid. Here,' and she thrusts a ceramic vase into my arms. 'Our venture has failed,' she says.

'It wasn't a bad idea, though.'

'To hell with it. Don't talk to me about it again.'

Anzac day is a great national holiday, a day for lots of drinking. Dusty ghosts who resurrect the martyrs of the past, no longer with us, kaput, and, after the parade, when cannon, machine guns, flags, patriotic speeches are all wrapped up and put away, the wankers rush off to the pub to wash the residue of desert dust out of their throats. For me it is a day of rest, a different day from the usual, a day which makes the migrant feel part and parcel of the system, you can be patriotic in any country, and it is a comforting feeling to admire the brand new weapons as they file through the opening formed by the compact crowd and to think of what could burst forth from that pacific and bedecked ironmongery should it rush to the front in our defence. That is why I begged Lella to come and pick me up early in the morning so we could go together to Martin Place to choose the best spot and then to have our photos taken with the Scots soldiers in their kilts. It's ten o'clock and Lella hasn't come. She won't come. I really didn't feel like getting up. It was so nice to stay in bed that it took quite an effort to get out of it. When you get up at dawn every morning, one morning just like any other, maybe until you die, and your sleep is troubled because you're besieged by problems, days of martial remembrance are of secondary importance. The dwarf at the factory is what torments me. The situation at work, one foot on the ground and the other on the precarious edge of uncertainty! The dwarf has become a nightmare which accompanies me to bed. She is becoming increasingly insolent day by day, faint praise, a retort, a nasty little trick which I can't avoid because I'm not burdened by a servile character. My fellow workers suffer from a petechial servilism which manifests itself by means of petechiae, it's written in the dictionary. In their case it's manifested by a gushing unctuous eruption supported by gifts, flowers, little chores at home, knitting, cakes, tomatoes, fresh eggs, string beans and lettuce from the home vegetable garden. All this she gratefully exchanges by giving overtime and easy better-paid sewing work. But for me the situation is getting more and more complicated, I've been demoted. In the beginning my pay packet competed with those of the fastest machinists, then it slowly slipped back, becoming thinner and thinner as though eaten away by termites. On Fridays I approach the counter to collect my pay timid and confused as if I were getting a handout from some charity. That's the state to which the dwarf has reduced me. This morning I woke up with bile in my mouth. Usually I give vent to my rage by cornering Lella against the wall or the edge of the table and throwing up everything I don't dare say to the dwarf's face. A bitter revenge. Lella isn't the dwarf, nor does she react, she listens in silence, inscrutable like a mummy, until I calm down.

Talk. Shout out my negative virtues. If only I could use my hands instead … Sometimes I want to die … And who'll cry over you, stupid? Just forget it. By the way, Helen wanted to die too. She really did … Now she's got a boyfriend, that ridiculous fellow with the short coat and clodhopper's trousers, Australian for a hundred and fifty years, preserved in plastic bags and moth balls until she became shipwrecked on this blessed isle. The caveman and the duchess or the duke and the cannibal woman, depending on which way you look at it. Just try to find out nowadays who is high class and who is low class, who is at the top and who is at the bottom of the social ladder. But this sidetracks the issue. I want to get to understand the new woman Helen has become in the two-week span since I last saw her. At midday I nibble something all on my own. I don't like to eat on my own when it's a holiday. I devour thoughts and sandwiches. I miss Lella, I miss Beniamina, whom I detest, I miss Sofia, Zio and his friends from the next chapter. They leave off where I begin, I leave off where they begin. It's the insane wheeling of a mad rollercoaster. Sofia comes and goes between the Miami Hotel and Falcon Street and does not give interviews, make appointments, receive visitors, for fear that news of her latest address could reach Nicola's ear. I've heard on the grapevine that Beniamina has gone to live with Claudia at Five Dock in a house with a swimming pool and three toilets, two inside and one in the laundry. So it's impossible to get in touch with either until they give out their addresses. Five *p.m.*, I'm taking a walk round by the park and unexpectedly end up in Helen's neighbourhood. I go up just to say hello and to learn the latest news. But Helen has disappeared, vanished without trace, without even a note to say goodbye. There's a little Chinese man in the flat now—minute bum, very thin, delicate little hands, head like a plucked bird, the whites of his eyes yellow instead of white. He's very polite but knows nothing of the previous tenant. At the agents they know even less.

'I don't know,' the Greek boss says, 'try looking round in the streets. She lives in the neighbourhood.'

Sure, maybe at the funeral parlour. So, I think bitterly, nothing lasts forever. As I go away I get pins and needles on my skin, like a sudden chill, there must have been a drop in temperature, a storm is about to break, papers and cans are thrown against walls, shutters banging, trees groaning, people running all hunched up. Hail as big as the pigeon's eggs which are growing at the base of my spine. An instant and I'm soaked. I hail a taxi and tell the driver to take me to Newtown. Maman is busy tending her tables. It's packed tonight and Maman is crying because according to her the business is going to rack and ruin.

'Lellina? She hasn't shown up here,' And then: 'Good God, you're soaking wet. Go and dry off in my office ... You'll get the place a bad name.'

Dry and revived by a slug of amber liquor drunk straight from the bottle, one of the many bottles piled on a silver tray in Maman's private drawing room, I go back to the cafe, order some toast and a cappuccino from the waitress and sit down at a corner table. At that very moment the painter comes in, thumbs stuck in his belt, goes to the bar and talks to the barman. I see him shrug his shoulders then slowly scrutinise the customers' deathly pale faces. When he gets me in focus and is sure that he hasn't mistaken me for some other woman who looks like me (I had put on my sunglasses and lowered my face over the plate—unfortunately it didn't work), he comes towards me chest thrust out and huffing like a bull, thumbs still thrust in his belt like a pistolero.

'Where's Lella?' he asks me, standing with his legs wide apart. He has been waiting for her for more than an hour outside the police station and the water has got into his car.

'I'm not her nursemaid,' I reply curtly. 'And don't sit here.' He was about to lower himself into the chair. 'This table is reserved for a party of French people.'

I am lying. He goes off muttering under his breath but not before throwing me a sideways thoughtful glance. He once shouted me a dinner and a strip show, that fateful night when we met up with Giacomo D., and in memory of the event, he feels he has the right to pester me if our paths cross. All those men Lella runs round with, from whom she bludges movies, outings, meals, money, follow her all excited, just as faithful as followers of Jesus Christ, patiently waiting for the moment when they can catch her off guard and screw her.

When I finish the toast and cappuccino Maman comes along to tell me a secret, an enormous wig on her head, fake beauty spot on her chin, violet lipstick thick as grease on her fleshy sensual still-fresh lips. She is old, she says, wants to go back to Lebanon, her cedar-perfumed homeland, and enjoy her old age. When I feel alone and desperate I too want to go back home with its smell of tarallucci biscuits and vino, the laughter and the friends. But everyone has to bear the cross they deserve. You can't have everything. Either feed your belly or nourish your spirit. Better the belly. Nostalgia can play itself out, if you don't get obsessed by it, that is. And as for me I couldn't care a damn about past troubles. I no longer have interests, stimulus, ambitions. I live as if I did not exist. Maman rushes off called by the cook. I get up and, heedless of the stares of the other people, fold the scarf that I always spread under my buttocks when I sit in Maman's cafe for fear of picking up some vagrant germ.

I am shouting and do not realise that I am doing it. I shout and get angry easily.

'Stop it, stupid,' says Lella.

I shout that I have only one chair which in any case is not mine but belongs to the Greek spinster. The gang is right, if you mind her you end up all in knots, you get screwed. She's got a screw loose, irresponsible, couldn't care less about others. I do not deny that she is an artist, altruistic, a kind-hearted type who cleans up after the farts of the disinherited, but despite this, despite her artistic merits, I cannot bring myself to share my bed, the furniture, the few square metres of airless room, without ventilation, without a ray of sunshine, narrow, smelly, damp, without freedom, where the two of us wouldn't even be able to move and with the added risk that we will not be allowed to cook since there are two of us. The Greek woman expects me to pay extra for the use of the gas on the pretext that I am Italian and it is common knowledge that Italians like to eat well, they cook, use gas, since they rarely go and eat in milk bars or fish and chip shops.

'Well then, you've turned up out of the blue … with your bags … without so much as a warning … and where are you going to sleep … who's going to put you up? … Where can I put you?' I say, shaking the bed which barely manages to hold itself together with string and sticky tape.

She takes offence and pours it all out. She's always known that I am a hypocrite, a stinker, a traitor, a daughter of a b---, a bigot. Her lips tremble. I yawn, grab a rag, start to do the dusting. I take her bulging calfskin case, real calfskin, from the middle of the room and put it out the door. The case still bears destination labels for Greece, France, Switzerland, Italy, Belgium, Holland. She gets as furious as a tiger. That I should play such a dirty trick on her.

'Lend me a pillow, just for the night. Tomorrow I'll look elsewhere,' she says, peering at me anxiously.

'There's only one pillow, just like there's only one chair, one blanket, one pair of sheets, one pot, one fork knife and spoon. Go on, check it out. Who's going to buy utensils with all this moving about …'

'I realise you'll have problems with your landlady,' she mumbles.

I'd rather be skinned alive.

'What's the big deal in putting me up for one night? I wouldn't have bothered you if I didn't know you like I do,' she says.

'Yeah, and what am I like? Tell me. I don't know myself. It happens, you know.'

'A leprosy-ridden bastard, that's what you are,' she blurts out. Something in my ironically moving tone of voice has struck her. 'You … you …' she stammers nervously. 'You, with your narrow limited life, you believe that you're in the eye of the storm, you believe you've achieved the agony and the ecstasy, eighteen-carat suffering. You don't appreciate a belly laugh, a drunken bout, a free-for-all among men and women. You keep yourself disdainfully aloof, leafing through one book after the other, and there's nothing that can get you to change your skin, to give vent to your hostility, to shake you out of your petty intellectuality. You … you don't live. Don't tell me that you're satisfied with this lousy life or I'll spit in your face. You're vegetating. You're wasting your time. You're slowly bleeding to death. Get all those mental blocks, all those fantasies, out of your head and wake up to reality. Reality is enthusiasm, sex, enjoyment of one day at a time. Don't programme a shitty future by dreaming about it. Give yourself a good shake. If you go on like this your sexual organs will be first prize for the worms in an Australian cemetery. You're not going to tell me that you emigrated to sacrifice your virgin graces to the worms. Oh, if I were in your shoes I'd shoot myself … and … what's all this rubbish you're writing down in your notebook … what's the use of your writing? It's incredible, your typewriter doesn't even work properly. Broken-down decrepit old thing. And these sheets of paper, use them to clean your bum, seeing that toilet paper is so expensive. What do you know of life? You don't screw, you don't drink, don't take drugs, don't sniff, you're not part of the gang. Get out of your shell. Observe people from real life, not from the shit-house keyhole. Sure, you're a very observant type, you've got an iron-clad memory, but you make a mountain out of a molehill, you store and pile up rubbish like a scrap-iron merchant ... ha, you don't really think you're a writer. Ha, ha, ha ...'

God, when she brays and shakes her head like this I could kill her.

'Take your clothes off, go on,' the order comes out of the blue as if it were the most natural thing in the world. I stare at her dumbfounded. She's busying herself with her photographic equipment, a determined expression on her face. 'Get a move on. I want you naked, now, with that look of horror on your face,' she bursts out.

'I'm not photogenic. I come out awful in photos,' I barely manage to say.

'I'll touch it up, OK? Or maybe you don't want to because you're jealous ... yes, jealous of me.'

I look at her even more dumbfounded than before.

'You're not taking me seriously as you should. Don't you know that I could do the mad-woman act and do you in tonight?' she says with a grimace. 'You little prick, you can turn out your silly little abortions of stories. Make room for me, you great, tragic, worn-out prick. I'm all on fire. One day I'll photograph the moon's cunt, the moon's prick, because I'll never stop looking for them. I mix with people of all lands, people of all races. I'm not afraid of being contaminated and in the end I'll find what I seek. In the meantime I'll hoard all these experiences. Your idiotic goings-on. Jesus, you make me sick. I'll give you something absolutely original to publish. An autobiography of my first twenty years, cut short at age twenty ...'

'My dear, you're not in a position to dictate anything to me,' I cut her short. 'You've got to leave New South Wales, or have you forgotten? Actually you'd be better off jumping on the first plane for Europe.'

She stares at me astonished, an expression of genuine terror on her face. I understand her, it's exactly the same terror I would experience. But, damn it, you play around with one bastard, fine, you take advantage of another one who's willing to be at your beck and call at all hours, right, but when you pull the chain on them make sure you pull it good so they go right to the bottom … a piece of shit often comes back up to the surface …

'How can I possibly disappear if I haven't any money … You got any?' she wants to know.

'Hold on, am I your mother or something? You're talking about deportation. Can you imagine me, yours truly, escorted back to Italy by the ears. No, I'll never return to Italy in these circumstances, the very thought is enough to bring on an epileptic fit. First of all I've got to make something of myself, a nest egg, money, money, those who go back without money …. Listen, I'll let you photograph me all decked out in ribbons, with make-up, passionate, whichever way you like, as you prefer, and I'll even rack my brains to come up with a sensational caption worthy of a thousand and one fucking nights to go with the photos, which you can sell door to door, at newsagents, bookshops, to your acquaintances, but go away, disappear, buzz off. Go and sleep at a motel, OK?'

'It's no use,' the wretched woman is insistent, 'here I am and here I stay. Give me something to drink instead and take that look off your face. Cheer up. No one will find me here. Haven't you changed your address too? If the police wanted to keep track of all those who come and go in rented rooms giving a different name each time they'd have a job and a half of it. Anyway, I swore I was a minor, from Persia, my parents had died in a road accident, and I pretended I didn't understand English. My landlady, who really doesn't understand a word of English, fainted …'

'But the Yugoslav guy who shot at the window said you're Greek, told them your name, that you have friends …'

'Aw,' she brays. 'He was stoned up to his eyeballs. Jibbering like an idiot that he wanted back his matchboxes with the marijuana. Anyway I hadn't seen hide nor hair of his marijuana. Hadn't a clue what he was on about. Do I look like a drug addict? Tell me.'

'No, you look quite normal,' I say, collapsing on the bed.

She bursts out laughing. 'You should have been there. It was really funny. I'll never forget it as long as I live. One minute Mirko was on about wanting his marijuana back and the next he couldn't even remember why he was there and why he had fired. I kept on saying, me foreign, me don't speak English, me don't speak English ...'

It had happened while Lella was watching television with the Greek girls. All of a sudden the glass in the lounge-room window had shattered with a loud bang. The girls, screaming, had thrown themselves behind the divan, followed by Lella and the landlady. Luckily the landlord wasn't home—he works evening shift in a biscuit factory. A few seconds later there was a second shot. This time Lella clearly saw the cluster of shot strike the wall above the fake fireplace, then silence, a weird unnatural silence. Lella crawled to the window on her hands and knees and looked out into the street. The street was empty except for someone running away down the street and the Yugoslav guy on the footpath still with the gun aimed at the house and jumping about tearing his hair in desperation because he'd missed the target. And since people never mind their own business, along comes the paddy wagon with siren wailing, and since the Yugoslav is still hanging about the scene of the crime the police put the cuffs on him and drag him inside the shot-up house. There is a confrontation, accusations, counter-accusations, questions. Lella pretends she doesn't understand. The Greek woman, who hadn't fainted when the shots were fired, faints at the sight of the police in her home, the little girls, one six the other eight, act as interpreters. Among all that babel of intersected languages—Greek, Slavic, Turkish, English—Mirko, the Slav guy, bursts into tears. He doesn't remember anything any more, goes into a severe state of shock, thinks he's a baby again, calls out to his mother to change his nappy and give him a lolly. Bewildered the police call the lunatic asylum and ten minutes later two strong male nurses rush in, wrap up Mirko and take him away. That left the little girls who didn't make any sense, the Greek woman who had fainted and couldn't say anything, and Lella who in the meantime had gone all mongoloid, foaming at the mouth, so they couldn't get any sense out of her either. The police go away telling Lella that she will have to be interviewed in order to help throw some light on this intricate matter. As soon as they're gone, she opts for a change of scene, takes her case, goes out through the back gate without so much as saying 'goodbye' to anyone, and comes straight to me. Where else could she go, anyway.

'Why run away? Why get me mixed up in it?' I ask.

She gives me that sneaky smile of hers, that smile which is supposed to mean many things but which just makes me mad.

'My dear,' she says, mimicking me, 'look out if they get their hands on you when there's drugs involved. It's a tough job proving you're innocent even if you are, and then you'd be doing a disservice to your community, putting it to shame. Would you do that to your own kind? Would you like to read in the press that we kill innocent angelic naive people, people without stain or blemish? And then, the very least that can happen to you, seeing you're a migrant, is deportation … jail … or the madhouse for those who don't speak English …'

'You're blowing it up out of all proportion,' my comment is accompanied by a long loud raspberry. Impossible. Unbelievable. 'I don't believe it.'

'Well don't then or we'll end up talking about it till morning. I want to sleep. Turn off the light.'

In the morning while the lady lies comfortably in bed I serve her coffee with a drop of milk in it accompanied by rebukes and much advice, enough to set her head spinning, or if not spinning at least to make her think about her behaviour while I'm away.

'Try to make as little noise as possible. Keep the blinds drawn. Walk softly—even if we're above the laundry someone could hear you. Don't smoke like a chimney, the room already smells like a men's toilet. Get rid of the ash in appropriate receptacles (shells and bottle bottoms), make sure that the matches are out. Don't burn my notes. Don't mess up my papers or I'll put your eyes out. Don't worry about them being stupid things. They're my follies and they have the same value as yours.'

I leave the house apprehensive, exhausted, anxious. I'd hate to change lodgings again. That eternal searching, disgusted by what you have to take. How healthy it would be to sleep in the pews of a church. She has no perception of this sort of mannered romanticism. It's like shouting yourself hoarse in front of a mule. She went back to sleep after drinking her coffee. I prayed that I wouldn't find her when I came back, that maybe she'd decide to take refuge at Maman's, dear understanding Maman, or with some prince charming or other, she knows lots of them. I was so absorbed in my prayers that at one stage I faltered, astounded at the requests directed to God Almighty. I rush along with the furies snapping at my heels, soup, bread, food to go with the bread and a ton of bitter mouthfuls to keep my job at the factory because I'm human and a woman. What does it mean to be a woman? I get hysterical, hysteria, womb, weakness. Crap. Haven't I more strength and character than thousands of maggot males put together? There, if I were only cunning, with it, and had a degree in Anthropology or some such, I'd throw myself into an article by some famous old male writer who lets himself rave on about feminism just to get rid of the complex created by the fact that a woman can have ten orgasms to the male's single desolate one. This morning I'm feeling rather jumpy. Thanks to Lella who has upset my solitary routine, or the book I read last night which has got me up in arms. A book written in the first person where the male writer fucks all over the place making abundant use of nymphomaniacs, and all sorts of women good and bad, just to fill his six hundred pages, which is a waste because had he condensed it all to ten pages it would have turned out a masterpiece. To my mind there is nothing more effeminate and ridiculous than a man who writes, especially a man who collects the Nobel prize for literature by writing about women.

All through the day while working the heavy sewing machine I think about the book I'd like to write, if I knew how to write, if I kept company with educated people, if I'd completed all my normal schooling just like those damned so-called poets ... But I'm a machinist, a factory worker, I work on the machine, I sew. I hate the work and unfortunately I've associated the work with the people around me, with mind-bending results. I do not cherish false hopes. I keep battling on. I don't owe anyone anything except maybe some spittle which I'd willingly dispense. I have to sort out these tangled details which fight each other in my innermost secret being, an operation which takes up the first five minutes once I've started up the industrial machine, after which all flows smoothly. Pressed by the hum of seventy machines, the murmuring of seventy voices, the smell of seventy bodies, the plot of the book I'd like to write, if I knew how to write, begins gradually to take on an indistinct shape. I formulate an idea, a phrase—I don't know if I'm explaining it properly—initially squeaking, puffing, sweating grey matter, and then all in a gush, waves, landslides, mountains of water overflow the dam erected round my mind. In the days and months spent at the D. & A. factory I could have produced voluminous novels—romances, thrillers, science fiction, autobiographies, pornography. If only I could have paid a secretary to sit by me at the machine, or even if I'd just had a recorder to record my thoughts, I would by now be acclaimed as not only the best but the most prolific self-educated woman writer.

On the way back home I am in a euphoric state. I am the winner in my dreams. In my dreams there is no need for me to suffer. I buy a couple of bottles of chilled beer. It's a very hot day and a cold drink is just what we need. I buy the beer because I'm thinking of dear disinterested Lella all locked up. She's better than I am, I bet that if I were in trouble she'd go through fire ... fire ... fire ... an alarm goes off in my head. God, I hope she hasn't set fire to the furniture out of spite. I rush up the stairs four at a time, find the door ajar, no one in the room, the furniture changed, the ceiling painted in green and black stripes. For an instant I'm petrified, thinking that I've come to the wrong pad, my pad sweet pad. These little houses all look the same from the outside, and inside as well, so if you walk about engrossed in your thoughts there's nothing easier than to walk into one rather than another. But it's my palace all right, wretched and narrow as it is, with its faded patched curtains, the lino lifting at various points, the dripping tap, the bit of sponge I've put in the sink to silence the drip. Yet I don't recognise the room I left only this morning. There's one bed too many, forming an 'L' with the other one, blocking the entrance as well as access to the dressing table mirror unless you stand on the mattress. The table has disappeared, replaced by a bamboo hat stand—silly because neither of us wears hats—on the fridge little flags from various countries stuck in two duck eggs painted Greek style, a silver tray with a roast chicken and a salad made of cucumber, yogurt, garlic, some round wholemeal buns in a straw basket, the walls completely covered with huge enlarged photographs in which repulsive carcasses wave their flabby members and withered jellyfish shine blood red in a reddish sunset frame. Many photos have the setting sun and a red berry bush in the background which throw into contrast the bloodless flesh of the unnatural falsified models. The most realistic photos are those of animals, sheep, cows, birds, dogs, caught by the shutter whilst miming the sanctity of acts which should constitute exclusive human prerogative. I don't know much about photography. I confess that I'm not even able to take a photo of a tourist standing in the Opera House plaza. She's probably a great photographer, poetic, I adore and respect her, but if she wants to make me happy she's got to take all those animal and human cunts and pricks off the walls because they make me uncomfortable. Yes, it's an interesting display, a dynamic exhibition, I say it without jealousy, without envy, but exhibiting in this way is like casting pearls before swine.

Silence in the house and it's dinner time. At this time the Greek woman dines, seated in the middle of the kitchen to see who comes in and who doesn't. But this evening I haven't seen her and that's strange. I go down the stairs without making any noise and eavesdrop at her bedroom door.

'Oh, the bull's balls,' I hear through the closed door, 'how natural they are, and how beautiful, strong, glossy is this Aborigine.'

No comment.

Hold on, Lella is at the bottom of this, it's her indisputable trademark. I turn the door handle just a little to see without being seen. And there's the

Greek woman gaping like an idiot at the spread-out photos. And there's Lella exciting her disused sex glands.

'I'll give it to you, seeing you like it so much,' she is saying.

The woman places the photo a few centimetres in front of her glasses, a smile of pleasure spreads over her horse-like face. She reminds me of my aunt when I set foot on the ship. I was sorry, desperate, full of fear at the unknown before me and was making a tremendous effort not to burst into tears while watching my brother go away, his shoulders shaken by sobs, along the wharf, impotent, more impotent and useless than that last minute renunciation of mine. She kept asking if the Australian sea was salty and blue and could compete with our own sea. Yes, I'll put it in writing, the sea is the same, maybe cleaner, the people are defective, only one eye in their half blind bum. I cough politely to warn them I am there, that I am part of the scene. The Greek woman gives a start, awkwardly bends over the table to grab the photos, cover them with her body. In her haste she has come down with all her weight on one side only, the table shakes, lifts, the photos fly and the woman finishes up on all fours on the floor.

Cheeks puffed with the effort to keep herself from laughing, Lella suddenly says, looking as if butter wouldn't melt in her mouth, 'Rosa poses for me, she's used to it, there's not need to be so formal.' And she winks both eyes at me.

'Yes, you haven't shown any of mine?' I say.

The Greek gets up, face as red as a beetroot. 'I was looking at the photographs as documents for sociological research,' she says faintly.

'Sure, I understand, no one is better than she is. She uses the camera like a psychiatrist uses mad people.'

She looks at me intently, as though seeing me for the first time, in fact up till that moment all we'd ever said to each other was 'good morning' and 'good evening' and often I didn't even say that since I went in and out at a run, head lowered, in case she stopped me to demand another increase on top of the gas bill or whatever. Now she fidgets shyly, joined hands in her lap. With a sigh Lella rakes the photos together with her foot then picks them up.

'Well, then,' she says, turning her back on us, 'thanks for the roast chicken, the salad …'

The Greek woman follows her up the stairs talking about tomorrow's weather, it would bother her if it were to rain … her teeth ache when it rains and she gets that insistent nagging pain in the ischium nerve which gets inflamed when the weather goes bad. By confiding in Lella about all her aches and pains she tries to re-establish that rapport which I have interrupted. She hasn't understood how volatile Lella is, incapable of comforting a spinster—suddenly she slams the gate on you, wipes you right out, even though she's been ready enough to show concern about mucus, caries, arthritis, conjunctivitis, to organise your funeral if necessary complete with bell, book and your portrait drawn in charcoal. When I didn't know her so well, when I didn't share with her my meals, my sleep, my problems, I used to think that she was the type who could kill herself over the slightest thing. Now I'm not so sure. She drags me into our room and slams the door shut on the Greek, then, remembering something, flings it open again and without so much as an 'excuse me' thrusts into her hand the photo of a naked man.

'She should go hang herself. She doesn't need talk. She needs a stud,' she says.

Since Lella has been sharing my mansion, or, to be more exact, the Greek woman's mansion, the three of us have been getting on in a rather odd way. Lella is patiently waiting for the room with the verandah—which at the moment is occupied by a drunkard New Zealander—to become vacant. The Greek has told him he has got to go. I'm going through a period of crisis. Living cheek by jowl with another woman, even if she were the best friend in the world, makes me go crazy. I always get up at the crack of dawn while she sleeps on like the idle rich, without worries, at her own pace. Around ten she starts to yawn, stretch out, amazed, surprised at the good fortune which has befallen her. She goes to the bathroom, uses the lavatory, has a shower. Then down to the kitchen dragging her towel behind her where a servile landlady serves up breakfast. It really seems that the woman has adopted Lella, seeing in her the lost pleasures of an afflicted arid youth years past when they lived like pigs in ethnic ghettos, worse than now. In any case Lella repays her by teaching her all the vices. She didn't smoke, now she smokes cigarillos. She used no make-up, now she does, spreading two tubercular stains on her cheek bones, brushing her eyelashes with cod liver oil, bleaching her moustache, her sideburns, she has gone on a diet to get rid of the surplus kilos, what the Greek doesn't eat we do thus saving on the grocery bill. She loves Lella's advice, a simple smile puts her on cloud nine, and she doesn't care if her mentor pinches the iron, the toaster, chairs, salt, derides her, makes fun of her, steals. They go out shopping arm in arm, buy transparent nighties, undies with a heart-shaped hole, with silk frills and veils, and if they have lunch in town it's not unusual for them to take in a blue movie without thinking twice about it. The days flow easily on. Time passes unnoticed when it's spent senselessly, insincerely In any case I was no longer alone, Lella was no longer alone, the Greek woman was no longer alone, we watched television together, we would drink a glass of rosolio together with the Greek woman's friends who would come visiting with their children. But there are nights, terrible nights, when, eyes wide open, disgusted, I look at my reflection in the flyshitted dressing table mirror, my face pale, heavy, unhappy. God, I think, I've really reached the end of my tether.

Sofia rings me up at the factory, her thin child's voice, excited, tells me she'll come and pick me up at five with a lovely surprise. Surprise, there are two surprises, her phone call and whatever she's got to show me. She tells me not to give her the slip, like sneaking out through the garage, or she'll never forget it. That's just what I was thinking of doing. I usually avoid going round with her. It's a gamble. Just when you're sitting in the club bar minding your own business and drinking a Bacardi and Coke, Nicola is likely to turn up suddenly with a black look on his face and you see Sofia tremble then leap off her stool and run round the tables with

Nicola in hot pursuit. Believe me, it's happened more than once and it's not at all funny. I racked my brains to come up with some excuse which wouldn't offend her, I thought of an attack of appendicitis, paralysis of the right arm, an epileptic fit, my big toe mashed up under the needle, lowering myself out of the window ... The dwarf comes up, swaying from side to side, her lips pulled back.

'There's someone downstairs asking for you, urgent. Looks like there's been a death in the family, her grandmother. Do you know that poor girl's grandmother? She's desperate. Must have been very close,' the dwarf's eyes are moist.

I pull the plug on the machine. The other workers mutter sympathetically, as though it were my grandmother who had died. I shake the dust from my hair, from my blouse. I don't even go to the dressing room nor to the toilet. I am so uptight that if I could give vent to my feelings by breaking up the machines I'd do so right under the dwarf's nose, and I'd also smash up Sofia's non-existent grandmother who dies whenever it suits her.

Outside, in the sunshine, Sofia takes me by the arm, afraid that I might get away from her. Brazen smile, well-tanned, looking lovely in a skirt with a yellow flower pattern and a sky-blue top. Waiting at the kerb a taxi with its door open and a gent around sixty, looking a bit uncomfortable, holding the handle of the rear door.

'You'll see, a real gentleman ... very rich,' she mutters greedily.

In fact he really looks a distinguished type, used to handling lots of money, more European than Australian, refined, well-dressed, no red nose or beer gut. I like him, but I don't let on.

'Listen,' I stop short a few paces from the taxi, glancing circumspectly all round, 'are you sure Nicola hasn't followed you?'

If he finds us with the old man he'll stick a knife into us for sure. And maybe in order to defend herself Sofia will accuse me of diverting her from the straight and narrow so I'll be the only one to get knifed.

'Why are you reminding me of that madman,' she screams, pulling to a sudden halt and casting roll-eyed glances left and right. 'Don't mention him. Not at moments like these.'

The old man comes over, curious, she shuts up at once and introduces me, he acknowledges with a slight click of his heels. We get into the taxi. I try to make myself as small as possible, to cover the part of my face on the window side with my hand.

'Beniamina will burst with jealousy,' Sofia sniggers, cheerful once more. 'I've pinched her escort.'

It's no news to me, it's an old, old, story. The other girls feel sorry for her, they see themselves reflected in her. Each one thinks she is the most fascinating, the most charming of our group and then Sofia is unlucky with men, they say. Now she explains with rancour, in a low voice, how she did for that bitch Beniamina by ringing the old man and telling him in the strictest confidence that she suffers from intestinal colic, only it's not really colic. She says that it's colic but there's a stink, a stench, of infected genital organs. 'I've put such a fright into him that as soon as she goes into his apartment, he'll jump about all over the place to avoid the slightest contact with her.' Beniamina has to go into his suite in any case since she works as a chambermaid in the same hotel. Her come-hither behaviour had aroused the interest of the rich old man who owns a great mob of sheep and cows at Tilba Tilba and doesn't know how to spend his money. Beniamina boasted about it to her bosom pal and look what happened, Sofia licks her whiskers like a satisfied she-cat, unable to sit still for laughing. The trick she has played on Beniamina has got her all excited, so much so that she's thinking of dropping a word in the manager's ear so Beniamina will get the sack. 'Serves her right. She made a very bad mistake in telling me about him then in introducing us. Greedy, stingy, wants a rich sugar daddy, does she!' She can't wait for the evening to end so she can run and tell Beniamina all about it. She detests Beniamina because she works so much. Works worse than an animal, at the clothing factory by day, five nights a week at the hotel, Saturday and Sunday in a pizzeria at Manly until three, four in the morning. Works on statutory holidays as well. How can she do it? Sofia would already have kicked the bucket. When does she sleep? Who knows.

When we get to the hotel, Sofia pushes me out of the taxi in a hurry. 'Hurry up, move, you snail, run to the lift,' and she runs off ahead of me, 'if she sees us there'll be hell to pay. She's quite capable of making a scene in public.'

In the lift she presses the button for the fifteenth floor. The old gent is paying the taxi and doesn't notice that we're disappeared. On the fifteenth floor, while we wait outside his suite, a door opens and out comes a swollen foot, a triangle of black satin skirt and a piece of white starched apron. Sofia looks at me in fear, there is nowhere to hide. But it's not Beniamina, although she has cellulitis-swollen feet and ankles like Beniamina.

'Hi,' says Sofia, 'we're waiting for daddy to bring the keys ... What's up?' she says touching me on the arm. 'Have you changed your mind? We'll have a good time, promise,' she repeats, not at all convincingly.

I'm not convinced either, especially when I see the old gent come out of the lift, spinning a key chain round his thumb, tie loose and a relieved look about him as if he had just got out of something that he didn't relish in the least. He obviously thought that we had got lost in the hotel's maze of corridors. An inexplicable look of stupefaction comes over his huge face when he sees us calmly waiting for him at his door. As usual Sofia doesn't notice a thing.

'We ran on ahead,' she says with a silly knowing smile, 'so as not to embarrass you.'

'Embarrass what, who?' he asks astounded. 'What on earth do you mean?'

'Ah, well, I made a mistake. We all make mistakes, don't we? I apologise,' she's bold enough to say it smiling spontaneously and running her tongue over her lips. 'The old fool's touchy into the bargain,' she whispers.

Anyway he behaves in a proper manner, steps aside to let us go in, invites us to sit down in the comfortable velvet armchairs, closes the heavy curtains. It's still daylight. The sun is just setting on the horizon. He politely asks us if we like the suite and what we would like to drink.

'Just some orange juice,' a deflated Sofia barely bleats out.

There is no orange in the fridge. He rings through to the restaurant to ask them to send up the drinks and a menu. Sofia throws me another mute worried look. I shrug my shoulders. Anyway I would like it if Beniamina did show up. Instead of a threesome it would be a foursome in honour of the old gent. A foursome three-quarters continental and one quarter local complete with the baaing and mooing of the Tilba Tilba sheep and cows. Sofia gets up worried, cigarette trembling in her mouth, ashtray in hand, walks indecisively the length of the room, finally asks where the bathroom is and locks herself inside. She's in there for a while before the maid turns up. Lucky for her it's not Beniamina this time either. Maybe Beniamina is sick or has taken the evening off, I point out to Sofia as she quickly comes out of the bathroom. 'And maybe it's raining gold nuggets,' she comments.

Reading through the menu she lets herself go, orders three different types of hors d'oeuvres, two servings of oysters for both of us, lobster, smoked and cured ham, French bread it must be French, she says, hot and buttered, mineral water Italian, of course and a calzone pizza. The waitress has no idea what sort of pizza it is, she's never heard of it. She stands there poised, pen in hand, huge protruding teeth shiny with saliva.

'What do you want pizza for?' I butt in.

'Keep out of it.' Sofia threatens me with the menu, jumping up and down just as if she had been suddenly struck by an attack of the Saint Vitus dance. 'I want a calzone from the Manly pizzeria where Beniamina works,' she says.

'You're obsessed over Beniamina. Watch out or she'll punch you up good.'

We debate the matter as if the man who is providing such lavish hospitality simply isn't there. In fact he's not saying a word. Silence. I feel that there's a rather uneasy atmosphere in the room. The waitress has enough written down in her order book to feed a regiment of starving people.

'I really like the pizza they make at Manly,' Sofia mumbles. Then she agrees that it's better to forget it and sends the waitress away.

We sit down at the table. The old gent has got the colour back into his cheeks and only occasionally does a look of alarm come into his blue eyes. He seems uncertain whether he can trust us. Sofia whispers very softly into his ear. He orders her to open her mouth and examines her small, white, perfect teeth one by one, then, in a more polite manner, he orders me to open my mouth. I find it hard to understand what's going on. I find it strange, to say the least, that he should examine us like horses at the saleyards. Throughout all this he's kept an inscrutable expression on his face. Disappointed, Sofia leans towards him again and this time I do as well ... and hear the bitch telling him not to be taken in by my smooth face, because I'm older than she is, nor by my white teeth because I wear dentures. I feel like laughing but somehow I can't get it out. Jesus, she'd be capable of telling him that I've got cock's comb, that I stink because I'm infected by chronic syphilis, that I have bad breath, that my nails fall off, that I have a cataract and my eyes weep in the morning. Without thinking twice about it, I grab a fork off the table and stick the prongs in her bum which she keeps turned towards me. She jumps and screams like a chicken having its feathers plucked. There's a knock at the door. The food has arrived. I recompose myself. So does Sofia, thrusting her chest out and throwing me murderous sideways glances. She's lost her appetite. She picks at her food like a bird. A heavy atmosphere, pregnant with disquieting reproaches. Strange way of having a good time. Pull yourself together, Sofia, it's not like you to dwell on an act of spite by a friend. You needed that prod with the fork, and I'd give you another one up your nose. Let me tell you that you're just a walking chamber-pot ... But to get over the feeling of hurt all she needs is a glass of wine and a puff at a cigarette between one mouthful and another. She's drunk some wine, she's sucked oysters, she feels obliged to throw up a burp. Even though our host is struck by this, he doesn't show it. To burp like a Turk is part and parcel of custom, of folklore even.

'We don't do that in my country,' she asserts abruptly.

'I like you. You're not a frivolous type. She's a half crazy drifter, thinks I'm interested in her but she bores me,' he says, his cheeks red.

Sofia shrugs her shoulders as if to say, promised you, didn't I, that we'd get a good laugh out of this. Australians don't have a sense of humour nor do they take kindly to criticism. They're full of complexes. Sugar him up. You can have him. He's all yours. Didn't you say you preferred older men?

She's not wrong, really. I've always liked the oldies. Thanks. But it's the old man who gets the full benefit of the 'thank you' accompanied by a dazzling smile. Sofia gets tummy ache, feels sleepy, becomes agitated. She wants to rest on the bed for a while. As soon as she goes off, he draws his chair close to mine, begins to pet and hug me. I literally leap out of my chair, bang against the wall just where the nineteenth century style lamp is fitted. The lamp falls to the ground and shatters.

'Nice burst,' he exclaims in English, pushing me against the wall. He's on top of me and he weighs a ton. He has a really big erection.

'Please,' I implore, 'please.'

Mamma mia! Is this the savage desperate defence that patched-up virgins put up when sex has now become taboo after nausea? They all try it on, whether they've experienced the miracle or not. I thought I was more progressive, emancipated, free, a committed feminist. But, good God, it's that time of the month, my stomach hurts, my back hurts. Sofia is also menstruating. I'd like to know why she always gets it when I do, maybe she gets it twice a month because she's weak. We'll probably have to put up with the old man's verbal abuse. Anyway how can we get it through to him now that all we wanted was a chat over a good meal so we could penetrate the Australian soul? Sofia won't tell him, that's for sure. She is the sort of woman who can be bought for a plate of pasta and beans, a worthy pupil of Beniamina. Meanwhile he is kissing my chin, my throat, little sweet tender mature kisses. Respond, that's it, be fondled, love, be loved, break this isolation, this barrier of suffering and inertia, lacerate resignation, abandon yourself to fantasy in the arms of a refined man with naive blue eyes.

All of a sudden he pulls himself off me, grabs my ears and shakes my head as though it were a bell. 'Are you a lesbian? Tell me. You're two lesbians. You wanted to play a trick on me.' Yet another shaking, another pull, my ears nearly fall off in his hands. Tell him what? My guts are complaining. I should not be manhandled like this straight after meals. I am a delicate, sensitive type who ought to be treated gently. I hate to be forced. This way you can stuff the much-vaunted equality between male and female. It does not make sense. It has no purpose. It's like allowing a pig to rape you, to let him masturbate in your flesh. I'm the one who has to give the go-ahead, and I did not give the old man any encouragement, nor did I get drunk, so his heavy advances are quite out of place. His attack has exhausted me, has suddenly electrified me, to the point that I might consider giving in. Sofia bursts into the room, eyes popping out of her head, malicious. The old man leans against the wall on an elbow and sighs.

'Australian men are like little boys,' she says, giving emphasis to her words with a regal air. 'If he were an Italian, Greek or Turk, he'd already have had the pants off us by now … You might as well have it off with a dog … the more I get to know them the more they disgust me. You know what I think about it.' She's talking in Italian, of course.

'No, I don't. Anyway you should explain to me why you always drag that nut Nicola along with you.'

The old man's eyes look at us in turn.

'Oh, him. He persecutes me. He's too jealous. He wants to marry me, has been begging for ages. I can't get away from him. It's quite a sacrifice … But you know it would be a sacrifice with anyone, they're all obsessed with virginity. The only solution would be to get yourself patched up over and over and over again …'

I cut short her avalanche of lies. 'But you're the one who's running after him. Nicola would have dumped you ages ago.'

Sofia becomes angry, forgets where she is, throws her half-smoked cigarette on the carpet and stubs it out with the point of her shoe. At this point the old guy springs to life, waving his arms like a windmill, begs, implores, orders, demands that the matter be settled to his satisfaction. He has never found himself caught up in such a disgraceful situation. Are we lesbians or aren't we? We'd better tell him. Do we want money? Yes, he's understood all right. Do we think that fifty between the two of us is all right?

'Fifty what?' Sofia asks greedily.

He does not reply, wavers, looks like he wants to take back what he has just said. A shadow comes over his ruddy friendly face, a shadow which grows increasingly bigger. I am afraid that he will break everything in sight. I'm sorry for him. I'm sorry for me. I'm sorry for Sofia, and to be fair I'm even sorry for Beniamina who is running around with a tray on one of the hotel floors. Eventually the old gent shakes himself, giggles as if he had made an unexpected decision, rushes into the adjoining room, puts his hand in the pocket of his trousers and pulls out a roll of banknotes, peels off a fifty dollar bill, smoothes it out, waves it about, and puts it down on the dresser. Sofia envelops me with a pleading glance, a desperate glance, she doesn't know which way I'll jump, whether I'll back her, or the old gent, or whether I'll stick to the virginity routine. Since in our group they were all self-avowed virgins, the latest arrivals were even more vehement in advertising their saintly state. And silly Sofia also brings up the subject of her virginity every now and then. I don't care whether she's ever been one or not, it's just that ever since I set foot on this blessed land I've had it up to here on the subject, so much so that I expect to blow up from one moment to the next.

'How'll we get out of it with the old man?' says Sofia laughing. I don't know why she's laughing. There's nothing to laugh about, if anything she should be crying. The old gent, not without some effort, has joined the two single beds together, gets out the pyjamas, flies past us into the bathroom and comes back with some towels, then he goes to the kitchen cupboard, loads himself with glasses, a bottle of liquor, a jug of cool water, goes back into the bedroom, unloads the stuff and claps his hands.

Sofia backs off towards the door, an idiotic stupid smile on her face which suits her to a T. 'You've misunderstood. Sure, we can excuse you given the circumstances, the delicious dinner. But we're not that sort of woman. We're minors. We're not allowed to stay out all night. Do excuse us,' she says putting her hand on the door handle.

'Whores. Lesbians. I'll call the police,' he hisses.

'I wouldn't advise it,' Sofia replies throwing open the door. 'We're the minors. Now I'll scream. I'll shout for help.'

'Get out, out,' he retorts, waving the towels in the air. He leaps to the door and slams it behind us. The bang echoes in the corridor.

'You're not used to high-class people,' pouts Sofia. 'I won't come and get you any more when golden opportunities like this turn up.'

It's not late. On seeing the ground floor bar Sofia suggests we should go in and have a drink. I refuse. We part in the street. She goes off muttering.

I arrive home sunk in the black gloom of failure. The lights are all on. In the breakfast room mad Mariolino, seated in Lella's lap, mimes for the Greek woman his millionth rendition of his dog's funny little ways. A Pekinese bitch, a four-footed creature with human feelings. It seems that she really did exist. She died of heartbreak. She was jealous, possessive, spiteful, had coughs, colds, convulsions of jealousy for her master who was a great lover. Mad Mariolino. Obsessed with cunts. A fanatic. A cuckold. Always quarrelling with women because they won't give it to him. They make his balls sweat. Finally he makes it and goes for broke. One afternoon while I was coming out of the Leichhardt bookshop he accosted me with these words, 'South American, are you? Giulia's friend?' And he gallantly offered to carry my bag of books. As we walked along, he told me about the feats of Fru Fru, a female bitch who died because of too much love. A small tear shone in the corner of his eye. I thought of the moment in which he picked up the story in one of those cafes in

Parramatta Road or Norton Street where our over-endowed deadly migrant men hang out. The first few months I was in Australia I would make a point of going there with Lella to have a coffee and at the same time observe and learn local customs. Wonder of wonders nothing became impressed in my mind like those plague-ridden sessions listening, between one short black coffee and another, to talk about prostitutes, whores, bums like this, bums like that, she's a great one, I did her seven times, she hadn't had enough. I'd be able to do it eight times. And I ten. Aw, I do it under the husband's noses, easy, while the fool plays the pokies at the club I fuck his wife in the car. Ha, see that pimp he's bought his house with the money his wife earned at Kings Cross. While eating and drinking they would spit out names, surnames, nicknames, vital statistics, colour of pubic hair, length of horns. It all seemed to me quite extraordinary and I would write even the farts down in my notebook.

How to describe Mariolino? The first thing which springs to mind is to compare him with the description of a turd given in the Garzanti Italian dictionary. A solid piece of cylindrically shaped shit—flattened at the top (my gratuitous observation). He's a turd and he will always be one. He's unhappy, he's saying, he feels lonely, in need of sincere affection, but he immediately starts to rave if his sexual prowess is thrown into doubt. His wicked coal-black eyes sparkle, his concave forehead bursts out hairless and his long thinned-out swept-back hair no longer manages to hide his bald skull. An ugly and vain man responsible for the bitch's death. They celebrated their birthday together in December.

Not long to Christmas now. My second Christmas. I am still suspended in uncertainty. Couldn't be any more broken-down than I am. My liver's fit to burst. The balls which have taken the place of my ovaries too. I've had it up to here with faeces, bile, trickery, exploitation, cowardice, barely sufficient but secure wages. Christmas. Prevent the Child from being born. I am the Christ become old and rusty on the nails. Prophet of evil. Christ gone wrong. An artificial abortion. In retaliation I eliminate His mother, the Holy Virgin Mary, egging her on to revolt against Father, Son and Holy Ghost. I dress her in skirts with such daring slits which show yet do not show what is underneath. Stilt-long legs for high-heeled shoes are the fashion, loudly acclaimed by the populace. This oh-so-couth populace that no one bothers to take down off the cross. We all meet on the summit of Calvary, to give humanitarian and artistic interviews, exchange points of view, nightmares behind our smiles and defeats, continual, repeated defeats.

I've stuffed my ears with cotton wool so as not to hear Mariolino. The bullshit filters through anyway.

'Oh woe is me,' he lays it on like a born actor. 'Who will look after me now that my guardian is gone?' He's talking about the bitch. The Greek woman is beginning to show signs of impatience. All those praises, even if addressed to a dead bitch, are not to her liking.

'She talked like a person,' Mariolino goes on. 'And I loved her, I really did. Why did I let her die, why?'

No one replies. Words fail us in rising to this particular occasion. Mariolino writhes in Lella's lap, his short legs don't even touch the floor. A gaily coloured bird chirps in a cage hanging by the window, the family cat dances attention upon it.

'Ah,' Mariolino gives vent to a tormented sigh, 'I still haven't got over my loss. I should try a change of scene … Take a trip … I'd like to get married. Here,' and he hits his chest in the region of the heart, 'here beats my undoing.' He throws a knowing glance at the Greek, hand over his prick, those who want to understand do and those who don't want to don't understand that it beats there as well.

The Greek woman does not seem in the least perturbed. Her eyelids are heavy with sleep. She mumbles something about the prayers she has to say before going to bed, prayers that take an hour or so of her time. She yawns. Mariolino yawns. Everyone yawns long and wide.

'I'm not boring you, am I?' he exclaims, cold and arrogant.

'It's been a pleasure,' says the Greek, getting up.

Mariolino jumps up with a pirouette-like motion. 'Can I call on you again?'

'Whenever you like.'

'We still have a few things to settle, we two.'

'I don't understand,' she says uneasily.

'Take your time. Take all the time you need,' Mariolino replies, looking her over from tip to toe with a slight bow of approval. He puts on his little check hat and clicks his heels together. After which Lella and I escort him to the front gate. He pulls up short in front of the gate.

'She seemed rather cold to me. An iceberg, I'd say. I don't think she'd be compatible with an ardent character like me. As you both know, for me sex is everything.'

'But you acted as though you found her repugnant,' Lella reproves him harshly.

'What do you mean?' Mariolino stammers in a blue fit. He is on the verge of getting hysterical. 'I'm educated, intelligent, likeable. Where will she find a better man? I've made an enviable position for myself. I have a car, two flats, one here and one in Italy, all paid off … As for you … you could have warned me that she's so ugly. She's not rich. She's not plump. No style, no personality, no grace. She's got hairy legs, a moustache, thick eyebrows, a yellowish complexion, her tongue hangs out like a dog's, she's no spring chicken. Never laughs, what's she in mourning for … the death of her prick?' Trembling with suppressed rage, he lifts the lapels of his corduroy jacket to protect himself from the warm south wind and goes off without saying goodbye.

As for us, we've learned that the Greek woman is a type who is difficult to please while Mariolino hankers after unspoiled eighteen-year-old dowried maidens of noble family.

We're going out with the house painter and his mate, also a painter. On Thursday there is an exhibition of paintings by young Jewish artists at Paddington. Lella has the invitations. We are on the ground floor, right in the midst of all the confusion, with the two painters who are holding plates of savouries. They scrutinise the canvasses from a distance of a few centimetres like jumping fleas. With brush in hand they can paint in a more inspired style and at cheaper prices. Lella whispers in my ear that we look out of place with all those fat bejewelled women about and that we had better go off to the opening of the new casino. On the way we stop off at a pizzeria for a snack.

At the casino we meet Beniamina, Claudia, Carmelo and mad Mariolino who from a distance scowls offended and resolute. A couple of pros in long dresses, badly bleached hair piled up in a knot with hairpins dropping out, join our group attracted by the look of the painters. To spite us the two bitches (Claudia and Beniamina) commandeer the attention of the painters and the pros. We see them gesticulating. Our escorts blush to the roots of their hair. I'd really like to know how much Beniamina's getting. The old sow has a really great gift for arranging close encounters of an illicit kind. Free drinks and savouries here too. Five dollars lost on a bet. Lella gets high. The painters disappear with the pros. The evening which had begun so badly ends up the same way and when we return home we find the landlady out in the corridor in her nightie hopping mad and ready to let fly.

'You scum,' are her welcoming words. Our behaviour is getting her a bad name in the neighbourhood. This is how we thank her, by giving her a bad reputation. It won't be long before the Greek community won't talk to her any more.

We went straight to our room without saying a word. For quite a long time we put up with screams, insults, swearing, threats of eviction. When Lella couldn't take it any more she flung open the door and threw everything she could lay her hands on down the stairs: the bamboo hatstand, pots, pans, mattresses, the bed. Sobbing, the Greek woman protects her head with her hands at the same time trying to calm down Lella who has always been her favourite, her slightly crazy artistic goddaughter. She takes it all back, absolutely everything. She is sorry she lost her temper. She was worried for Lella. This life of revelry could ruin her health. She offers to carry up the bed and the mattresses, to bring a cup of tea or coffee, but Lella has already pushed me inside and locked the door. For a few minutes there is a soft sobbing, then silence.

'I want to throw up,' says Lella.

'Go right ahead.'

'How quiet it is. How peaceful. I don't want to go to sleep now,' and instead of throwing up she uncorks the bottle of ouzo which the Greek woman had given her. I drink a small glass of water with a bit of ouzo to keep her company. 'Athens,' she mumbles. The city where she was alive. Study, friends, people with whom you could measure yourself. Her roommate, a final year medical student, very beautiful and lesbian. Used to take drugs. She got blennorrhoea. Genuine students' stuff. Went overboard. To wrack and ruin. Now she's convinced her womb is all twisted and mutilated. Discouraging. Shameful. It all comes out. She wants to keep talking on and on.

Two o'clock. I get into bed. She lies down beside me. She's trembling. I put my arm round her shoulders, I'd like to comfort her but I'm so much in need of comforting too. All of a sudden she tickles my tummy, my nipples, wraps her legs around mine … A bubbly sensation even though it remained impressed on me like a fiery brand, a feeling of repugnance, the embarrassment of her caresses, the disgust at her manipulations. Afterwards I looked at her for a long time while she slept, lips sullenly drawn, child-like relaxation, white skin, nicotine-stained fingers grasping the pillow. What do I know about her? She hates men, she hates women. She strikes a masculine pose, masculine gestures, blusters and brags like a little castrated man.

At dawn she's asleep or pretends to be. I move quietly. Another day. Living is becoming an increasingly frustrating business. I'm tired of battling against injustice. Fear of the dwarf is softening my brain. Loathsome imbecile. Disgusting working class. There're those who invent Jewish grandparents just to make money and there're those who die at the presses eight months pregnant. There're those who have an abortion and those who send their babies away.

Merde.

And the Australians, will anything good ever come out of them? Mean, petty, ignorant. Australian women wander from puberty to the grave staggering from one pub to another in a frenetic search for humanity through the sexual act.

My thoughts are disordered.

It's frightening. Exchange the smoke screen for a little bit of courage. I enter the factory with my heart in my mouth. On the machine a whole week's sewing which has to be done all over again. I'll kill the dwarf this time, I really will ... and then I'll lose my job, work, work, work. If I lose my job now that there's a recession, what will I do? I haven't a friend who will give me a crust of bread. Work. Animals. Pack asses. The women especially have the sensitivity of Sardinian mules. Make me take back all that stuff about what's going to happen next, welfare aid, my love for this young, healthy, naive country. The dwarf struts along, finger raised menacingly, in all the splendour of her four foot six inches. A wink here and there at one of those women who never tire of working. The row of working bitches wag their tails joyfully at her passage. A female Christ would be willing to die if it meant saving the dignity of everyday living, but is there one woman here worthy of salvation? If I have to sweat blood to survive I'll sweat blood right to the last drop sucked out by modern pumping machines like they use to milk cows, but don't make me suck up to the dwarf supervisor who rules the family budget with an iron hand and boasts that she has a TV set in the toilet so she can watch television while sitting on the dunny. No I won't do it, I'll never do it. It's a year now that I've been sweating blood for my weekly pay. And that's enough. I raise my voice in protest, stand out from the herd. 'I'm quitting, I quit,' I scream, but more than a scream it's a death-rattle.

Ah, I was really high after that piece of bravado! I sang as I walked across the park, my mind wiped clean. No regrets, no worries about the future. And yet, if only I could have guessed what the future had in store for me I would have shot myself. I was free. I revelled in the balmy breath of freedom. Humming I brushed past Turkish and Arab women, neckerchiefs covering half their faces, violet jumpers, pistachio green skirts over bright blue trousers. I brushed past a beetle in perennial mourning, a curly-haired moustachioed youth. I jumped over a drunk lying on the footpath. Sidestepped a dirty tattered woman under the influence of drugs. The little green-eyed Aboriginal boy was smiling at me.

A note stuck to the mirror, 'I've had it. I'm off to Surfers Paradise. Lella.' The Greek woman had rushed up the stairs after me. I don't open the door. She can go to hell. I know less about it than she does. I feel more down in the dumps and at a loss than she does. And anyway while I was away she probably read the goodbye note over and over again, probably watered it with a flood of tears. The note's still wet. All of a sudden I'm aware of the cruelty generated by poverty, not that poverty which is a consequence of riches squandered in the sun or vanished because of financial disaster, but poverty of spirit spawned by an empty existence, the aimless struggle in a country which often offers only suicide or madness. I feel thirsty. I have a drink of water. I stand as still as a stone in the middle of the room. The room incarnates expectations without dreams, without myths, without hope. Write. Moments like these are the best for writing. I take the cover off the typewriter which a year's idleness has covered with mould, a cockroach jumps out of the keyboard and my inspiration disappears. I leaf through the illustrated calendar given to me by the woman at the greengrocers. August, the feast of Santa Rosa. Silly name. My thoughts turn to name days. I've never liked Rosa. Makes me feel stupid. If I were to change my name I would automatically become the personification of a motive for action. I feel a great tiredness in my bones. If you're tired, sit down, I tell myself. Go on, sit down, who's stopping you? I drag the chair up to the window, dust it off. I could remain seated forever in the chair for what it costs me, or tie myself to it by the back-rest so I won't burn up a lot of kilojoules or physical energy which means that I would eat less, walk less, use up less shoe-leather, spend less, begin to save. Good, you're getting acclimatised. Soon you'll see snakes slithering over the walls, bats hanging from the light, frogs laying eggs on the dresser, gnomes raping you in the mouth nose and ears. You'll soon become the carbon copy of that great army of people who don't eat so as to stop shitting. Good. Great. Go on, act crazy. All you need is for them to haul you off to the madhouse. Pull yourself together, you idiot. Hang a dozen or so canary-filled cages at the window. Go look for sparrows, plant cauliflowers in the garden, get busy making paper flowers, embroidery on canvas, knit jumpers. Think of the future if you want your microscopic destiny to survive. But pull yourself together, for God's sake. Talk to the wind, the stunted lemon tree, the garbage bins, the oh-so-decorous weatherboard dunnies in the back yards. Shout out a greeting to that dirty old man pissing against the wall in the darkened street.

When did it happen, and why? Twelve months. Twelve years? A hundred and ten years ago? There were seven of you, four were lesbians who used to hold each other by the hand. What a laugh! Where has Helen gone? It did me good to laugh in her face every once in a while.

I go knocking on the doors of clothing factories. There's not much work around. I don't see any of my dear friends. Then Saturday, at dusk, the two sluts come to see me. Claudia is a picture of health and freedom from worry. On her head Beniamina wears a black turban sprinkled with little brass-coloured stars and twinkling like a Christmas tree. They tinkle and jingle all over with bracelets and pendants which they have obviously stolen from the chain stores. They ask after Lella. Lella is in Surfers Paradise. They seem to be delightfully impressed and amazed at the news. Especially Beniamina who never takes the bus and has never gone on a trip.

'Join us,' Claudia invites me. She's just dying to introduce me to Armando, the rich guy from Salerno. Her new protector.

I change in a flash. Say hello to Armando as I get in the car. A quick dash and we're at the Vesuvio. A lot of the tables are taken by uniformed Alitalia pilots and hostesses who are on strike. We eat and eat. Put on a drop of spicy sauce. Have some fresh assorted fish. Peppered mussels, prawns, trout in the bag. Our escorts smile with their mouths full. Once they've paid for the dinner they expect the right to screw us. They laugh in the restaurant mirrors. I laugh and enjoy myself. I'm laughing now, I'll pay later, later I'll fuck or be fucked. Better to fuck than be fucked. The faces of the two tailors display a grasping hunger for cunts, a far cry from vermicelli alle vongole and two finger thick steaks. Armando displays the satisfied air of a man who's made it and can thus afford to keep a girlfriend. Claudia tells me in confidence that Armando's wife is neurotic and that he hasn't touched her for years, they live together like brother and sister, and that Beniamina has lowered herself to washing Carmelo's clothes, just so she can have someone who pays for her supper, and that Carmelo is a fleabitten old goat without a roof over his head, that is he's got a roof, a two-bedroom flat with a balcony which he has rented out while he goes round begging everyone for a place to sleep. It gives me indigestion to swallow gossip all the way to the dessert, to the coffee. When the bill comes the two men split it up between them. Beniamina turns away for fear that Carmelo might decide to ask her to pay her share. Then we rush off to the Apia Club to exercise our legs. On the dance floor ugly dwarfish men cling to the bums of lanky droopy-breasted women who at the end of the evening desire the impetuosity of European bulls. The male vocalist's tremulous, forced, sentimental voice puts me in a mood of ferocious malcontent at the thought that wretches like him bleat about love, honour, our mothers back home, and sip their drinks with little fingers raised while engaging in idle malicious gossip. My pupils are clouded over by such beauty. My ecstatic gaze flows over the turning dancers, the chaste maidens who won't accept an invitation to dance unless the request is first made formally to father, mother, grandfather and grandmother. Behind us a wedding reception is in full swing. Clodhoppers in hired dinner suits and bow ties, matrons bandaged in shocking pink, pastel green, faded blue, red pig-blood organza. In their ringleted hair and necklines are fresh rosebuds. They keep turning their heads round like spinning tops, throwing challenging glances as if to say admire our good taste, our inborn elegance, our flair for fashion, and may the merciful God consign them to the deep. I dance with Sergio who's a bit of a queer. Lella, I wish you were here to take a photo. I dance divinely. They should make me Miss Ballerina or whatever. Beniamina, in Carmelo's arms, her trinkets tinkling to the beat of the music, dispenses greetings and smiles to the people seated at the tables nearest to the dance floor. Carmelo, for his part, waggles his bottom like a high class uninhibited prostitute. Every now and then his rear end connects with mine and I am pushed up hard against Sergio. 'Darling,' the queer whispers in my ear. Sure, darling but not a virgin. You don't find virgin cunts in this country unless on the postcards sold to tourists. Carmelo and Sergio bet their last cent to see who'll be the first to set foot on the shores of Italy and marry the immaculate maiden. Nothing wrong with it if they don't use as a yardstick that sow which Mimmo the pizzaiolohas in tow. A swarm of forcefully ejected turds, they're either talking about money or about virginity.

It's Christmas. I'm crying. It's something to do with the festivities. My tears are like a waterfall. The dams have broken. Taut fists in my eyes to stem the flood. I cry and make noises like the surf against the rocks, or rather like the sound of the seagull's cries. I cry and yet desire to comfort the crazy little girl who used to believe in Santa Claus. Christmas eve, Christmas, New Year's eve. A year. Preposterous. I'm having a breakdown. So as not to go mad I go to the Domain to listen to the mad orators, then I go to the rocks in the Royal Botanic Gardens to read a book.

The first day of the year. It's not yet midday and Carmelo turns up dressed to the nines. He's come to take me to lunch. I waver. Blush. They have invited me out of pity. They're sorry for me. It's as plain as day. Don't accept. Refuse to go. Tell him to go to hell. Tell him you couldn't care less about it. Go. I would have to make an almost heroic effort to reject the girls' kindness. Send Carmelo back empty-handed. Hurl insults. Undermine that superior ability they claim in being able to adapt to any way of life.

'Have you decided to come, or not?' Carmelo asks impatiently.

'I'm coming.' Because I am a woman of straw. My desperation is like a straw in the wind. And anyway I hunger after turkey, cassata, panettone, confetti, Christmas carols, greetings. Beniamina and Claudia are busy with the lasagna. In the meantime Carmelo, Sergio, another long thin tailor, and I are swimming in the pool. At Carmelo's command Claudia hands us a bottle of chilled champagne and some glasses. As soon as she turns her back Carmelo rakes up some muck about her. She's not as tough as Beniamina, she gives it away generously to everyone. The word goes round from one friend to the other. Sergio's had a go too even though he's half gay, but the tall guy hasn't since he's a confirmed queer.

'Her mouth's just right for a screw,' he exclaims in a burst of disgust and clucks his tongue against his palate. 'Pity her cunt's on sideways.'

At this latest remark the queer and the gay guys burst out laughing weakly.

'Giacomo D. dumped her, you know,' he goes on in a conspiratorial tone. 'She would have stayed on despite all those airs she gives herself, as she's convinced that one day Armando will decide to send her to Rome with a case full of money to open up another travel agency with herself as manageress, and the stupid woman is even convinced that he'll eventually divorce his neurotic wife and marry her. But all he wants is to get rid of her because she's become an embarrassment,' he finishes with a satisfied air and just to show how smug he is about it he shows off by doing a couple of somersaults in the water. By gossiping away like a housewife Carmelo does manage to achieve something—to set Claudia and Beniamina at loggerheads. The two detest each other, although this is also partly because Claudia has the devil's own luck in attracting well-to-do men.

My impression that something is not right is confirmed when we sit down at table. A richly spread table, the men have spared no expense, dried and fresh fruit, wine, orangeade, lemonade, chinotto, champagne, Sicilian cassata, apple pie, peach pie, and a tray of golden crusty lasagna. Everyone has a serving of lasagna on his plate, a glass of wine. No one talks. They eat with lowered heads. My first few mouthfuls of lasagna godown the wrong way. Suddenly there is tension in the air, irate glances from the two women. I stop myself from reaching for pepper and salt for fear that one of the two might explode in pyrotechnic rage, whingeing about who's bought the bread and who's bought the oil. Damn the New Year, without money, without paid holidays, I feel less than nothing. I can't even bring myself to say my piece. I'm really doing myself no good at all.

When I set foot in this country, anonymous and unknown, I was prepared to find a haven in any corner, as long as my basic human rights were recognised, but as time went on I quickly learned, right from the first moment of need, that in migration there is no refuge and that you don't even find God. To a certain extent I can understand Beniamina and Claudia, even more on the skids that I am. The all-consuming desire to go back with a small sum of money. To start all over again. To feel at home. This country will never be home. It will never be a refuge for anyone who isn't a sheep.

During the meal the reason for Beniamina's anger at Claudia comes out. From her complaints it appears that Claudia doesn't treat her as is her due. After a week's holiday in Alice Springs with Armando, she had the gall to bring her back as souvenir a common basket of shells which ended up straight in the bin. Yet at one time they were the very best of friends. The bond between them has been ruined by Claudia's good luck which brings her rich generous men with handicapped wives who don't cause a fuss. Claudia handles more money, has more clothes, enjoys a rich and varied diet. With Armando's help she puts her wages straight in the bank, an enormity which has reduced Beniamina to the point of imbecility, and to get even she has cut down on her weekly expenditure. She no longer eats meat, her fibrous physique can't stand it, yet she doesn't refuse Claudia's steak. Coffee contains caffeine, strains the heart, so she recycles the used coffee grounds which should be thrown away. In the bathroom torn up magazines are hung on a nail instead of toilet paper, no more deodorant to get rid of the smell of the windowless bathroom, nor sea-blue liquid in the cistern, nor Baygon against the cockroaches teeming in the cupboards. She takes a bath once a week with bran, cuts cotton wool out of sanitary napkins, bludges one and two cent pieces off everyone on the pretext that it's a hobby and has filled up three fat moneyboxes. She smokes OPs. She would like to bludge the food she eats and the air she breathes. She hides her own packet of cigarettes behind her bum and grabs other people's without so much as asking. She bludges off you, me, every Tom, Dick and Harry and grants sexual favours only if she's paid in some way. Her aim is to beat the bank book deposit record in as short a time as possible and then to buy herself a prefabricated cottage back home with pots of geraniums on the balconies, terracotta tiles, a fire place, a little bit of garden where she can grow lettuce, cucumbers, beans, tomatoes, where she can keep a pig, some chickens and maybe raise mink. In the meantime she complains of migraines, rheumatism, pain in the joints, swollen feet, dry losses because of the strain under which she works. The tepid piss which comes out she drinks for tea. In the morning she squeezes her tits to obtain a drink of milk. She wrings vitamins out of mice. Reads by the light of the street lamp on the corner. Catches the bus two stops further on so as to save five cents. Searches for cress and edible herbs in the parks. Writes to ship-board waiters but not to her family. Always suffers from aches and pains and blames it on the climate and social discrimination. She claims tax rebates for an elderly distant relative and a couple of idiot cousins. Cries over the miserable desolate life she leads. When sick she goes to the hospital as an outpatient giving a false name and address. In her room is a broken mirror where she looks at her reflection all night through. When I think of the mirror I get the urge to smile.

Beniamina would be an interesting person if she weren't so insistent on snowing us under with the greatest possible number of educational sexual experiences. She modelled herself on an old drugged prostitute who, one boring rainy Saturday, knocked at the long guy's door presenting herself as a vestal of domiciliary screwing services. What a great opportunity, thought the group of men present, sex lessons free and although the vestal was, to say the least, jaded and corpse-like, it didn't detract from the surprise, rather it added that little bit of incentive in stimulating the dulled senses of a rainy Saturday. Flattered by such a typically Latin reception, the vestal giggled, dainty hand covering her mouth, and when Carmelo sampled the goods by pinching her bottom and squeezing her breasts she hastily jumped aside because they hadn't understood, or perhaps she hadn't explained, that each sexualogical lesson cost twenty bucks per student, including the women, no discounts for women, she said. She counted eight heads in the living room and came up with a total of one hundred and sixty bucks. The Latin males completely lost interest as soon as money was mentioned and came up with puerile excuses such as stomach-aches or not having digested their meal properly. Only the queer was sincere. He was just a queer but he would allow free use of the carpet. In the end Carmelo had it off with her for ten dollars. After that episode Beniamina cornered the market for domiciliary sexual services and she is now the liberator of female sexuality enslaved for too many centuries.

But to get back to Claudia and Beniamina … Claudia is falling in love with Armando and he with her, it seems, while Beniamina, out of spite, won't even give the two lovebirds the time of day. After all she's gone through to help her out in her troubles. Pregnant three times in eight months. The first time by a waiter on a ship, the second by a wharfie who used to beat her up. So she helped her to run off. But in this country everyone does it, there're those who run off by day, others by night. People run off with a mattress, chairs, fridges, washing machines, hired TV sets, other women's husbands.

Sergio and the tall guy rush off as soon as they finish their meal. They're going to a party for homosexuals at Bondi. The Christmas panettone lies intact on the marble bench top and it won't be touched until Armando arrives for the ritual toast. Armando is late. He had promised to come at dusk. And dusk has come and gone. The old year is going away hands in gloves, maybe it's going north, maybe south, maybe west, maybe east, or maybe it's not going anywhere. If only I too could go away like the old year.

'Love?' huffs Carmelo out of the blue. 'Sure, that thing which starts from the heart and comes out at the anal opening. Love makes fools of us, love makes us suffer, and then, damn it all, there's a girl here dressed to the nines, all made up, perfumed, a stunning girl who won't even give out a hint of a smile. Gees, what apathy. What a bum evening it's turning out for me.' He punctuates this last remark by hitting the table with his fist.

Claudia's eyes are filling with tears. She must be thinking that Armando's met with some sort of mishap. He's never been late for an appointment.

Carmelo draws near to her, arms outstretched, willing and able. 'What say you give in, eh?' he says, putting his arms round her waist.

'Don't touch me, you shit,' she snaps at him.

'See,' he says, opening his arms disconsolately. 'She can't take a joke. Gets all hysterical right off with that sideways cunt of hers. Anyway, who's going to touch it? Might as well give it to the worms.' He whistles so as to regain his composure, shakes himself, twists around, goes down on his knees, does some exercises, then disappears. He's gone to thrash about in the pool with all his clothes on. He angrily flails the water with scythe-like strokes, then he tries breast-stroke, butterfly, floating on his back. When Beniamina joins him he climbs onto her for a piggy-back and spurs her back and forth. Playing about in the water, they don't see Armando come in.

'Oh, you're here,' he exclaims, surprised. 'Where's Claudia?'

'She was here, crying,' I tell him, pointing to the empty kitchen.

Armando knocks on the door of Claudia's bedroom.

'Go throw yourself under a train,' she screams from inside.

'She drives me mad,' he whispers to me in an embarrassed tone. 'She acts like a child.' And he bends over to look in through the keyhole.

Carmelo, who has come in without making a sound, observes the scene, sniggers, then gets right up behind Armando and swings his leg back in preparation for a well-placed kick. Beniamina, who has just come in, choking with laughter, barely manages to restrain him.

'Have pity on me,' begs Armando.

'Get a divorce and marry me. You've promised me a hundred thousand times. I'm sick and tired of picking up the crumbs,' Claudia is foaming and raging inside, throwing things against the door.

'Yes. Everything you ask for. I'll send you on a little trip to Italy even. I love you, I love you. Please open the door, you can't do this to me ...'

The door flies open, throwing Armando off balance and into Claudia's arms.

Midnight. The green veil which separates the entry to Beniamina's room from the kitchen ripples in the gentle breeze wafting through the open window. Beniamina's sleeping place is king size, a rest-a-pedic mattress right there on the floor. There isn't a decent sheet. They're torn down the middle, two different colours—faded pink and faded blue—sewn together. The menstrual chart, a packet of contraceptives, a doll made of red wool with little black eyes, hang from the only lamp. There's three of us under the sheets. I'm waiting for Armando to finish so I can go into Claudia's room. I'm wearing one of Beniamina's nighties, low neckline and covered in frills.

'Turn on the light, Rosa,' the idiot orders all of a sudden. I obey. Without thinking twice about it Carmelo jumps on Beniamina. They're having it off right under my nose and with the light on. Instead of turning me on they turn me up, especially the sight of Carmelo's bony, plebeian, hairy bum. He has little tufts of hair poking out of his anus. And Beniamina's ankles and big feet! The air fouled by cigarette smoke. I feel the panettone, the lasagna, the champagne, the melon, the wine, all come up. Beniamina is down on all fours. Carmelo gives it to her from behind. She shows her appreciation, likes it more than the previous positions, and gives me the nod (she's got the decency not to say it in so many words) that I can make use of the services of Carmelo superstud. But I don't have that abnegation and generosity which a whore has towards her own kind.

To tell the truth I like a whore to do her own soliciting. After that, they do it like monkeys, dogs, one in the mouth and one in the crown of thorns position. All without a break. They look like two tame rabbits. No, Beniamina looks like a dove striating sparks from her open mouth. The lifting of the greenish veil interrupts the performance only for a second. Having finished his number Armando waves goodbye with his little hand lifted over the broken mirror. I go to join Claudia.

The sun is high in the sky. Its light flows through the curtains. I get up. My mouth bitter with the taste of cigarettes. I find a woman sleeping in the shelter of the porch. To look at her you'd say she's got 'madhouse escapee' written in block capitals on her forehead. In fact they call her Irma the mad Neapolitan. Having noticed my presence she flutters her eyelids like a bat would flutter its wings in the full glare of the sun. She's pregnant. Her belly and her bottom joined together encircle her waist like a doughnut. On the top of her cottony head of hair spreads a mauve-coloured velvet ribbon.

'Hello,' I say. 'Do you live round here?'

'No. I indulged in too much elbow raising at the club last night and my escort dumped me. I didn't know where to go. I thought about it for a bit and then I got the idea that my dear friends Beniamina and Claudia wouldn't refuse to take me in.'

'Out on the porch?'

'Oh, everything was shut, in darkness. I didn't really want to wake you up,' she says in a dismal tone, then bursts out laughing, a gay couldn't-care-less laughter, as though not having a place to sleep is the most natural thing in the world. 'Happy New Year,' she says jumping about like a flea. 'Happy New Year, Happy New Year,' she shouts, going into the kitchen. 'It's me, Irma. I've run away.'

And she had run away, on New Year's eve, from the hospital where she had gone to have an abortion and then had changed her mind. The doctors were keeping her under observation, having discovered that she was an excitable, emotional, impressionable type who probably wasn't pregnant at all and maybe just had a stomach full of water.

'Fancy them saying such a thing! Accusing me of being paranoiac, schizophrenic, and in English too! In Italian they've got to tell me these things! Can one of you explain to me just what the hell paranoia and schizophrenia are?'

'It depends on environmental compatibility,' replies Beniamina.

'You approve of me,' says Irma drawing a big sigh. 'You're a friend. You respect your fellow man. You understand that I was in danger at the hospital. You understand why I've run away,' she says in a plaintive tone, face drawn by the urge to cry. She passes from tears to laughter, from joy to grief, from worry to nonchalance, just like a mad person. If she hadn't run away from hospital you can be sure she would have run away from the madhouse, from a speeding ambulance, from a blue, from a hearse. She throws the same sort of fits as Mariolino and it seems that they know each other very well even though they avoid each other like two mad dogs. Irma doesn't consider Mariolino worthy of her favours, Mariolino doesn't look upon Irma as his equal, both have assimilated all the intolerance, the rejection syndrome of those driven crazy by the climate. Irma boasts about having broken up a family with six children, four girls of marriageable age and two biggish boys. Mariolino is single but provides gratuitous and flattering appraisals for both married and single women such as defloration of the hymen in the cradle and progeny of dubious descent. They are constantly coming and going from police stations to lay charges against phantom enemies, always taking someone or other to court. They suffer from persecution mania and to obtain help they make constant nuisances of themselves with the sixty or so welfare organisations that provide assistance for society's misfits. In short, all bum organisations with fine-sounding names that are utterly useless in a country where charity should be unheard-of. Take life as it comes—that's the enormous reality of the inhabitants of the lucky country. On at least three occasions Irma has said goodbye to friends and acquaintances. She's gone back home three times and three times she has returned after selling the movie camera, binoculars and opals which she took with her each time. Naples brought on a homesickness for here where a girl like her can really enjoy herself. It's no accident that wherever there's a wild party raging, there she is, accompanied by hefty brylcreamed lads who hope to carve themselves a career by pimping for her. Or that you see her wherever there's rape and violence. You come across her with an arm in a sling, an ankle in plaster, pregnant by God knows whom. Always weak and jaded, always pregnant, introducing you to the expectant father to whom the news always comes as an absolute bombshell.

'Yes, this time I've decided to keep the baby,' she says.

'But when is it due? Have you counted the months properly? You haven't made a mistake, have you?' Carmelo asks, giving her a slap on the ribbon which slips to one side landing on her ear. And so it goes on like this all day, talking back and forth about abortion, marriage, and pensions for unmarried mothers.

A few days later I meet her on my way to the bookshop and she's hurrying down the hill, belly deflated, wearing a very tight very short piqué skirt.

'Hey, hello,' I shout out to her.

'I'm working part-time at the Padre Pio pizzeria,' she shouts back without slowing down. 'Come and eat a plate of tagliatelle. On the house.'

When everything is rationed, even bread, you don't pass up invitations to a meal. There's an air of poverty about this year. The same as in 1950, you hear people mutter. And who is poorer than Lella or me? She came back, skin smoked like a pig's scalp, pimples all dried out, eyes shiny and lots of ideas in her head. She should keep her ideas to herself, they don't give us our daily bread. The Greek woman has fitted padlocks to the cupboards, the washing machine, the fridge. We have to do the washing by hand and we've also got a rash on the soles of our feet. We wear thongs when we step into the bath. While taking a shower I gave her a serious and disconcerting talking-to about our current situation. I made her swallow all the crazy ideas she had brought back with her from Surfers as well as the marijuana seeds which she planned on planting in the Greek's little garden. First thing next morning we rushed to register at the nearest Employment Office. This way cigarettes, rent and chips for breakfast lunch and dinner are guaranteed. I remembered about Irma and on the pretext that we just happened to be passing by Padre Pio's we offered to wash dishes in exchange for a meal. Wednesdays and Sundays we look through the job ads.

There's that certain smell wafting about the room. Lella is taking a drag— where she gets the stuff only a clairvoyant would know. She lets me have the last puffs although she holds onto the pin. She loves me. I get emotional at the thought. At least someone loves me in this filthy existence. All right then, I love you too, Lella Karaposi. Draw on my love, support yourself on my faltering limbs. I am smoking and reading a book about lesbians and I'm all freaked out and I can't wait to grow in your arms like a tendril of ivy, to open your corolla like an immaculate first communion lily, to glue myself to your lips like a drugged dogfish, to stick to you like a valuable postage stamp. Bite me as you would an apple, a plum. Let's make love. Drain a little desolation out of me. Pull me up high and dry. Dispossess me. Exorcise me. I'm floating, I'm drifting, my views have all gone by the board. Anyway, what use are they to me when the lamps are put out. But God shit, don't tickle my orifices! You disappoint me, you really disappoint me, what's all this licking? This finger play reminds me of my childhood. And anyway, why the shit don't you look me straight in the face? It disgusts you to look at me. You lose your touch. Your lap, eyes, hands are ashamed. You exist and you don't exist. I don't exist either and I don't resist. This isn't what I want. This isn't what I'm looking for.

'Excuse me,' I say, pushing her away roughly.

'What's come over you? Why are you doing this?'

'Forget about that,' I reply.

Lella is upset. The genius is angry. It's not that she's behaving strangely, but she looks alienated, annihilated. She's cheating on my emotions. She is showing interest, and she's never shown any before, in my literary aspirations, asking whether my hopes are up or down. Bullshit. Go hang yourself with your own troubles. You've been excluded from the Greek woman's affections. She's threatened to throw us out. And don't talk to me as if you were Plato thinking he's talking to Socrates under the porticos. The room stinks, the floor is dirty, the sink's full of hair, not to mention the bars on the window, the lock on the telephone, the mail which doesn't arrive, the jobs not found.

MacDonald Town. I've moved. Other Greeks, Italians, Turks, Lebanese, Aborigines. It's the third, fourth, fifth move, I've lost count. I live with my bum on the edge of a volcano. Ready to leap up at the least hint of lava or landslide. The most difficult thing is to put down roots, to get used to these odd characters who rent us rooms. MacDonald Town, an old house at the far end of the little park. Right next to my room a nosy couple from the Abruzzi. I've fallen out of the frying pan into the fire. From my minute kitchen on the verandah I can just get a glimpse of the children playing in the park and the old drunks sitting on the benches. There's a public lavatory on the edge of the roadway, there's always a red brick lavatory with two entrances in the parks. The toilet in my park catches my attention more than the others because the entrances are boarded up. Lellina has explained to me that children of all ages used to be lured there and raped, and she's also warned me not to walk alone in the dark in the vicinity of the station. She, on the other hand, has found a place in the posh suburbs, out Rose Bay way, in a big, white house where there's a beautiful balcony with a view, to look after a millionaire and his German shepherd. Lella has started to smoke a pipe, has resumed her medical studies at the University of Sydney and on Saturday mornings teaches Greek at the Marrickville Greek Orthodox Church to children of Greek families. Sometimes I don't smoke because I don't have enough money, and I wouldn't have enough to eat if it weren't for the Abruzzese couple.

They feed me and lovingly guide me through the tortuous paths which lead to domestic labour. They are very proud of their profession as cleaners and they would like me to join the partnership. A continual scraping of hotplates like this, scrub pots and pans like that, brush my teeth, wash my feet and neck with a sponge, my outer ears with a scourer.

Don Luigi is the husband of the hyena with curlers in her hair. He has a fat bum, always wears shorts and long socks, always canvas shoes because of his bunions. He quickly caught on to the fact that I like people to bow and scrape before me and bow he does before my heaven-sent cunt. In fact I get the impression that I have come down from heaven to liven up their miserable dull daily toilet-cleaner routine. They don't let me off for a split second. When I go to the toilet they take turns at guarding the corridor for fear I might disappear down the drain. I'm not used to this type of attention. I feel just a little bit disoriented, especially at mealtime. It's an impressive entry. The cook calls to dinner by beating the spoon against the soup tureen, Don Luigi makes his glass tinkle against the bottle of genuine wine. The wife moves forward, the husband a step behind her, with the pomp of the maître d' at a luxury hotel inspecting to ensure that everything is just right. When the food is on the table they don't wait for me to invite them. They draw up their chairs and sit side by side. They look at me right through the meal. I look at them, my stomach contracts and I have great difficulty in swallowing. Ah, the things we have to put up with in order to survive! We'd even sell what little dignity we have already lost. I say these things in grief and sorrow. It means revealing my innermost thoughts.

One afternoon Lellina happened to be present at the ceremony. The hyena, curlers in her hair as usual, drew me aside and said to me with a black look on her face, 'I don't like the look of your friend. She's chosen to come and bother us at mealtime. How ill-mannered of her! If we started feeding the tramps round the city we'd end up in the poor house. Don't let her taste the minestrone, okay?' The blood rushed to my head but I didn't breathe a word. Stingy me. Lella had a certain look about her. It must have been ages since she last sniffed the smell of good home cooking. I was thoroughly ashamed of myself. I'm sorry, Lella, it still stings me after all these years. I hope you've forgotten about it. At the end of the meal the woman cleaned my chin with the napkin and in unison with the man burped like a hog. They do it so I burp in reply. It's the best way of giving thanks. It's the type of thanks they really appreciate. I should have had the patience to burp as ordered. At the time I really regretted my inability to burp in an orchestrated and harmonic manner. A worn-out burp. A yes-man's burp.

I begin to get my bearings with regard to the couple. Twenty-five years in Australia. Only daughter married to a son-in-law they detest. They've never been to a movie, never set foot inside a club, never even been to a saint's or madonna's feast. They don't read newspapers, don't watch television. They live in the passive tense. My appearance has livened them up a bit. A puppet to manipulate and plagiarise. And I was dreaming of featherbedding my nest just like that mad painter Gauguin and lots of others did, a haven beyond humiliation, compromise, wrongs. Things never work out for me. Tomorrow it'll be another hole, an abyss. Now Don Luigi is paying court to me, suggesting that we should run off together and then there'll be wedding bells. He passes me notes with all the details, maps with the proposed destinations marked in red. Arid, desert places as far away as possible from his wife. But the beast has got wise to his schemes. She's with me more often, nicer, more attentive. There must be something I haven't cottoned on to. She asks after my health with a great deal of concern, if I've ever been ill, if my periods come regularly, says what a lovely face I have and if I were to have a baby what a lovely baby he would be, born with a silver spoon in his mouth and with his future assured. They'd make him heir of all the millions smuggled into Italy just to spite their rebel daughter and grasping son-in-law. Of course, the seed would have to come from Don Luigi and I would have to contribute my belly for nine months. What a marvellous example of rough vendetta Italian style! And what a splendid pregnant female I would make, carefully fed on cornflakes, honey fritters, vegetable and meat broths. Months of living in the lap of luxury stretch out before me.

The couple is already looking after me as if I were expecting. When I nibble on fine food and sip red wine, red because it makes the blood strong, it doesn't even enter my head that the hyena could poison me in a sudden fit of jealousy. She is so sure that I will give in to her husband and get pregnant, and she is even surer still that when the baby is born—just like Don Luigi: short crooked legs, dog-like nose, coarse vulgar face—I will hand it over to her and disappear from the scene. Crazy. A baby; some hope! Jesus, what have I got into? At night I wake up all of a sudden, in a cold sweat, after dreaming that the newborn babe is torn from me at birth and immediately swallowed by the hyena while Don Luigi looks on laughing his head off

To take my mind off things I've started writing again and I go out with guys I meet at the pool. Usually if they're European they approach me. We understand each other, speak the same broken English. I must have committed a mortal sin when I invited one of them to my room. An insult to the couple which can only be washed away in rivers of blood. They've cut off my food and won't give me change for the telephone. They set the Greek witch against me, who is pleasantly surprised at the support she gets from my compatriots. It's a madhouse, I feel as if I'm living with a bunch of crazy people in the throes of menopause. The couple has come up with something new. At three in the morning, when they get up to go to work, they bang on the wall with their clogs and, shouting through a funnel, they demand my unconditional surrender.

'Give in, you pig-headed female!' thunders Don Luigi.

'He'll rape you with my consent,' his consort's voice booms out. 'I want to sleep. I want to sleep. I'll have the law on you,' I always scream back.

I went to the police, though, when Don Luigi made me fall down the stairs. Everyone knows the police can't do anything. I was advised to take him to court or to move house. Another move. Transport my bits and pieces to another cesspit, another brothel. Never. So I swallowed my independence and rang the girls at North Sydney. Crying like a walrus, I begged them to come and help me. I didn't have to tell them twice, they came en masse and it was a good thing they didn't bring the men as well.

They had all squeezed into somebody or other's brother's flat top truck. As soon as I saw them get off the truck, some holding clubs, some brooms, I leant out of an upstairs window inciting them to revolution, mayhem and massacre. My God, I could hardly believe that this army of furious women were my friends and had come to save me. I ran downstairs to the door. They swarmed up the stairs and then into my room, breaking chairs, tearing open mattresses, turning on gas and water taps, flinging the contents of tubes of tomato paste and tins of tomato puree all over the place. It took all my strength to calm them down just a little. We emptied out the drawers and loaded everything onto the truck. In that noisy devastation neither the couple nor the landlady put in an appearance. Unchallenged we left that purgatory. Carla took the wheel. Next to her rabbit-nosed Victoria. The rest of us got in the back and the girls held a meeting to discuss how to look after me. The three sisters, Anna, Sara and Carla had already decided to take me in. I liked their parents, country folk from Procida, practical, sincere, simple people. I was touched by the offer and was on the point of replying when Beniamina, who had latched onto the expedition, came up with a better idea. Since her liaison with Claudia had by now come to grief she had teamed up with rabbit-nosed Victoria. They had just rented a large room with all the amenities for thirty-two dollars a week off Milsons Point Road. It was a huge room and could take another bed. Further, since we would be splitting the costs three ways I would manage quite nicely even if I was unemployed. Sofia strongly supported the proposal. She had moved from Falcon Street, and was now living in the same building. Even though I was dejected and a bit weak in the head because of my recent troubles, the idea of joining Beniamina, with Sofia as co-tenant, made my hair stand on end and gave me goose pimples. The proposal left me utterly speechless but no one noticed the tragic aspect of my change of humour and my silence was interpreted as consent.

The chapter of my second year, in certain respects, was rich and full of life. The past year had been arid, unfruitful, and had made me swear and curse the day I set foot on the ship to come here. Now I lived in North Sydney, in a house kept clean by the caretaker, in a classy street, where even the air was clean, where the wind brought the smell of the sea, where there was the smell of flowers and the chirping of birds which I hadn't heard for a long time. The sea, just crossing the bridge, more than made up for it. And the girls. Beniamina wasn't around very often, busy with three jobs which kept her out night and day. Victoria worked as a telephonist, sometimes on night shift so she slept during the day. She was quite the opposite of the other girls, an idiot face without any warmth at all in it. Sofia doesn't work, she has never worked and she enjoys herself more than all the others. The only thing she wants is a pay phone within earshot.

I think about the importance placed on the telephone. That ringing at the oddest hours outside our door. That ringing which invariably caused a rupture of the collective code we had adopted. Our lives were entirely centred around telephone contacts. When the phone rang we would push and shove, each one attempting to be first to grab the receiver, thus achieving supremacy over the others by becoming the depositary of the secrets whispered from the other side. The call must surely be about an appointment, a deal, the hoarse voice of Zio Lino, Peter C. announcing that he would come to visit loaded with little gifts. New acquaintances, new friends, Lino's mates. Sofia was a veteran, she could sprint like an Olympic champion and regarded it as her duty to swoop down on the talking prey, hitting the others over the head with her fists and elbows. Her victim would almost invariably be Victoria, woken up all of a sudden and heading for the door. A punch from Sofia would knock her down again. 'Hello, hello. Yes … yes, yes. Hello,' she would say over and over again all out of breath. And maybe the call wasn't for her, or even for one of us, but for one of the drunks in the corrugated iron shacks behind the laundry. For those four New Zealanders with burnt-out faces, fringes of hair over their foreheads, who once worked as truck drivers, but were now just alcoholics and castrated into the bargain. Cheerful fellows, always ready to offer us a beer or a bunch of dwarf wattle-blossoms picked by the back fence. They held us in high regard, heaven knows why. We would often meet up with them at the corner pub or at the Luna Park jetty where we used to go fishing. When they were sober, which was hardly ever, they came with Sofia and me to Balmoral Beach and we would set them to gathering mussels in a plastic bag from the nearby rocks where they were big and plentiful. We would always eat peppered mussels and small fried fish.

Zio Lino finally makes his entrance. Beniamina and Sofia were always talking about this relative: a cultured, sensitive and generous man. When he rang to welcome me to his nest of nieces, I was so overcome with emotion that I was about to come on the telephone. He said just a few phrases but delivered them in a gentle and gentlemanly manner. Then Sofia jolted me from my erotic fantasies by jerking the receiver out of my hands. It's incredible how her base nature is aroused if you put your nose into her affairs.

'Excuse me if I've butted in,' she tells Zio, laughing like someone possessed, 'but Rosa was about to faint … no, certainly not. I'm not out to show you up in a bad light … You're getting mad. You're getting angry. You're shouting … Sure … What are you saying? Ah, yes, I'm your little darling pet. Did you buy me that snakeskin belt we saw in Pitt Street? You haven't bought it yet? I'm worried, sure I worry. You never keep your promises … No, Rosa's not here. She's gone off. Yes, she seems a sensible sort of girl, but … she's a virgin and she doesn't drink. No, I'm not joking. Jesus, what's there to joke about? No, I tell you she can't hear me, maybe she's a bit deaf and she limps with her left foot. Hey, talk louder. You're willing to shell out two hundred dollars to deflower her? Give me the two hundred dollars, Zio Lino, I'll get myself patched up. What!? Watch what you're saying! All right, when are you coming? Thursday night? Don't forget the snakeskin belt and the cannoli alla siciliana …'

OK she signals me forming an 'O' with two fingers. Sofia has won out. Uncle's little visits are quite profitable, there are always a few dollars to be got out of him and then if it's Saturday morning and Beniamina is off work, they divert him to Flemings and take out one or two trolley-loads of food. Zio Lino is a fairly fine-looking man, a firm solid profile, as they say. He's good-looking, has shifty eyes and a certain air of depraved decadence about him which classifies him at first glance as a long-time, highly experienced connoisseur of whores. To see him out in the street he could easily pass for a well-to-do family man. To look at him you get the impression of an ex-votive offering so polished that it blinds you. He hands the bag of cannoli straight to Sofia.

Beniamina is very disappointed. 'Oh, I don't like cannoli. I'd rather have some rum baba.'

'They give you heartburn,' retorts Sofia.

'Be good, girls. Don't quarrel,' Zio says in a conciliatory tone.

'We wouldn't quarrel over a few measly cakes,' Beniamina teases him.

'Right, we're fond of each other,' Sofia adds, with slightly malicious overtones.

'When you act like this, I feel like choking you. What's happened to you, you tarts?'

'Don't talk like that in front of Rosa. Lord knows what she'll think of us,' a dignified Beniamina interrupts him.

'So, what's she supposed to think. She doesn't think anything.'

We had got dressed to go out. We are waiting for Zio but he has other ideas and stretches out on the sofa covering his face with a newspaper. The girls quickly lose patience and start begging him to get up, imploring, then they shake him, take the paper off his face, put it back on, take it away from him, tear it up, cover him with the pieces, spray him with perfume, pull the hairs on his chest, comb his eyebrows, and seeing that all this doesn't work—he doesn't give in, doesn't move an inch, seems to be sleeping—Sofia kneels by the sofa and massages his prostate. Zio's immobility alarms her, she throws Beniamina a questioning glance and then turns to me. I shrug my shoulders.

'In that case, we'd better go,' says Beniamina. The *Galileo Galilei* is tied up at Circular Quay and she's determined not to let it sail until she's had her bimonthly clean-up of cooks and sailors.

'I'm tired,' complains Zio drawling his words, 'I had a meeting yesterday which lasted till dawn.'

Beniamina whistles. Sofia makes a loud rude noise.

'You don't believe me, as usual,' Zio protests.

'No, we don't. You're as lively and rosy as a cherub. You're a liar, but we're better liars than you are. Come up with some good excuses, damn it, after all we haven't seen you for ages. And then you've got the nerve to make us take a taxi … it'll cost us five dollars,' Beniamina croaks with a broken voice to try and move him to pity. She's virtually doubled the price of the fare, supposing that she was really thinking about taking a taxi in the first place. More likely she would have made us walk over the bridge. Zio thinks about it. 'Go on, make up your mind,' she won't let up.

Zio tries to strike a decisive stance but only manages to make us sorry for him. The swollen wrinkled bags under his eyes, sensual lips set in a fatuous grin, that of an unappreciated man who succumbs to threats and blackmail even though he fights strenuously not to give in. To go or not to go. He's gone to stand in a corner at the far end of the room, slips his hands in his pockets, in his eyes the inquisitorial gaze of a corrupt discriminatory Australian judge. There is a strong smell of wattle-blossom, the vases are full of them, we have to put them out in the corridor at night otherwise we would wake up feeling terrible or perhaps not at all. Hot February summer, I wanted to commit suicide.

Zio's eyes look straight up to the seventh heaven, the promise a good whipping. Whip the women every once in a while. Torture them. Sodomise them. React. What am I afraid of, anyway? Who is this other woman? What's she made of? What's her name? I'll have it off with her, I've got to have it off with her. Yes. No. Yes, I think I'll definitely have it off with her. It was preordained. I believe in fate. I read the horoscope every day. I'm a bit of a sucker, an easygoing, tender man. I often forget insults, don't mind them. I adore the executioner, offer him the other cheek. I love to suffer. Yes, I wallow in suffering. I'll take her to bed, well, you got something against it? Obscenity is ecstasy in me. Shit, feeling mixed with watered-down fuel, that's what it is. The grief these little whores cause me uproots the joy of innocence, or maybe it's old age, think about it, no it's not, yes, no, maybe it's the present syndrome, suspicion of what the future may bring, old age looming up, go on, own up to it, you ugly pig, who do you take after, nobody knows just what a burden you are carrying. They have you in their tight little fists and they aren't bothering to hide it. I started when I was just a lad, fifteen, the mother of a friend of mine. Oh, God, my heart's bursting, go on have your session, isn't there anyone who will enlighten me?

Not far from the word spoken in the dark Zio Lino's thoughts are formulated. They assail me and, incredible as it may seem, they rush out of his Adam's apple, his fingers, his heel, his belly button, like evanescent matter from the body of a medium in trance. And he stinks, whiffs of stench trying to get out into the open air, gathering together a little higher up, at the intersection with the traffic lights, like soaped-up clouds. Right, now I'll get to the bottom of it. Memories come flooding back covering me with cheeses, salami hung on street stalls, ricotta, fruit and vegetables, Siamese cats, chirping chicks, varicoloured parrot feathers, a noisy crowd, sellers' voices, buyers' voices, fleas being fertilised on a stool for betting purposes, a clown eating fire. He is there and so is she. On his face the ragged smile of senile impotence. She had red hair then and was much fatter, wore a long dress, Roman Empire style, made of transparent material with frills. She was holding an enormous cane laundry basket and they were talking nineteen to the dozen in Italian. It was clear as day that they had stopped to chat so as to enrich the dose of insults they were busily tossing to each other. It is not the fidelity with which these victims are conjured up in my memory which makes me associate that man and that woman with Zio and Sofia that day at the market, but rather the clumsy yet concerted attempts he made, livid with rage, to shield himself from the holocaust. He was at the mercy of red Sofia then just as now he is at the mercy of blond Sofia and of Beniamina. Still standing in the corner of the room to which he has been banished, he takes his hands out of his pockets and torments the buttonholes of his coat.

'The reason,' he begins after thinking the matter over very carefully, 'please keep quiet ...' he says giving them black looks. But no one has moved a finger. When he began speaking the girls sprang to attention, their arms folded. 'The reason is to be found in your behaviour in public ...'

'What? Do you want to insinuate that you're ashamed of going out with us?' screams Beniamina.

'Zio, all we have to do is pick whichever guy takes our fancy, and anyway who's forcing you to go around with us, did we point a gun at your ribs, a knife at your throat, send you menacing letters, if you don't like it, cut,' Sofia is screaming even more loudly than Beniamina. They were like two bombs ready to go off.

'I don't know what to make of you,' Zio says in afflicted tones. 'I'm fond of you. I've known you, Sofia, since you were a little girl, I'm fond of you too, Rosa, I get to like people at first sight, but these women get drunk all too easily, dear beautiful girls they may be but once they're drunk they're real bitches, and I'm the one who gets the worst of it, I have a reputation, my good name, I'm an important personality.'

'Bullshit,' explodes Beniamina. 'I've had it up to here.' And leaning towards me she whispers so's the others don't notice, 'Don't let him impress you, he carries on like this because he's got it on the short side,' and then loudly, 'Okay, let's go. Don't give him the satisfaction of thinking we can't do without him.'

'Wait, I've forgotten something,' Sofia hurriedly ransacks the drawers in the wardrobe where Beniamina keeps her panties. She carefully picks a pair with the elastic still firm and goes to change behind the cane screen which divides the living area from the other half of the room used as a dormitory or rather a hospital ward given the new row of beds with their white bedside cabinets. This hospital ward look is reinforced in the visitors' eyes by the toilet which Sofia also uses and the display of all sorts of catheters, glass phials, little candles, knitting needles, thermometers, hot water bottles.

'I'm ready. Let's go,' she exclaims.

'What are you doing? Are you going?' asks Zio, suddenly becoming vulnerable and lost. 'What about me?'

'You always spoil our fun,' Beniamina accuses him.

I must say that when they used to talk to me about this uncle of theirs I actually believed that he really was one and I couldn't wait to meet him. Someone who works at the Consulate can be useful to you in many ways. I'd even formed a fanciful picture of him, which was later shattered, since you can't create fantasies about a cunt-struck woman-chaser continuously tribulated by weak demonstrations of a virility which is neither overpowering nor real. He just didn't have it and yet, strange as it may seem, almost a legend had been created around him as the man who had made it over a million times. Over a million in a sort of hurried broken-down way, including those done standing up and of a few seconds' duration. While I was engrossed in these reflections, Beniamina trotted off determined to phone for a taxi, which would have cost us thirty-five cents extra for the call. Well, Sofia and I were keeping a very tight rein on our money, not because we are misers, but just so we could survive the rapid price rises, inflation and so forth, and that gesture of a filthy rich type who can afford to have the taxi come to the door, paying for the luxury with our life and our indigence, made Sofia really sound off. She lashed out at Zio Lino like a mad woman and accused Beniamina of exploiting unemployed women who were not on the dole. Hers had been cut off until further orders and you can imagine how she felt, lame, blind, paralysed, buried alive. She was one of those girls who spend and squander, dress in the latest fashion and support themselves with an income of dubious origins, but who do not disdain the fortnightly cheque from a paternal government since it was guaranteed income. Zio gave in there and then, took pity on us, the poverty of us Italian citizens has this effect on him, an employee of the Consulate. He promised to come with us and slipped her a couple of notes on the sly, but he made it quite clear and swore an oath on it, that once on board ship he would go off to the left, we to the right acting as perfect strangers. Zio was terrified, and he wasn't wrong in anticipating that things would get out of hand in the congenial environment of an Italian ship full of kitchen hands and sailors on the watch for homesick girls to whom they could unburden themselves.

We split up on the gangplank, set up camp in the kitchens and, while Sofia and I ate ham rolls, Beniamina shut herself up in a cabin. We spent half an hour in drinking and masticating. Three-quarters of an hour passed, an eternity, Beniamina had disappeared without trace. She had sneaked off without so much as saying, excuse me I'm dying to do it. Sofia was showing signs of nervousness, she was about to go off her head, at least that's what it looked like to me, she walked along the corridor sniffing and scraping at the crew's cabin doors, making a tremendous effort not to batter open with her head the ones that were locked. Her indiscretion in the matter of her friend's affairs was rewarded, she caught her lying on a bunk, legs up, with the ship's boy bent over her pumping the neck of a Coca-Cola bottle in her vagina. Sofia did not get upset, did not utter a sound, she retired silently, nor did she utter a word when Beniamina rejoined us. She gave her a distracted sort of look, neither profound nor superficial, but which nevertheless gave to understand that it was her particular sort of look. We said goodbye to the crew, adding that we hoped to see them again in three or four months, and climbed up on deck. In the big saloon lounge Zio was relaxing in an armchair with a double martini and a bored look on his face which immediately changed to one of indignation as soon as he saw us. And to think he had stated quite clearly that we must not bother him on the ship, we must not approach him even if the ship were to go down.

'Zio, dear, won't you offer us a drink,' says Beniamina in a very merry mood. You just need to see her, all shook up, mellow eye sockets, to get the idea that she must have made it at least six or seven times.

'I forbid you to call me Zio when there's company present,' he whispers. Anger makes him blush deep red all over and twist his ears.

'But what company are you talking about? Who the hell cares about what people think, you don't want me to swallow that, do you? Don't let's start the whole stupid thing all over again. Don't you see that it makes you ridiculous? These belated scenes of jealousy do not suit you one little bit, and anyway what have we done wrong this time?' Beniamina asks cautiously.

'Don't raise your voice,' Zio whispers vehemently, glancing quickly round the saloon.

'You're the one who's drawing attention,' Sofia reproves him.

'Let's order our own drinks,' I say. Zio would have paid anyway and the whole situation was really getting on my nerves. If he was worried about his reputation why did he take them in tow?

'Yes, be good, girls. Go and sip your drinks someplace else,' says Zio stiffly.

The saloon was beginning to fill with people. By way of reply Sofia sits down in a huff, imitated by Beniamina and myself.

'What a grind,' Beniamina exclaims, hardly bothering to hide her smile.

'What do you expect?' he says, pointing his chin in her face. 'For your information I don't like it one little bit when I'm framed.'

'Framed?' Beniamina echoes him in astonishment. 'Oh, you mean cuckolded. You're going off your head, Zio. There's something gnawing away at you, confide in your little nieces.'

Zio takes a hardline stance, his lips tightly drawn, he won't open up, doesn't want us near him, won't pay for our drinks.

'Zio, I'm hungry,' says Beniamina in a wheedling voice, 'won't you take us to eat a pizza?'

'I'd rather take you to hell,' he explodes.

'Do you know I'm looking for a job,' says Sofia.

'Oh!' Zio looks impressed. 'And what type of job?' he asks sceptically.

'Any type. The cost of living is going up day by day. It's no longer an easy thing to steal clothes in the shops, when you go to try on a dress they take note of it. It's a real problem, I've got to get my clothes somehow,' Sofia sighs.

'Not all the shops do it,' Beniamina encourages her. She's an expert, even though a few months ago she got pinched at Centrepoint together with one of the girls from North Sydney, and that time she had to apply all her procuress wiles in order to convince the policeman that he had to do with two innocent teenagers. And now she has to keep to the straight and narrow because next time they'll throw her in jail.

'Zio,' Sofia calls out languidly.

'Yes dear,' he replies absentmindedly.

'Introduce me to some rich friend of yours.'

'Good God, what an idea!' he protests, horrified. 'You're not their sort,' and he takes her hand in his. 'It's just that you're a bit of a scatterbrain, my little darling.'

At last he orders our drinks, throwing circumspect glances all around. It seems that an appeal to his hip pocket is always preluded by mawkish mutterings of this kind. He likes it. Makes him feel important. When the occasion presents itself he is not loath to introduce the girls to some visiting businessman or invite them to dinner to provide female company for his friends, thus showing the same spirit as Giacomo D. Only Sofia always plays the fool and embarrasses him.

'You could do it for her,' I intervene in a vague sort of way.

'Go on,' Zio prompts.

'She's got the wrong idea about you, Zio,' Beniamina interrupts. 'We've got to teach her the ropes. She hasn't understood yet that you are a real gent.'

'Maybe, but she's got better thighs than yours,' says Zio unexpectedly, stooping to pat my ankles. 'Thin and muscular, just as I like them.'

'Zio, Rosa is a virgin,' Sofia admonishes him.

'Sure, they're all virgins to start with,' says Zio in a meditative mood. On the way back Zio, at the girls' insistence, stops to buy a bottle of dry white wine. Almost none of the pizza places has a licence and Mamma Santissima on the Pacific Highway is no exception. The place is deserted. Zio heads for a table in a secluded spot, behind some pillars wrapped in ivy. He uncorks the bottle. As soon as they've got a bit of wine into them Beniamina and Sofia begin to go off their heads. Beniamina intones a desolate anguished song, something of a tear-jerker. She's probably been unexpectedly struck by one of her mortuary crises.

'Virtuosos, these nieces,' exclaims Zio, leaning back in his chair, glass raised, wearing the blissful expression of someone determined to have the time of his life.

'This is nothing,' retorts Beniamina, 'I'll now show you the monkey's dance,' and she begins to writhe about in the narrow space, red-faced because of the wine sloshing about in her stomach. Sofia, not wanting to be upstaged by Beniamina, also gets up and throws her arms around Beniamina. They stagger around together like two tipsy partridges, rubbing up against Zio who keeps on lifting their skirts, undecided about which of the two dancing cunts to grasp. The only waiter in a red jacket and the proprietor watch the act with amusement while leaning against the counter. Then Sofia suddenly frees herself from Beniamina and drops down on Zio's lap.

'Zio, darling,' she begins in a malicious voice, 'I must tell you what happened on the ship, otherwise I'll blow up.'

'Later, later,' cuts in Zio, squeezing her breasts and then pulling one out, heedless of the others present.

'No, now, or I'll forget,' screams Sofia, thrusting the breast back in her dress.

Beniamina draws near to her, a suspicious look on her face, ready to jump on her, I think, tipsy as she is. But Sofia merely gives her an inscrutable look and leans her head on Zio's shoulder.

'Sofia, Sofia,' Zio shakes her, alarmed. Sofia looks dead.

'She's acting,' Beniamina's voice is heavily disdainful.

'Slut, at least I'm loyal. I'm not engaging in malicious gossip. I'm only pretending.' Sofia is all het up.

Zio shuts her mouth with a napkin and she bites his fingers, so Zio gives her a push which slams her to the floor and he might have taken to kicking her in the stomach if Beniamina had not suddenly begun to wail shrilly. A wail which makes an enormous impression on me, I have to admit, because it means death and destruction, emigration, alienation, frustration, discrimination, useless struggles and emasculated rebellion. She sobs and slobbers and wants to make it clear what a good girl she would have been if Mum and Dad had been alive, if there had been some wise person to guide and counsel her. She cries perhaps like the Madonna cried at the foot of the cross, I think in a state of shock. Zio solicitously makes her swallow a little wine. 'More,' she demands and says that she feels empty and dejected. We leave the pizzeria in haste. A couple of blocks from the flats she begins to cry again but more overwhelmingly and violently. She seems about to have a fit, to faint. She is suffocating in her tears. Once out of the car she says she doesn't want to sleep in the big room with me, she wants to sleep in Sofia's room all on her lonesome. We help Zio undress her and put her to bed, and a second later she's snoring like a trombone. Zio stays a few seconds to talk to Sofia and me, then he's off as though the devil were at his heels.

'Where do you think Zio's gone?' asks Sofia.

'How should I know,' I reply.

'To have it off with Beniamina undisturbed,' says Sofia. 'Did you really believe all that act she put on?'

The days go by and one afternoon about five o'clock I get a big fright. If I do not rapidly adapt to my friends' irregular way of life it won't be long before they find my jaundiced yellow corpse. I'm in Sofia's room drinking some vegetable broth when there is a loud persistent knocking at the door. Sofia goes white and trembles without even asking who it is. There's no need to ask, at least for her, she could easily guess who it was. The silence and the trembling which have come over her begin to affect me as well.

'Who can it be?' I ask in a feeble voice.

'Open up,' thunders a loud nasty voice. 'You know who I am. I've got a knife this time. I'm going to skin you alive.'

'Mother help me.'

Sofia clings to me although I am more frightened than she is. It was one thing to hear about and have a good laugh, from afar, over a virgin-obsessed maniac prone to using a knife, knife thrusts given until now with the tongue, but who would have assured me that we'd get out of it unscathed this time? If only the virginomaniac could at least use a gun, I would have preferred it to the knife, as I would have appreciated being hit with a chair on the nape of the neck or being strangled like a chicken. And anyway I didn't want to die still full of vigour and unfulfilled dreams. Yes, I wanted to live, even if in the past I'd wanted to die millions of times and I'd never had the courage to kill myself. My experience of life had been so brief, so incomplete, and I now found myself at the centre of the world or at the end of the world without having revealed myself. The goals for which I had lived, for which I continued to live without really wanting to live, were not important enough, and yet I didn't want to die by the hand of a virginomaniac.

'I'm off out the window. You fix things up with the madman,' I tell Sofia and without further ado I rush to the windowsill, to lift that damned window so I can get out into the street.

'No. You must stay, you've got to help, he'll kill me. Jesus, fine friend you are,' Sofia implores in a broken, tear-filled voice, clinging to my legs which are hanging down from the windowsill. I push her and try to shake her off, but she won't let go, I punch, knee and pinch her, but she is so afraid that she doesn't even notice the blows, mutters something which I only just hear, she's convinced that my presence will cool off Nicola.

When he's got a virgin in front of him he's all full of compliments and on his best behaviour.

'All right, then, I'll open it if you won't,' I agree, uncertain as to whether Nicola will respect me as a virgin. But before going to the door I grab a saucepan off the stove. If he really has a dog's sense of smell, he'll most likely greet me with knife thrusts. Instead of Nicola at the door there is Leonardo, the chimpanzee-like boyfriend of Rose from North Sydney, wiping the sweat off his face because he's laughing so much.

'I've scared the shit out of you, ha, ha, ha,' he sniggers.

'Where did you get such a damn fool idea,' Sofia barely manages to get out—she is still bent double from fear.

'Here,' he holds out a half-full bottle of cognac. He was just passing by, he explains, and thought of bringing us the bottle.

I'm woken up in the dead of night by voices muttering in the kitchen. The light's on. It sounds as if one of the girls is in trouble. I don't understand what sort of trouble, but she must be someone from outside, though a close friend. I hear them mention genital prolapse, bacterial flora, Doderlein's bacilli, fungus and parafungus, trichoma, lactic acid, dry mucus, over-heated vulvae, bacteria, parasites, gonococco, streptococco, pneumococco, staphylococco, and since all these infectious diseases ended with the name of a tropical fruit which contains a refreshing liquid (*cocco* is Italian for coconut), a great thirst comes upon me. I get up, walk barefoot, swaying like a sleepwalker, pass among the girls who are petrified at my sudden appearance. Through my half-open left eye I see Sofia, Beniamina, Victoria and a Greek girl to whom Zio Lino had given some money to get herself patched up since she was going to get married and then, I don't know the whys and wherefores, the wedding didn't take place so the lamb returned to the fold. I go up to the fridge, take out a can of lemonade and, still acting the sleepwalker, bring it to my lips. Then I go back to bed. Now the whispering has become louder, like the buzzing in a beehive. 'Are you awake Rosa?' Beniamina calls out. I do not reply.

'Rooosa,' Dutch Victoria's throaty guttural call. I don't reply to that either. The next moment Sofia is by my bed telling me off for digging into their secrets. I'm as silent and motionless as a sleeping fish although I'm really wide awake, hardly able to stop myself from laughing, thinking that if she begins to tickle me I'll put on a really bad show. Sofia touches my hair lightly, then turns and goes away. I hear them whispering for a while until I hear Sofia state quite loudly that she has never experienced an orgasm and to do so she would be prepared to hang from the lampshades or waddle over pins … and so on until I fall asleep.

Zio Lino rings every day at lunchtime. Most of all to ask if I would be willing to be deflowered for two hundred dollars. Irritated beyond words I yell at him through the mouthpiece not to keep bugging me every time he calls.

'Yes,' Sofia agrees with him. 'She's a really vulgar and ignorant girl. Pinch her on the bum when you see her. Yes, sure, she'd deserve it if someone were to fix her … you're right … you're always right, Zio. This one's a country bumpkin. She's uncivilised.'

I've drunk a glass of Strega and a Bacardi and Coke and my head's spinning. I'm sitting on the sofa. The gang has just gone out and Lino has just come in. I can't bear to look at him. He looks ill at ease too, or maybe it's just the impression he makes on my tender heart. As usual Zio has brought some cakes and there is a smell of rum around, rum dripping on the floor, torn nylon stockings and dirty clothes. I've eaten two baba. It's Beniamina's fault that we don't have enough to eat. She's the one who keeps the kitty. We never see any fruit. I'm certain she cheats on the shopping. And to think that in this huge room there's not the least bit of cheer. All we needed was Lella's heroic decision to come sneaking back and ask us if we could put her up for a couple of nights. Beniamina, as long as it meant saving, would take in a whole tribe. With four of us in the room, like sardines, with continual quarrels and cursing at each other, there's always shouting.

It's in this Christmas season climate that I decide to make a concerted effort to find work. The only thing I can do is sew. But to go back to working on an industrial machine for nine hours a day doesn't appeal to me at all. The best thing is to phone the editor of the Italian biweekly newspaper who has read some of my writing and has found it interesting and innovative. I mention this to Lella who immediately looks disgusted. What have I said that is so unseemly? There must be something wrong or stupid about me which I haven't caught on to. As soon as both she and Sofia are out of the way I ring up. When the editor is on the phone I panic, gasp and stammer mentally, at last I speak, I've got to say some damn thing or other, I can't stay there gasping into the mouthpiece forever.

'Good morning, sir. You probably don't remember me but I remember you very well. My name is Cappiello. I like to write. I'm looking for a job.'

'Yes … yes,' he replies tense and alarmed. 'What's it got to do with me?'

'Well … I really wouldn't know, I'm only asking you if you can give me a job.'

'Oh! And what can you do?'

'Well, nothing really. I've never been inside the offices of a newspaper.'

'You must have worked here in Sydney,' he interrupts. 'What did you do?'

At this point I jam completely.

'Well, what sort of work did you do?' insists the editor.

'If you really want to know I used to work as a machinist,' I say all in a rush.

'What did you sew?'

'Look, the work I used to do was of an entirely different type, what's the relevance? I write. I like to write '

'Yes, yes, and what can I give you?' A pause while he puts his thoughts together. 'Listen, you don't by any chance belong to one of the Italian associations in Sydney?'

'No.'

'Not even the Neapolitan one?'

'No ... Jesus, I never thought of it ... You aren't thinking of getting me to write about associations, madonnas, saints ... ?'

'Yes,' is his short sharp answer.

'And ... what sort of writing?' I stammer.

'News, just local news ... On such and such a day the X club held ...'

'Oh ... Ah ...' I say. Then it dawns upon me that this is not enough, I must thank him intelligently, in a manner more clear and coherent than the drama going on in my brain and which I would maybe never have appreciated if the editor hadn't given me the nudge. Maybe it's easier than it looks. Luck comes to my aid, last Sunday I happened to turn up at the feast in honour of Saint Catherine in the park next to the Apia Club and words can't describe the exuberant mood of the crowd, no, I'll write about the torrone, the loaves of bread shaped like animals, the coloured balloons, the statue of the Madonna covered with dollar notes and supplications, and the singers specially imported from Italy. 'Look, you know the Santa Caterina feast last Sunday? I'd like to try and write about it, what do you say?'

'Yes, excellent idea. Have a go at Santa Caterina,' says the editor.

I want to write an article full of passion. In the evening I keep turning it over in my head while sitting on the toilet because it's the only private corner in the entire flat, and I discover that the creative fires won't turn on. I've already spat twice on the handwritten sheets of paper. I can't use the typewriter in front of the girls, who knows how many laughs they'd have behind my back and at my expense, they're looking for penises and money not idiotic goings-on of this nature. I retrieve, submissively, a sheet which I had crumpled up and thrown onto the wet floor and read it over again. 'Brothers rebel' is the peremptory phrase which jumps out of the first line. Not bad as an opener but it had a false ring about it. What has it got to do with brotherhood? If you meet these people in the street they avoid you, that's the truth. I recommence reading haphazardly, between the lines. 'Do not allow them to stifle the promises you made to yourselves when you left the old life behind you. Shake off ...' At this point I stop, gloomy and unhappy, incapable of carrying on. What do they have to shake off after thirty, fifty years of migration in a new world? Years without number still rooted to fetishes. Cholera of ethnic culture. Culture they call it. A past which kicks the present. And I can't see myself writing a straight factual report. Lella's right, with my malaise I can only present a misted-up picture of reality and get the punctuation wrong, but if the sun shines through the window, I have to write that the sun shines through the window and if the madonnas purse their lips, that's what I write, even if it's not correct. So that's the way things are after half an hour's meditation on the toilet and three sheets half full of scribbling, ready to go to press.

The girls have caught some infection or other. Catheters of various sizes and litres of drink for frequent urinating are back in fashion. Sofia and Beniamina confer in dialect but Lella and I have our ears up like radio antennas and one word is enough to get the drift of the subject. They are very angry with Zio especially Sofia who does not have a bathroom and he makes her suffer the affront of washing his penis in the little sink for washing the dishes. This morning they have gone out early, one to St Leonards to visit her regular gynaecologist and the other to town, to Macquarie Street, to the Greek gynaecologist. Lella and I pretend not to notice, not to understand what is going on, not to see the tense faces around us, and spend as much time as possible out of the house. Lella is available and has no commitments. She has lost her Saturday morning job at the Marrickville church, she has lost the roof over her head, the salary which the millionaire was giving her and the company of the Alsatian. It seems that the eccentric old millionaire became infatuated with her, but that he was also in love with the Alsatian, and insisted on several occasions that she should have intercourse with the dog, claiming that it was the same as doing it with him.

We no longer have the consolation of chatting with Maman. The authorities have closed her cafe-brothel. Maman has disappeared from circulation and Lella is broken-hearted at her disappearance. She had developed quite a sincere and filial affection for the old harlot.

Underneath it all she is full of slobbering frustrating sentiments towards adopted mothers, to gratify her contorted restlessness and the intermittent suffering she goes through because of her free choice to be an orphan.

Once the other two have gone out, so do we. First we waited until Sofia had gone a fair distance. Since she's headed in the same direction as we are we don't want to run the risk of meeting her at the station ticket office and being obliged to buy her ticket for her because, as usual, she would have come up with the story about losing her purse or forgetting it just so as to scrounge a few cents out of us. Once we get off the train we shout ourselves a double ice-cream, lemon and chocolate, in spite of Sofia, Beniamina and company, and then at the Hyde Park stand we order hot dogs, chips and milkshakes which we eat by the fountain. There's a spring breeze, people lying on the grass and men walking their dogs. A heavenly quiet interrupted by the sudden appearance of mad Irma from behind a flowering shrub closely pursued by Mariolino shouting and gesticulating. Lella and I just manage to hide behind a tree.

'Cocotte, you're a cocotte of the worst type,' screams Mariolino stopping at a fair distance from Irma.

Irma looks at him, uncertain whether to take offence, she doesn't know what 'cocotte' means, probably thinks it's a bird, because she looks up at two cawing crows in the sky and laughs.

'You don't know any French, cocotte in that language means prostitute. You are a prostitute,' Mariolino says clearly and imperiously, at the same time backing off because Irma has caused bodily harm for lesser insults.

'You impotent bastard, you do it in your pants at the mere mention of sex,' she retorts at the top of her voice. 'You impotent bastard,' she repeats, '… and watch your language … don't talk dirty … talk polite, or I'll kick you in the balls …' and she advances towards him with clenched fists.

He backs off a little more, taking cover behind the flowering bush. 'Come here. Closer. Take me on if you've the guts for it,' he incites her from the depths of the shrub. 'Come on and I'll throw you on the grass and fuck you in front of everyone, you and a hundred thousand other women.'

By way of reply Irma turns to the small group of onlookers who have stopped to listen, screaming in Italian, or rather in the Neapolitan dialect, and striking a solemn pose just like Moses must have when pointing to the ten commandments. 'He doesn't have it, what do you think? He's lost it. He doesn't frighten anyone with his little stories about cutting the pubic hairs off women of every race and religion and displaying them all tied up with coloured ribbons. They are hairs of old decrepit alcoholics, women whom even a dog wouldn't touch.'

'Keep quiet,' begs Mariolino, peeping out from amongst the flowers. In his voice there is the terror that someone might understand and believe Irma's lies, 'Quiet, you lying cocotte. Breaker-up of families. Prolific rabbit. Murderess of innocent foetuses …'

'Why do you deny it? He denies it,' she says addressing the group, 'he denies spending his nights playing patience to the point of going blind over the cards and devouring Little Red Riding Hood, Messalina, The Golden Ball, Snow White and the Seven Dwarves.'

And you can see that she has really lost control because she rushes at full speed towards Mariolino. Mariolino, who was expecting the move, takes flight towards the group of onlookers and runs into a drunk, the usual type, hat tilted right back, always carrying a tool bag, fly also always unbuttoned so if and wherever the need arises he can relieve himself without needing to bother unbuttoning.

'Fuck, fuck, bloody bastard … Fuck, fuck you bloody bastard … fuck, fuck, fuck you, you,' he says in a sing-song voice, grabbing Mariolino by the shoulders, holding him still and spluttering all over his forehead the plug of tobacco which he was chewing.

Mariolino is a dwarf compared to the huge drunk so he swings his legs and flaps like a infuriated chicken, calling for help, but not one of those present lifts a finger. He would really have had a bad time of it if mad

Irma, moved to pity, hadn't intervened. She goes up to the big man and tugs hard at his coat.

'Fuck you bloody lady,' the drunk explodes, letting go Mariolino who falls on the path.

'Fuck you too ... you slob, go home and take a bath,' Irma replies vigorously, tripping over the insults because she doesn't know the correct way to say them in English.

The drunk makes a gesture with his thumb as if to say up yours and with his other hand he raises his hat, bowing slightly. 'Fuck bloody wog, fuck wog, fuck, fuck, fuck, wog, wog, fuck ...' he repeats ad infinitum, disappearing into the empty sewer of his infinite void.

Now crazy Mariolino has drawn near to Irma and is comforting her. All the rage, the spite, the hate have been swept away by the common insult they have endured. Gesticulating they go off arm in arm, more friends and enemies than before. At that point we too come out of our hiding place.

'Mad Irma, good on her ... and to think that she's on social security because she's an exemplary mother of a family ... She's got no problems obtaining her daily bread. If only I too could go off my head just as easily so I could claim compensation for the damage caused by the bad climate and by the hair-raising sights we see every single day,' Lella complains and then smiles, childlike.

From the distance comes Irma's shrill voice, 'A man who's always saying he's going to die ... and never dies but is forever chasing after cunts with renewed vigour ...' some incomprehensible words reach our ears. Then we hear distinctly, 'Go on, kill yourself ...'

I have a cold, maybe I've got the flu, my bones ache all over. I feel sick and utterly alone even if Lella dances attendance on me with boiling hot tea and biscuits. I don't like to lie sick in this huge room. It's as if I were already dead. They're all present in the room, the North Sydney girls, the patched-up Greek, all doused with perfume and very elegantly dressed.

Sofia is wearing a long hair wig stolen from the chemists down the street. Beniamina a gipsy skirt, big round earrings and a turban with little bells. They were planning a dinner with Zio Lino and his mates, been planning it for weeks, but Lella and I knew nothing about it. The wretched women kept us in the dark over all the preparations, they don't trust us any more and won't even tell us a little white lie. When the horn sounds they disappear without even having the decency to say goodbye or to tell us to drop dead from envy because they're off to enjoy themselves where there is fine food, wine and piles of money. I doze off and perhaps dream a dream beyond all illusion, all recall. Images nested in my fears, fear of existing which clouds my dreaming. At a certain point I scream. I am awake. The telephone is ringing. It is Mariolino reminding us that it is Sunday. A mild spring Sunday, marvellous for going out with trusted and sincere friends. And he is the only friend. The best. The most sincere and loyal friend, the most sensitive to women's problems, the most knowledgeable … the most, the most … the list goes on and now there's no stopping him.

'The most deprived and licentious bastard son of a bitch on Australian soil,' Lella, who was there next to me, finishes off the discussion and hangs up. Before two seconds are up the phone rings again. 'Let me answer,' she says. 'I know how to put him in his place.' I back her up in order to restrain her in one way or another. I wouldn't want her to make him so furious at a distance that he'd be prompted to rush here and make a scene in person, with all the disastrous consequences for our reputation here at the flats. At Lella's abrupt 'hello' he releases a flood of chaotic senseless phrases, genuine protests which rise to the ceiling, and now the corridor is full of him mutilated, patched-up, offensive, begging, slowly enclosing us in its vapour. It would be better to cut him off there and then, but Lella does not have the firmness to interrupt him.

'You two … you …' the tone of his voice lowers, it seems like the sound of rain on the windowpanes, birds chirping in the forest. 'You've got it in for me. You hate me. What have I done to you? Christ on the cross … I'd give an arm for you … I'd have a leg cut off. I admire you … I prefer you to the other women. I speak well of you. I heap praises on you, I heap praises on your artistic voluble natures. I appreciate everything about you. Accept you without reservations even if I do not understand you completely. And how on earth could I? You have a fixation about photographing copulating cadavers. I am willing to pose naked for you without even asking for a cent in exchange, perhaps because I'm in love with you … and how do you repay me. I understand and analyse each person's tragedy, but you exaggerate out of sheer malice. When you treat me like this my guts get all tied up in knots and then in the evening I can't digest. You want to see me get sick. Tell me, do you want to see me ill?' His voice breaks out in a sob. 'I am alone, more alone than you women. Yes, we are all alone and damned, and maybe life wouldn't seem so bad if I had someone to hold close night and day.' Enough to break your heart, to hear a cockroach crying and being all emotional. Yes, because he sniffs out the tragedy that lies in each of us and sings it out to the city. He sings, despite being tone deaf, the soledad which is in each one of us, the fury in each of us. His song overwhelms me, weakens me, makes me hungry. And I am hungry, a slow hunger, of a fleeting shadow, of disconcerting things, of unexpected, unplanned, vital flashes. His song is broken, stagnant, old through centuries of emigration. His heart is cold, it no longer remembers the dream. He no longer remembers if he is a man, if he has travelled by land or sea, if he eats white bread or black. He was a man without secrets. Now his nerves are in tatters and he is only a poor madman.

Finally Lella manages to stammer that she has caught the flu off me and that it is impossible for us to go out. At this stage he offers to send us his private doctor.

Sofia has disappeared. She has been missing since the night of Zio's dinner. No one knows exactly where she has hidden herself, not even Beniamina. Perhaps, at long last, she has decided to throw herself off the bridge. We get into her room through the window. Her things are there, in disarray, the wig thrown on the bed, the open suitcase on top of the wardrobe, some change on the dresser and the bottles of pills for her headaches. We are depressed. On the credit side we are never bored. Something always happens, absurd, upsetting and at the same time entertaining. Even if it were just a yearning for a simulated flight or a fantasy created by the desire for escapism which stirred the deepest nightmares of those of us left behind. As infinite as a hallucinatory phenomenon which pursues, persecutes, throws down, lifts up, flings into the fray … and panic, fear, satisfaction, pride in the intimate approval of the heroic decision of a carbon copy. A copy of us which confronts the situation head-on, throwing itself head-first from an anonymous little bridge, or by cutting its veins in a hospitable park, meeting place for queers, and surrounded by those lifeless young people who cough and vomit out their souls. We engaged in endless discussions, at times broken-hearted, at times animated, about the chances of this neophyte in suicide ending it all in a painless manner. Of giving herself a dignified departure, identity card and comb in her handbag. It was all so moving. The sorrow of never again seeing dear Sofia was so delicate and distinctive that it made my eyes sting. Anyway they were talking about it in their own fashion; far from being offensive, of giving rise to scandal, they treated it as if it were a piece of banal social gossip, about who was now going to assume the difficult task of simulating abortions and suicides in order to bludge a few dollars from silly old Zio or that idiot Peter.

Zio pops in around lunchtime as usual. I've always thought that he came round at that time because he considered it the polite thing to do. He heralds his arrival with the same sacred fear, a fear of approaching death. There is no one at home. The old woman doing the cleaning sends him round the back where I am busy reading. He has a tired look about him, worried, remorse eating away inside and weighing him down like a millstone, if you paid any attention to what he said. But I couldn't give a stuff. He came in just as I was reading the most interesting part, and anyway, what sentiments could this gossipy spying little old woman with a mouth as large as a crater have? A splendid day today, whiffs of wattle in full bloom, the grass browning in the burning sun, smell of parched earth, puffs of salt sea air and the cancan in the neighbouring pub. Zio orders two beers from the man in the kitchen, giving him a good tip. I spit out the chewing gum, shut the book, take a sip of cool beer. The foam forms little bubbles on Zio's very thin moustache. He is now convinced that it's all over for Sofia, that she is sleeping her eternal sleep, all curled up like a cat which feels cold just as she used to do when she went to bed. He wants the father and then the police to be informed, but anonymously, so he wouldn't be implicated, so we wouldn't be implicated. I smile.

'Why are you smiling?' he asks with a pained expression on his face. 'You're a strange sort, you are.'

'No,' I reply without thinking, 'or maybe yes, I was smiling at that funny shadow which passed over your face.'

Silence falls. A crow caws, others reply. Human cries, shrill, sounds of hungry newborn babes, calls sometimes rough sometimes incisive which hit your brain like a blue flash, a rainbow of voices which are transmitted from one beak to another. Who knows what they are bawling about. I would give my eye teeth to know. At first I thought they were magpies but then my English teacher said they were crows. Zio looks like a crow with that jutting lip and sharp nose which stands out on his lean profile. But I like crows, Zio I like less. I like him even less when he has that caressing look about him which makes a blazing midday seem tender but which is not tender. Two stones roll off the low wall and fall on the grass with a thud. Red petals fall from the waratah tree. Spirals of wattle pollen. Dry air. My heart, always hidden, was, in that moment, as if it had its roots bared. It offered itself. It wanted to be swallowed up. It was on a lattice trellis. Take me, squeeze me, caress me, that damned heart was beating at the rate of a hundred and twenty a minute.

'I can't stop myself,' he breaks the silence. 'I'd like to kiss you, touch you.'

'Why me?'

'You arouse my curiosity,' he says, livening up. And then he sniffs, his cheeks trembling as he sniffs out the beginning and the end, oblivion, chaos. He is about to go, he too is about to quit the scene. There is nothing else, not even the names, to exhume them would be useless and damaging. The past, the present, the fleeting moment a lamenting museum echo.

Why me? I ask mutely. Why me? I reply mutely. Sofia who has disappeared because of the wig. Sofia is not a practical person, lacks propriety. The air has become like melting pitch. We go inside where it is cooler.

During the dinner the girls, instead of letting the businessmen relax at the sight of their merry serene young-cunt faces, had interrupted the man-talk irrespective of whether what they wanted to say was on or off the point, by talking about the ever-increasing cost of living and how very difficult it was for them to keep up with it, a strategy calculated to rouse the compassion of hard-headed businessmen who landed in this country with their trousers in patches, and whose only creed was to exploit the ignorant as far as possible, but which really had the opposite effect. After such a heavy session of domestic economy and appeals for charity, the girls expected to be treated to a shower of flowers. It is right that they should be just a little bit coy. It does no harm. But everything has a limit. To restrain oneself does not mean to be inhibited, to get stuck, on the contrary it means to stimulate, encourage, titillate the jaded senses of men whose god is money. When one of them who was seated next to Sofia thrust his hands between her legs, first of all she threw a fit, then turned on him like a viper spitting poison, and not being happy with having made a scene in a fashionable place, grabbed a glass full of wine to throw in his face. Zio expected Beniamina, who was a bit tipsy, to intervene with her sure-fire extemporaneous act, with recriminations and tears to flood the table and the dead called to witness. Instead she remained inscrutable, her face like impermeable wax did not show what she was thinking. A miracle. And then the collapse of Sofia when the wig came off and ended up in the soup. She ran to shelter in the restaurant toilet and there was absolutely no way to get her to come out either by threats or supplication. And now Zio is convinced that she has killed herself because of the shame. The other side of the story and the conclusion we reached, reported to us by the old woman who does the cleaning has, you could say, a happy ending. Coming home from her nightly drinking bout at the pub, she saw Sofia in a big flash car with the inside light turned on pulled up on the footpath in front of the flats, in the company of a red-headed man. The fellow she had quarrelled with during the dinner had red hair, and now there she was in his lap while he was making her jump up and down as though she were on a seesaw. The old woman swears she heard Sofia's head thud repeatedly against the car roof. But we don't really think that Sofia was banging her head against the car roof, not that at any rate, because the old woman is always drunk. I do not tell Zio this, preferring to leave him to stew in his grief.

The light is dim inside. The hum of the vacuum cleaner in the corridor. It is the only time we have been alone together and he does not ask for an iced coffee, does not want anything to drink, and when someone keeps repeating he doesn't want anything, it should really mean that he doesn't want anything, instead he wants me. When he hugs and kisses me on the sofa, I conjure up the images of my solitary nights, the unravelling of my interminably short sleep, the vigils and indifference of infinite suffering. Lino is an attractive man, after all. And even if he has got it on the small side, even if he's not sincere, even if he's superficial, inspires no confidence, he was after all almost a relative who prised me away from myself. I whisper hoarsely to the back of his head to give me a couple of seconds' grace so I could have a shower since I hadn't washed since last evening. He is against the idea saying that it's OK, smell of sweat and all. But I am more stubborn than he is and persist with my intention of freshening up and putting on a drop of perfume. 'Well, go ahead and wash if you really have to ... but hurry up,' he angrily pushed me away from him. A certain yearning has come upon me, a rash type of desire which makes your sex glands crackle. I really couldn't have been more than a couple of seconds under the shower. A splash of water, a rub of the towel round the shoulders, and back I went. He could have enclosed me in his hand and instead there he lies, in disarray, across Victoria's bed, in moist abandon, as petrified as a stone statue on Easter Island. He looks at me with the expression of a dog who has just been beaten. 'I couldn't wait for you,' he says apologetically. 'Yes, I know, it's criminal. Come, lie down beside me. I'll do something else to you … I'll … I'll …'

A bloodthirsty look must have immediately come into my eye. 'If I wanted someone to slobber all over my thighs I would have trained a Saint Bernard dog, at least he is faithful and has a quicker tongue than you have,' I throw in his face, unable to restrain myself. Shithead, irresponsible wretch. It was as though he had deprived me of a chocolate ice-cream cake.

'How tragically you take it,' he says with a note of compassion in his voice. 'You have no sense of humour.'

'Sense of humour, you call it,' I scream.

'Well, isn't there a funny side to it? What do you want to do, take me to court?' he throws out, exasperated, waving his arms. 'Anyway I've got to rush now. There's a friend waiting for me in the car.'

All that day and the day after I was so angry that I didn't even indulge in the usual chatter with the girls. And the more I witnessed Lella's euphoric state, her seriousness of purpose in working towards a degree and leaving our room, the more I sulked.

Just as Sofia had disappeared on the sly, so she came back, after having unleashed the deluge of water, tears and emotions. It's raining cats and dogs, there's hail too. The windowpanes rattle like castanets. It's Sofia banging and making that noise at the back door to attract our attention. Her fine blond hair is all stuck together, crackling like liquid sound. She gives no explanation. We're relieved to have her among us again.

Friday, pay day for Victoria and Beniamina, we unemployed are also excited. We buzz round the fortunate ones in the forlorn hope of obtaining a loan or perhaps the odd cigarette. No loans tonight, but we're smoking like chimneys, taking the cigarettes from the packets strewn all over the place. It's eight o'clock. The spaghetti pot is boiling on the stove. The smell of the bolognese sauce prepared by Beniamina fills our nostrils. We always eat so late. I'm really hungry. I've lost a couple of kilos. Tonight we'll eat even later. Sofia is pregnant. We have to get the money together for the abortion. We know Sofia is not really pregnant. We've agreed to put on a great act for the benefit of Zio and Peter. Beniamina, Victoria and the patched-up Greek have spent a fortune in telephone calls to make Zio come running and to try and track down Peter. They've got them well and truly frightened. Sofia wants to throw herself off the rocks. Sofia is cutting her wrists. Sofia has bought poison. She is hanging herself. She is not sleeping. She doesn't connect. She doesn't know who she is. She's reduced to skin and bone. I come and go between the kitchen and the living-room. Zio comes into the kitchen to see if dinner is ready. He takes the fork and rolls up some spaghetti. He is nervous. A shrill scream from Sofia makes him drop the fork together with the spaghetti. He bends over, picks the fork up off the floor and shoves it back into the pot as if nothing had happened. All of a sudden I remember that he washes his penis in the kitchen sink when there are no washing facilities in the room where he has his rendezvous. My empty stomach is grumbling, but I'm no longer hungry. I leave the kitchen area, exiting by the front door. I wish the earth would swallow me up. To dig a deep hole with just the force of my foot and bury myself in it. They have gagged me. I have lost myself. I don't even know who I am, the she-devil, the adventuress, the borrower of others' mannerisms, is drifting, shattered into a thousand pieces, every piece pregnant with things unsaid.

A room on the North Shore would have cost too much. Lovely place, luxuriant green, a haven for rich people. Riches, comfort, security were abstruse terms for me. I would have had to start wiping my bum with my hands, because I couldn't buy toilet paper any more. To snap again at the damp greyness of walls on which the sun never shines. On impulse I took a grotty room at Glebe. The verandah had broken windowpanes and no electric light. I wanted to start writing again. It was the only way I could feel alive. I loafed without a job but the inspiration to write would not come. The day-to-day exigencies, the stresses, combined to hound me, crush me, annihilate me. To ward off and cope with poverty I would have to have had testicles of steel and the stomach of an ostrich. Pretend to be in a house on the heights with the sea nearby, a maid, a washing machine, private lounge-room, an ensuite, a servant to undress me and comb my hair at night. I had to pretend that I slept in a soft four-poster bed with the bell-button in the bedhead. I had to force myself to be gay, willing, superactive and to love that cold nasty room. Toilet and bathroom were halfway down the stairs. Every time I opened the door I ran into the mad half-undressed fat woman with her singlet tucked into her bloomers who came down from the upper floor. And if I went to the toilet or to brush my teeth I would find her seated on the toilet with the door wide open. 'Hullo, Rosa! How are you? Nice day, today,' she would say to me. The rent swallowed up three-quarters of the government cheque, what little money was left disappeared in no time. I had my back to the wall. I worked my accounts over and over, more ingeniously than an accountant, in order to be able to buy cigarettes. In the streets I would lose myself in flights of fancy. Glebe was the Negro quarter. Negroes, not Aborigines. The Aborigines I used to meet in Redfern had their hair not so curly, skin not so dark, many had light eyes and golden brown hair, nearly all were alcoholics. In the street sirens wailed day and night— police, fire engines, ambulances. The intimacy I longed for as a universal panacea turned against me. The silence was no longer premeditated silence, it was something negative. I was full of the sounds and the squeaks of the gate which was continually being opened and shut. No graceful soul knocked at my castle, apart from Mariolino and Irma. I welcomed them in, even if they annoyed me, because they soothed my stupefaction. They were two furnaces which spat burning embers on my apathy. That's right. I would let them in, invite them to sit down, act as peacemaker while they would pierce me through and through. I would sort out their troubles for them and their troubles would stick to me. I would add and subtract, sometimes in favour of one, sometimes in favour of the other. And when they went away with a spring in their step, psychoanalysed, I felt like someone sentenced to take hemlock. I would often see them coming when I was glued to the window and if I managed to act in time I would turn off the light and not answer the door. I would observe them through the lozenge-shaped windowpanes as they flew out of the car doors like two fighting cocks, Irma hitting him with her bag, he paying her back by throwing the street directory, the brush, the sheepskin seat cover at her. But he would never ever raise his hand to her, he would have had the worst of that encounter. Hidden spectator in the darkness, I would enjoy the sight, inciting them to tear the chrome fittings off the car, kick the seats to pieces, bite the wheels, eat each other's ears and nose, tear their fingernails, impale, crucify, throw punches at each other. If only they would catch cholera, yellow fever, leprosy, syphilis, medusae to testicles and ovaries, galloping consumption, dysentery. They looked like another race, an extinct race, mad survivors from the caveman age. A sublime lack of inhibition moved them, making them different, I envied them their vitality, I too wanted to be like one possessed so I could tear, rend, dirty, charge and discharge myself like a battery.

Sofia used to come. She came surreptitiously and all out of breath. She would immediately insist that we should go and have a drink at the ladies' lounge at the pub. A lot of things had happened at the old place since I had set up on my own. Peter was getting married. Beniamina was going out with an Englishman called Ross, blond and handsome as a god and two years four months younger than she was. Zio Lino had gone to Europe and come back with his niece Fabia, depositing her in the house of the North Sydney girls. He had given the strumpet a thorough briefing because she behaved like a novice just come out of the convent, swearing until she was blue in the face that she was a virgin, a saint, that she was intact and immaculate, and that no one had ever had it off with her. And then the word came on the grapevine that she had not arrived on the thirty-first of the month, the day she was placed in the care of the old folks from Procida at North Sydney, but three weeks before that. Three weeks spent in a third-rate motel paid for by Zio. She had a very beautiful oval face with delicate features, nose sprinkled with freckles, thick coppery hair, shapely legs, but her bum was a sight to see …

I told Sofia not to come round any more at night. I had found a job as a dishwasher in a restaurant-pizzeria in the red light district from five to midnight. The whores in 339 ordered their meals straight from the kitchen through their window with the grating and our window with the screen. The pros from 328 and those from 290 would come in person and ask for extra sauce on their spaghetti. They would come in their working gear, tight black leather costume, fur coat over their nighties or with nothing on underneath. There was the odd one with a clean face, who looked like an office worker or a student. Many were accompanied to their door by the boyfriend who would then come into our place to eat some lasagna or a cannellone. Our steady customers were transvestites or homosexuals who would pair off in the upstairs room to engage in intimate conversation. The cook, a simpatica but nervous woman with thyroidal eyes, varicose veins on her legs as big as ropes, old before her time, would fly into a rage on the nights when we were crowded, nights when things were like an equestrian circus, when we were packed with touchy homosexuals, demanding whores and lesbians making a hullabaloo. She would scream through the screen to those behind the grating asking how much they got per client because the two of us wanted to join up too. I would gladly have exchanged the brothel I worked in for a more lucrative one.

I ate for free at the restaurant-pizzeria and I was also beginning to see a bit of money. But I had a feeling it wouldn't last long. It didn't. Guided by Sofia the whole mob descended on the place to make fun of me. They would laugh and point at me as if I were a monkey in a cage. Damp with sweat, deafened by the rumble of the rangehood fan, covered with flour, by the stink of the food, dead tired but unbowed by the laughter directed at me, I would look at them out of the corner of my eye as they went out headed for the pictures, the club, the poker game at the North Sydney girls' place. I hung on grimly for a month then I gave up. I was homesick for the collective life. I went back to the old room with my tail between my legs one Saturday when I didn't have the money to pay the rent for the room at Glebe. The wattle blossom had taken on a more vivid yellow because it was the beginning of spring. Fights, grudges, false jealousies kept breaking out. I took to reading. I vegetated in black and gold. Things looked black to me. I was overcome by personal mourning. The gold of the wattles adorned the windows. Lella had gone away. She now lived over a garage in a spacious room with all mod cons. You got up to it by means of a wooden staircase covered with vine tendrils and radicles.

Sofia slept in the big room at Beniamina's feet so as to have a carnal contact and something secure to cling to in case Nicola broke the door down or smashed the window to get in. It was a humiliating, stressful thing. You felt as though you were manning a barricade. Sofia would forbid us to air the room. The heavy faded velveteen curtains were always kept drawn. Victoria and Beniamina did not go out in the morning if the old cleaning woman did not go ahead of them first brandishing her mop. The understanding between Beniamina and Ross was taking a nasty turn. Ross, English bastard that he was, did not appreciate our sisterly solidarity with its attendant risk of being knifed in the company of that nuisance Sofia. Perhaps he was right. Why did we do it? Sofia would never change. One night, in the middle of the night—we were asleep—Nicola started to bang on a window. We all jumped up on Beniamina's mattress and cringed together. If there was anyone able to stand up to that virginomaniac it was she. Sofia was so frightened that she was crying hysterically and her teeth were chattering. I would have given her a good hiding. Nicola was threatening to slit our throats if we did not hand over Sofia, dressed or undressed, in a faint or conscious, because he only had to say two tiny tender words to her.

'Don't believe him,' Sofia was whimpering and sobbing. 'He's a liar, a monster, worse than Judas, call for help, help, help, Mrs Gray. Call the police. Call the police,' she screamed at the top of her voice while clinging to Beniamina.

A door opens, hurried footsteps, excited voices, knocks at our door. Beniamina goes to open. It's the old woman's elderly boyfriend with a large rusty knife in his hand. The old woman rings the police. While we wait for the guardians of the law Beniamina puts the kettle on. Sofia locks herself in the bathroom to wash her hair. When we've already finished drinking our tea, out comes Sofia like a mermaid sprung up from the depths of the sea, hair all done up in curls, eyebrows all wet. She had discarded the role of Sofia for that of Jane, Tarzan's mate, having decked herself out to look the part. She was so cute and full of childlike wiles in her denunciation of the monster who was persecuting her that the policemen took it all in open-mouthed. She even managed to impress us so that we couldn't bring ourselves to expose her. They spoke to her gently, as you would talk to a very beautiful but naive child, so naive as to get herself into messes like this. The con-girl seemed to put on display the problematical virtues of our race, knifings, jealousy, beatings, the wretched condition of women treated as objects and as slaves. It's true that nearly all policemen are stupid and obtuse and can barely manage to write down half a sentence in their native language, but there in our presence they felt superior, immortalised by civilisation, as they listened horrified to these tales of feudal barbarity. We were smoking like chimneys. You could cut the smoke with a knife. One of the policemen opened the window and peered out into the darkness with the aid of his torch.

Sofia is fated to plant dynamite all over the place. The inexplicable thing is that those around her light the wick. She has given us such a stunning piece of news that Beniamina has become anxiety-stricken. She will appear on television, on channel 10, in a documentary on Sicilians. Sicilian Sofia is not. She is Sardinian, blond, sly green eyes. But they're giving her twenty dollars to badmouth the Sicilians, anyway there's not much difference between Sicilians, Sardinians, Calabrians and people from the Puglie. Her story, if it were true, contains all the ingredients calculated to bring tears to the eye. Forced to live on her own because her widowed father, later remarried, wanted to force her to marry against her will a man above her station, she feels a martyr to the hardships, the barriers, the ruptures, the shame of children towards old-style parents.

Her father is severe, her father is a terrible man, her stepmother is wicked, and add to that the jumble of humbug, the advantage of not being able to prove it, poor child ejected from the family hearth. Instead Beniamina says that her father is a saint of a man, too weak and malleable for a wild filly like Sofia, and that one day she'll break the old man's heart. Sofia has no heart, not even a conscience, she has cowshit, a prehistoric callousness. And now she wants a suit bought in a boutique, an imported handbag, openwork lace gloves, a hat with a veil that has come back into fashion, a pearl necklace because it goes well with her complexion. She appeals to us. We cannot remain insensitive to her fashion needs. We do not have any cash funds. Beniamina refuses even to listen although she is quite free with her advice. 'Go to the Consulate,' she says, 'go with Rosa. Go on, both of you. Tell them how poor you are. You're bound to get something.' Sofia doesn't want to go there. She has been there before and has never managed to cadge more than five dollars at a time. Then there's Zio Lino who is going through a critical stage just now. Whims and fancies of fifty-year-old men. He's right in the middle of menopause complete with sudden fevers, unexpected blushing, bouts of depression, temper tantrums. It's impossible to find him. He refuses to come to the phone. He is no longer concerned about his nieces. Yet the money has to come from somewhere, not from us, that's for sure, who are like paupers at Pilate's feet. Those who had some like Beniamina and Victoria kept it well hidden, locked up in term deposits so it would earn them interest.

We gave up the idea of cadging money from the Consulate and turned our thoughts to the numerous charities operating in the big city and its environs. Sofia shillyshallied, recalcitrated, got deeply offended, turned sulky. She refused to go cap in hand to one of these sibylline organisations, with its continual coming and going of mad people, idiots, unemployed, depressed, hysterical, peripatetic women, abandoned wives, fathers who rape their daughters, exemplary brides set on the path to prostitution. A menagerie of abnormal people over whose heads hung an ill-defined not yet approved project, that of cutting out their balls, their ovaries, and sending them packing, deporting them back to the country from whence they came. Sofia does not want them to cut out her ovaries and send her packing.

After much discussion they decided to get Fabia to pawn her trousseau. They all hated the snake en masse because of Zio. Zio would call for her every day at ten to one at the old folks' place and take her to lunch at a restaurant. On alternate weekends they would go driving out in the bush. The old peasant from Procida muttered and swore at his daughters because he did not want that tramp thrust under his roof. Actually she didn't make the slightest effort to get on friendly terms with those around her. She looked down on us girls with contempt and she would get Sofia and Beniamina good and angry. When she turned up on Zio's arm, she seemed to say with her crude nasty eyes, this Christmas prick is all mine, I get the official blessing you get the enema, I get the nectar of the gods you the cod-liver oil, I smoke cigarettes in a holder you get the unfiltered butts and catch lung cancer, I get the stamp of sanctity, the crown, respectability, the silverware, the crystalware, a nice little apartment where the rich people live. Rave on, rave on, I love to see you do it. And she was really having a ball. Then it all ended. Zio took her away from the old folks to a tree-lined backstreet in Neutral Bay where he shut her up in a barrack-like building similar to the Miami Hotel with long high-ceilinged corridors painted in brilliant hospital white, white doors, black enamelled notice, sink near the bed, no lift.

'Let's force her to pawn her jewels,' says Sofia, who becomes increasingly nervous as the meeting with the Australian scriptwriter draws closer. They're going to discuss the interview in detail.

'But she's the type that if she's out in the street she'll hold her piss for hours just so's not to pay two cents at the public toilets,' says Beniamina.

Beniamina has been fired from the motel and the Manly pizzeria. Due to Sofia's machinations, I think, because she's jealous of her earnings. In the afternoon, when Beniamina comes home from the clothing factory, she changes, putting on her frayed shorts. Sofia always wears frayed shorts round the house, displaying her thighs. On the evenings when Ross doesn't turn up with his little bunch of cheap flowers Beniamina and Sofia stay up till eleven, midnight, sitting on the sofa with their legs crossed and drinking watered-down coffee. They detest Fabia now even though in the beginning they had welcomed her as though she were King Midas, saying that she had that magic touch and changed everything she touched to gold. Now they say that she is a stingy bitch who wouldn't piss in a public lavatory to save two cents and that at the customs she still has trunks full of pure silk lingerie all duly sealed. When she goes dancing she displays on her fingers stones as big as potatoes and to have acquired all those goodies she must have managed a bordello back in Italy. But Fabia was different, maybe she had more liberal attitudes or maybe because, having come from the north, from a cold to a hot climate, the heat had affected her head. She didn't think twice about going round with the men. And they, being inhibited, fastidious, frustrated crawlers, did not hold back one single word. They told about all the things she did with the German mechanic, married, with wife and children in Germany waiting for their visas. When Fabia started going with the German she didn't know he was married and neither did we. The slugs spat out the truth when they started making fun of her. After that, when I ran into her, we would scowl at each other. She wouldn't talk to me. She made me quarrel with Maria from North Sydney. I didn't go to play cards with the oldies any more. When I saw her again she had come down from her high horse, pale and drawn, jumpy, incredulous at the return to the middle ages, at the epic of bolted uteruses, at maidens with their hair in tresses, at madonnas who coupled, bore children, were graced with dribblings from heaven by courtesy of the Holy Ghost. She demanded compensation. But among the many useless agencies for helping mad people not one was to be found which fought for the rights of unchaste migrant women. I must say that each woman defended herself as best she could in this sort of madhouse. I scratched my head till I drew blood. My scalp was covered in scabs. Beniamina worked like a Trojan and hoarded away money. Sofia was piggishly foolish. Victoria was something of a halfwit. The sisters were as ignorant as anything, they were always thinking of men, dresses and money. So life went on without change, with the magnificent opulence of TV sets in the toilets, foamy rivers of beer gulped down, married women working twenty-four hours a day, and a fair slice of the Australian population desiring to change sex.

'She can't keep her hands off other people's pricks,' says Sofia blowing on her nail polish so she doesn't have to look anyone in the face.

'Who?' we yell at her, curious. If there was anything sacred and untouchable, not to be circumvented, it was pricks constituted as personal property. There were ethics, a moral code. To break the rules was tantamount to being excommunicated.

'What have you done to Ross?' Beniamina screams in a burst of genius. Her flash of intuition has so upset and surprised her that she beats with her fists on Sofia's back which resounds like a drum.

'He's still alive. He's still alive,' replies Sofia, doubled up with laughter.

'I'm not at all surprised at you,' Beniamina bleats woefully. 'You're the only one of our group whom I wouldn't trust to look after a child's dick … but that … that I'll tear her limb from limb. Now talk, tell me every single thing. You and Fabia have had it off with Ross.'

Sofia shuts up, worried.

Beniamina's ire increases. She beats her breasts with her hands. 'I wouldn't do such a thing, that's for sure.'

Sofia ignores her but begins to rave on at no one in particular. She screams about the lack of trust placed in her, she declaims her utter sincerity, she shouts that she would die for her friends, she screams that we've formed a terrible opinion of her. She would never betray her friends. We've all changed since that hooker arrived from the North but she has remained immutable in her virginal devotion. She only drank two fingers of Remy Martin because they made her. Fabia was rotten drunk and so was Ross. When is he ever sober, she says exultantly. Two drops and Sofia is off. Doesn't remember a thing. It's no use keeping at her, she doesn't remember a thing, when she's off it's like she's in a trance. Drink hypnotises her. Fabia has corrupted Ross. English men have bad blood. They're unfaithful, mercenary. Who have you paired off with? Sure Fabia went to bed with Ross. It's easy to go to bed with Ross. He's always got it up when he's around her.

'I'll forgive you because you know not what you do,' babbles Beniamina suddenly.

'Hey, what's all this crap about forgiveness?' asks Sofia harshly. 'If there's anyone who should be dispensing blessings, I'm the one. I ask only my mother for forgiveness—she was the one who brought me into the world. Every night I ask her forgiveness and pity. Mother forgive me, I say to her. Don't crucify me, I tell her, when we meet in the hereafter. Don't reproach me because all I give you is anguish.'

'Where did you pinch that from?' says Beniamina. 'You're a thief of phrases. You pick them out of the glossies. I read serious stuff, educational stuff. Words—I create, mould, suffer them. Go on, take this, how does that grab you?'

Insults coming down by the bucketful, by the cartload. Big words, swear-words, crap. A drunken tongue, eyes puffed and contorted, it was like love tied tight with sailor's knots, sharp shells to cut unwary feet. Beniamina has always conned us, managed us as she pleased. And she, Sofia, even though her memory is not all that good, does not forget certain discourtesies, wouldn't forget them even if she lived to be a hundred. She recalls the funeral-like atmosphere and the rumbling of an empty belly. Tap water, mouldy bread and the odd slice of cheese to accompany it. Her unemployment cheque was not enough for two and Beniamina hid behind the pretext of the broken arm hanging round her neck. The broken arm was Zio's fault. They were engaged in play-wrestling, Zio fell on top of her with all the force of his ninety kilos, so the arm broke, she could not go to work, could not claim workers' compensation and the Unemployment people still had not sent her the cheque. In fact they waited two months to send her the cheque, just at the time when she returned to work and went to live with Claudia in the house with the swimming pool, without even thanking her for all the sacrifices she had made. And surprise, surprise, at that time Beniamina already had a tidy three thousand dollars saved up and then Zio was giving her around fifty dollars a week. Now she's probably got ten thousand because she is about to buy a unit together with Ross.

Sofia, that monument of laziness erected to support long thighs, outstretched arms, beautiful hands, full breasts, dazzling white teeth in the mouth of truth, exaggerated sincerity to the point of giving you a headache, very aware, very accurate, wanted to make a point, and she certainly got it across to us. She started working. The work she does is to her liking. One day she will become an expert repairer of Japanese watches, because that's the sort of work she's doing. Work which is just a little bit boring with little men, who are also a little bit boring, always bowing and coming up behind you suddenly with that silent walk of theirs and looking you in the eye with that characteristically inscrutable look. But she is happy, ecstatic to be assembling little cogs with tweezers, powdering her fingers when they get damp, wearing glasses. In the shop windows she has seen a black dress with diamante shoulder-straps that she wants to buy, she has seen an ermine stole that she wants to buy, she has seen a diamond necklace with matching drop earrings that she wants to buy, she has seen an antique Mexican fan, a dew-drop, a puppy, trains ships travel. Everything she sees stimulates her desires. She has found out that the most succulent and least tragic fruits of work are those of buying, buying, buying. How frustrating it is not to be able to buy things, grab them out of the alluring shop windows, to ransack a shop just by setting foot in it. Buy something for me too Sofia, otherwise I wouldn't know what to do with you. Today, Thursday, they'll give you a big fat pay envelope. Please have the strength to buy me a towel. Haven't you noticed, when you use my bathroom, that my towel is all torn? I don't have anything to dry my face with, my panties are in tatters too, I'm out of handkerchiefs, my shoes need to have the heels fixed.

On the day she collects her third pay, Sofia does not come home. At seven on Friday morning someone rings from the Mater Misericordiae Hospital at Crows Nest to inform us that Sofia Ponti was admitted during the night as a matter of urgency she was suffering from acute appendicitis.

'Go tell her husband,' I quip, thinking it's a joke, and hang up.

When I tell Beniamina she becomes alarmed, rushes to look for the hospital number in the yellow pages.

'Yes, certainly,' she explains unctuously, 'our friend's name is Sofia ... no, not Sofia Ponti ... Sofia Poni,' and to me, there next to her, 'The silly woman wants to get herself arrested. Yes, yes, yes, she's blond, twenty-one, Italian.'

So after several months I learn that Sofia is not Sofia but Concetta Prochetti. I chew over that name, reduce it to mash. Porchetta—piglet, Porca—sow, Pig, piggishly, Sofia, Concetta. I've been living with a corpse next to me. I've been quarrelling, squabbling, fighting, getting angry at a woman who did not even exist. Appalling. There, I see her again as she cadges the odd cent off me for train and bus tickets, drinks, ice-creams, wears my blouses, my skirts, washes in my bathtub, sits on my toilet, uses up my toilet paper, rummages through my personal effects, my handbag, my suitcase, a pig of a corpse, a she-vampire terrorised by the dark, Concetta-Sofia.

How like Sofia. Sofia is in that smock tied at the back which looks like a straitjacket. She has always been mad. That white garment, without sleeves, collarless, really suits her to a T. Sure she looks a bit exhausted, bags under her eyes, dried-up lips. They've just brought her down from the upper floors. Four people lift her off the stretcher and put her on the bed. There she lies still, a complete blank. No more Sofia, no more Concetta. Rotten intestines taken away. With what name will you wake up shortly? In what absurd dream, in what alluring illusion will you lose yourself? Anxiety grips us, focused on the eyelashes weakly fluttering at imminent reawakening. Grow up Sofia. How defenceless and harmless you seem asleep. A little girl. 'Make her happy,' says Beniamina arranging the roses in the vase. On the tallest stalk hangs the get well card with lots of kisses and infinite XXX's. We've smothered her with kisses on paper. And let there be kisses at the hour of death. Amen. One by one we place a kiss on her forehead. At Beniamina's kiss, Sofia flutters her eyelids.

'Hello, dearie. You look great,' says Beniamina.

'Take off. Get your stinking hide off me. Go and smoke a cigarette in the smoker's room and … don't come back,' says Sofia, pushing her with her arm.

'Poor thing,' mutters Beniamina. 'Sedatives have a deadly effect on her.'

'You're all right,' we say.

'I'll be fine if she gets herself out of here. I can't stand her,' replies Sofia, pulling the sheet over her face.

'But what have I done to you?' asks Beniamina. And she gently pulls the sheet off her face. Sofia holds on tight and she pulls.

'It's your fault,' Sofia accuses her from her hiding place. 'It's your fault if I was about to die. You others tell her too that it's her fault. Forcing me to work. Not lending me the money for the dress … and I was going blind over those damned watches … damn them. I won't go back to the factory. I'm going to have a really good time.'

'OK,' says Maria, 'but come out of there now and see what big bananas and what ripe pears we've brought you.'

'You've brought them because I can't eat them,' replies Sofia, uncovering down to her nose. 'Give me a sip of water. I'm dying of thirst.'

'You can't drink,' says Beniamina.

'You lousy skinflint, you won't even give me a drop of water. She's a filthy skinflint, isn't she?' she says turning to us.

'I'm offended. I'm going away. It would have been better if I hadn't come … And now I'll take the roses and throw them out of the window. And to think I wanted you to be the first to know about my plans,' she says casually, in a different tone of voice.

'What plans?' asks Sofia, turning green.

'The bank has approved the loan for Ross and me to buy the unit,' she announces triumphantly. And she goes on, driving the point home.' As soon as we settle we'll get married.'

Sofia is at a loss for words.

'Congratulations,' chirp the North Sydney sisters.

'Congratulations,' I say.

'I knew it,' Sofia is desperate, begins to cry. 'You had to get me upset, so my stitches will all come undone. You detest me. Why do you need to get married? Aren't you comfortable staying with us? And why marry an Englishman? They're all anaemic and drunkards. Your Ross can't read and write. Isn't it true that you write his letters for him in English? You're a hundred thousand times better than he is.'

'He left school when he was a little boy,' Beniamina defends him, embarrassed.

'It's certainly not to his credit. It's no excuse for not knowing how to read and write and he's no exception, that alcoholic friend of his can't write either, nor can Mike, the one who works at the docks. Find one of them who can write and I'll buy you a drink.'

'But English is not an easy language, you know ...'

'Oh, go to hell. Pull the other one. I'm not having the wool pulled over my eyes. You were afraid of being left on the shelf.'

'She's not thinking straight because of the medication, that's why she's talking like this,' says Beniamina.

'But I'm quite lucid, more lucid that you think. The fact is that you're getting married. All the other girls are getting married. Everybody has somebody. What about me?'

'You'll find someone too. You're the most beautiful,' Beniamina says, to make her happy.

'Yes, I know,' she agrees quite seriously. 'I'll get married soon. As soon as I'm better I'll start looking for a wealthy husband ... The tragic fact is that wealthy men are scarce and men are scarce in any case, the few men around who look nice, dress properly, have refined manners, are busy sticking it up each other's bum. It's my intention to scrupulously evaluate each and every proposal, to examine the pants of my suitors under a microscope, probe those who look a bit on the seedy side to see if they hide something that's not quite right. I don't want that sort of problem, it would make me really sad. Can you imagine a mate with a bottomless bum? It makes me sick just to think of it. I swear that if it's my fate to end up with one of those bums I'll shit in it morning and night, I'll use it for a chamber-pot. I'll mix it up real good, to satisfy it as long as it lives. But it must be embarrassing, though. God, I don't want to think about it, otherwise I'll get mad ...'

Ross is getting fat. We see him getting fatter and fatter as the days go by, because he now lives at the flats, in a minute room with a corrugated iron roof. Maybe it was meant to be part of our room—there's a communicating door covered by a curtain. Sometimes Ross talks to us through the locked door. Beniamina is getting fat and we don't know how she does it since we never see her eat. We never see her except on Saturday afternoons and on Sundays. When she has finished the day's work at the clothing factory, she has to run to take the train to the electric cable factory ten minutes' travelling from home. She comes home at two in the morning and gets up at seven. In the meantime the bank account grows. Beniamina explains that they are working hard, going without, so they can own their own unit. Ross likes this enormously. The English are more desperate than anyone else for Australian dollars and they are more stingy and lousy than you could ever imagine. He will make an excellent husband, just what Beniamina needs. He washes his own clothes and Beniamina's as well. On Saturdays he puts them to boil in the copper where the gas costs two cents a pop and every afternoon he comes in to make her bed. He does not drink, just a drop when she is not around. He does not smoke. Asks us for cigarettes. Sofia, Victoria, the North Sydney girls find him a burden. Sofia, who is still suffering from the after-effects of the operation, has become rude and quarrelsome and is always at him over his lack of English calm and composure. She lights up cigarettes in his presence and hurriedly thrusts packet and matches back in her sleeves. Actually when he's round the place none of us leaves cigarettes around, rather we smoke less.

Sofia has also become sad and taciturn. This gives rise to collective remorse. The appointment with the scriptwriter draws near and she does not have a smart dress. She goes through my and Beniamina's rags but nothing appeals to her. Every so often I go to Lella's to work through my English exercises while she studies. Her dedication makes me feel uneasy. Dr Lella Karaposi. How are you getting on among those books, Doctor? I see you're in great shape, Doctor.

Summer was now on the way. One thing was certain, Sofia had always fornicated with danger, with the forbidden in her little tear-filled world. If she raved we didn't care a damn. If she went away we couldn't care less. She went all over the place by hitching rides. Nicola following her with his tongue lolling out. Since I often accompanied her Nicola sent me a message to say that he would work me over the first chance he got. His gabblings made me giggle. If he thought I would be frightened by the threat of his double-bladed knife, now that I had worked out what made him tick, he was very much mistaken. He could frighten Sofia who, dizzy masochist that she was, was absolutely delighted at the interest he displayed in her. They balanced each other in their mad desire for destruction. I annihilate you, you annihilate me, and we're even. She would run away from him, she would look for him, beg him to come back, she would run away again. For a while he would keep out of her way flirting with some Australian woman or other, then the thought would strike him that far away she was most certainly betraying him right, left and centre, he would take to pursuing her again with renewed vigour and when at last he managed to seize her by her slimy tail she would break out in whooping hiccups, the most bestial and theatrical type you would ever hear anywhere. Making up, tears, troth-plighting, tears, promises, tears, miles of tears forming an artificial lake with her sailing in the middle of it in her little paper boat. The longer the tears lasted, the bigger the lake became, turning into a river which flowed down to the immense ocean. The immensity of Sofia. And I would drown in it.

No, summer is surely not a suitable season for dying, one could at least wait till winter which is the season for chrysanthemums. In winter you can quite happily expose yourself to the scythe of the grim reaper. It's the sale season. Old people die like flies. But in summer … I love the summer. Let me enjoy another holiday. Sofia is dragging me along by the lapels of my jacket. She had to prise me off the steps where I'd got bogged down, having changed my mind. 'You're fickle,' she says, 'you can't be trusted.' Believe it or not, that's exactly what she said. Calling me fickle! At the traffic lights we met up with the woman scriptwriter and the man who had kindly offered to pay for our dinner. Basically it was his idea to get Sofia on a TV show despite the fact that he was perfectly aware of the scandals she had caused and that she was not Sicilian. Before getting into the car Sofia gives it the once-over, inspects the car, inspects the roof, inspects the bonnet, and then gives the signal for departure. As I'd anticipated, she makes the scriptwriter fall in love with her. Who knows if she isn't just a little bit lesbian? Sofia is excited and keeps kicking me. Her excitement contaminates me, bloats me, strains me. Ears pricked, as sensitive as radar, I try to guess the decisions being made by the scriptwriter. I place my trust in that particular intuition which, all boasting aside, I believe I have developed—to a very high degree, I would go so far as to say. A touch of folly. Basically I wanted to pierce the poor scriptwriter's skull and by means of my mediumistic powers make her submit to my will. Would she or wouldn't she—but she would, I was certain of it—include me in the programme as well? Maybe I could say something about our Neapolitan folk traditions such as the *Tammurriata Nera*, the Piedigrotta festival or the shepherds' chants, seeing that Christmas was almost upon us. I would have borne the expense of the trappings, the catherine wheels, the confetti, the jars full of *lupini*, the *scetaviasse* instruments. Convinced that I had worked her over mentally, I proposed the matter to her verbally as we were taking our places at table. But the old crow treated my offer with disdain. She didn't think I was as interesting as Sofia whose father was a little pruning-knife-wielding Sicilian. A delicious tasty morsel for the television viewers, something ancient and at the same time modern.

Pity it was a figment of Sofia's sick imagination.

'But she writes,' said Mr X, putting his foot in it as well as his huge hairy hand on mine. 'She writes very well, you know.'

'Really?' The scriptwriter was quite surprised. 'She doesn't write in dialect by any chance? Why waste her talents? Has she ever tried writing in Arabic? What a sensational piece of news! A Neapolitan woman who writes in Arabic!'

I'll give you something sensational you fucking, big-nosed, tropical-climate bitch. Kneel down and kiss me there. Together with the migrant masses I am contributing to the process of your civilisation, to widening your horizon which doesn't extend any further than the point of your great ugly nose. I tear the weeds out of your ears. I give you a certain style. I teach you to eat, to dress, to behave and above all not to belch in restaurants, trains, buses, cinemas, schools. You probably don't know, but I'll tell you in confidence, for your information, that your country, which is now mine too, is based on a gigantic belch. Its flag flutters in the wind created by the toxic gases produced by your stomachs which are choked up like sewers. The myth about being happy and lucky is based on your drunken bouts. Go on, then, drink. You offend us. You don't like wine? You prefer beer? Waiter, a huge bottle of beer for the lady.

Mr X swiftly changed the subject. He began to sing the praises of Sofia's beauty. Sofia of the seven beauties, sure, she shone like a star. She was dreaming about holding out her hand to have it kissed, men bowing before her, granting interviews, cancelling and confirming appointments, giving orders to a swarm of secretaries and press agents. It was all going great. We were having our ice-cream. The coffee had been ordered. Then I saw Sofia go white and cringe in the shelter of the carafe placed at the centre of the table.

'Darling, you've gone white as a sheet,' said the scriptwriter. 'Do you feel ill?'

'It's probably the excitement,' said Mr X. 'Would you like to take a turn on the dance floor?'

The band was playing music from the thirties. Old men, fat men, thin men, young men were slithering and hopping in uninhibited resounding idiocy. Sofia swayed to the music in her chair.

'Yes I'd like to dance,' she accepted, getting up quickly.

Mr X chivalrously followed her. He was leading her by the elbow when Nicola broke in between them. A big baby, face darkened because of his deranged forelock, constipated by arrogance.

'Good evening,' he said politely.

Sofia had seen him come in, that's why she'd gone pale. She went through the motions of running off to look for a way to get out, but the room was small, the tables close together with little space between them, the dance floor crowded, the restaurant toilet displayed a lit-up 'engaged' sign, and so she remained standing there, half turned round, her trunk twisted, as if a magician had suddenly frozen her there, immobilising her in that grotesque posture with his magic wand. She must have realised in a flash that she was safe where she was, under the care of Mr X and the foreign scriptwriter. Certainly not under my care since I was more exposed to Nicola's curses and beatings than she was. She straightened up, approached him with faltering steps, intertwining her fingers in his and then introduced him to us in a shrill voice. She gave him to understand that he was in the company of important people ... television executives were observing us ... maybe tomorrow would bring fame ... she would certainly become an actress and he too, through her, would have the chance to become a famous actor. She would get twenty dollars for the interview. Okay, okay, it was peanuts, sure. But didn't he think of the rotten life she was leading? Wouldn't he think of her for once? Didn't he realise that if they were in it together they could get all sorts of fun out of it?

'Please, please, be understanding,' she begged in the end.

Nicola looked at us askance, one by one, disentangling his fingers intertwined with hers.

'Have you no shame?' he said in a very loud voice. 'How can you do such a thing? Your father would die of a broken heart.'

In a flash Sofia's cheeks puffed up like bladders and a tear rolled out of her right eye. She realised that her parent did not deserve a volte-face of this nature. It was worse than denying that she was flesh of his flesh, blood of his blood. Her father loved her, he suffered, only he didn't approve of her. How could he approve of her? One day she was here, another there, and one day she would be gone for good. Tra-la-la, tra-la-la, tra-la-la. And not even one of her twenty years was worthy of note. Seeing her standing there with that huge tear on her eyelashes, incapable of making a decision, the faces of the scriptwriter and X registered indifference, nervousness, irritation. Actually, I was on the verge of going into a fit too. But Sofia was fighting an uneven battle against common sense—her arid affection for her father, her mother, her little brother and sister whom she hardly knew, were all constraining her to the petty things of everyday living. Her dream had not yet been clearly distinguished from her inhibitions and everything was now collapsing, failing. And to assist the unavoidable collapse she said to Nicola, 'You advise me what's best.'

At that point the two souls performed a grandiose pantomime which made me smile, which I would never have thought possible. Nicola opened his arms wide and she found refuge there.

Casting me a challenging look over his shoulder, she said, 'You come away with us too.'

But I did not want to go. I was all right there. They could go away. I was sick and tired of both of them. There was no ulterior motive, nor did I want to usurp Sofia's role. That little restaurant was okay, comfortable. The evening had passed pleasantly enough. Damn it. Why did she always want to take me along with her? I could not stomach it.

'Come on,' Nicola ordered in a bossy tone.

'What are you waiting for?' said Mr X, very angry.

'Bye, bye …' exploded the big-nosed bitch in an attempt to send us packing, and her farewell came out so brusquely that she almost choked, bending over the jug, and choking, she coughed, spat, spilt its contents.

She was in such a tizz, face red, eyes popping out, that we just had to laugh. X was smiling, I was laughing and so was Nicola, Sofia was splitting her sides with laughter and in doing this she realised that she had well and truly blown it. Goodbye hopes, goodbye opportunity, was her immediate thought. Naturally she pretended that it was all my fault since she had to somehow externalise her resentment against me, against Nicola, against everyone, and she took it out on me. Coming up to my chair she shook it with such force and rage that I fell at the feet of the big-nosed bitch. I wanted to strike back, grab the plates, a blunt instrument, when Nicola pulled me up.

'I've had enough,' he said, pushing me. 'I'll give you two seconds to get out on the footpath.' I had had enough too. It was obvious that they did not want me at the table. I might as well cease imposing on them along with the other two.

When we got to the car Sofia ordered me triumphantly, 'You sit in the middle.'

'You won't cheat me this time,' I replied.

'Right,' said Nicola, giving her a backhander which slammed her down on the bonnet. Marvellous. He should jump on you, do an Indian war dance, smash you all in. These were my thoughts but my face was a mask of utter indifference By now it was child's play for Nicola, he helped her along with one hand and with the other he was pinching her stomach. Another man would have killed the faithless wench. He was far too kind, given that he knew she betrayed him. The titillation of betrayal fed his virility. Every man was welcome to dip into Sofia's font.

The game was becoming too rough for my tastes. Nicola had the accelerator down to the boards and was driving like a raving drunk, avoiding by a sheer miracle head-on collisions with the cars coming the other way. At a certain point when the car swerved Sofia banged a tooth against the dashboard. The blood flowed down her chin and onto her white dress. She did not dare protest for fear of getting more of the same. There was no escape. It was a desperate situation. I had to find a way out, free myself from them, reach a place of safety. When we got out of the car, Nicola grabbed her by the hair and in this way dragged her to the front door. She was kicking out backwards, red drops of blood splashing down from her chin, waving her arms back towards me so as to grab me and thus make sure that I would not take off. I sadistically stepped first to the left and then to the right so she could only clutch at the air. Her beautiful hands vibrated like a blind snake.

How I hated them. I hated her. She was a silly female sheep, a passive cow, a dazed bitch to take all this without even uttering a bleat, a moo, a yelp. Well, calm down then. I respect your stoicism. Excuse me if I jump to one side, if I go in the shade and the light strikes you full on. You desire just a very tiny little bit to swamp me with love and passion. To see me dragged by the hair and by the halter. Whether you know it or not, I don't find it fascinating, it doesn't attract me. That sort of thing is alien to my nature. I am alien, intolerant, allergic and couth. What do you think I've become, a woman resigned to her fate, a dishonoured bum in the bud, a person who turns the other cheek? If it were up to me I would put out ten eyes for one eye, ten teeth for one tooth, I would bite the hand that feeds me, I would tear out his balls like a bunch of radishes out of the ground. I would boil them and serve them up for my dinner accompanied by a nice sparkling wine. And you should also know that I would drink a glass of chilled champagne too and then eat two fried bananas, a serving of ice cream, cakes, salt biscuits, almonds, peach delight, dates, biscuits, nuts, dried figs, sugared almonds, jelly. Oh, yeah, I would gobble all that down and then some. You're on a diet, a diet of sperm. You carry your hunger with you, and that's your affair, your bloody business and no one else's. I'm leaving you so that between the two of us there shall no longer be any forced politeness, politicking, falsehood. Let's declare war on each other. But it will be you who'll be put in the firing line, you and Nicola like two puppet soldiers. Go on, keep your purgatory, your hell, your fireworks, your

trumpets, your drums. I rebel against all this. I feel like a young lioness …
I have to thank the extraordinary variety of food and vitamins which I
guzzle daily. Yet we still have heaven to thank if we have bread but not the
wherewithal to go with it, if we have water but no wine. And anyway, I do
not drink, why should I be talking about wine? And then, I have weight
problems. People think I am slim but I am not really. Tapered but not
very thin. My profile presents a bit of a paunch, a high-class lady's
paunch. They served us quite an abundant dinner at the restaurant. I
must remember to buy a gold chain with a fob watch to hang on my belly.
So I'll go round with a watch and chain. Ouch, these thoughts! These
thoughts frighten me. I'm tired of thinking, of doing nothing and
thinking, it makes me tired, it consumes all my energy, it frees me. No,
don't shout in triumph, don't misunderstand me as you usually do. I
don't mean 'frees me' in the sense that it sets me free. Instead it makes me
a slave. It buries me. Flow, ebb, calamity. There, it's precisely the alleluia
of affliction, it distresses me because you do not speak, nausea and
contempt are your familiars, stitched to your skin. And what wouldn't I
destroy out of contempt. These two, Nicola and Sofia are a scourge, the
day of judgment, the dead rising from their graves en masse, the
menacing finger of God and of his children, the settling of accounts, the
plague, the cleansing of sins, and I have no sins to atone for, crimes,
robberies, expropriations, cheating and swindling, ambitions, slander. I
am innocent and immaculate. Dragon's blood flows through my veins. I
do not kill the truth, do not steal shoes from the feet of the dead. I am
happy to go around barefoot. Good for me—I think in an eccentric, mad
way. And who is more wise and happy than a madman? Just yesterday,
while I was waiting for the bus, in the bus shelter in George Street outside
Central Station, a man dressed in white like the Pope popped out of
nowhere and began to shower blessings on the passing cars. I have not yet
reached the point of believing that I am a female pope. That fellow
probably had a better imagination than I did. And what an expression of
divine, inspired folly he had on his face, what tranquillity, what peace
pervaded his patriarchal figure. The passers-by were laughing.

I stop. Nicola and Sofia stop short as though they had come up against an obstacle. I see the sparks flying off the rails, hear the screech of brakes, see vans run into each other. Nicola lets go of Sofia's hair and a twisted sigh escapes from her lips, a storm of railway sleepers, splinters, glass. The evil force contained in that sigh slashes me with all its power. Nicola regroups. Instinctively I raise my knee, ready to crush to a pulp his proud masculine organs. His glance falls on his groin.

'Anyway,' he says, laughing like crazy, 'I've got nothing against you.'

'You're sick,' is my outburst. I immediately regret having said it and back off in fright.

'Wait before you pass judgment … just wait,' he says, still laughing.

'Hit her,' screams Sofia. 'You don't use that honeyed tone of voice and such refined behaviour with me.'

'Shut your face,' he orders abruptly.

'And why not?' she replies. 'Go on, tell her you've fallen in love with her, even … that you love her … that you adore her.'

'She's a disgusting woman,' he says as if he hadn't heard her. 'Maybe you think I run after her because I'm crazy about her, that I'm blindly in love with her, that I would take on the world for her. But it's she who rings me and tells me where she's going. She needs someone to watch over her …'

'Liar,' Sofia cuts in on him.

'Keep quiet or I'll give you a hiding out here in the corridor.'

I give her the well-known cuckold gesture. It appears that she doesn't appreciate it because she starts to foam at the mouth and to incite Nicola to do this and that to me. The rumpus makes Ross and Victoria come out and Victoria begins to rave without even knowing what it's all about.

'Picking on people who are weak and defenceless. Why don't you have a go at Ross who's big and strong?'

Sofia sniggers in that demented manner of hers. One thing she has always enjoyed is casting the limelight on the English miser's virtues, superiority and chivalry.

'Why are you sticking your noses into this?' she says. 'Who called you out? Go back where you came from.'

'Come here,' says Nicola, and caresses her swollen lip.

I am flabbergasted. It was the second time this evening that I had witnessed Nicola being mawkish. It was too much, she laid her head on his breast, whispering nobleman, gentleman, superman. And I thought they were an extinct species. Until this moment I didn't even know what a gentleman looked like. And Ross, whose concept of racial superiority went to the very marrow of his bones, saw himself confronted by green mice, and courageous men do not engage in battle with mice whether green, grey or dappled. None of us liked Ross. It was hard to get to like him, after he had revealed himself to be worse than Beniamina. Sofia actually hated him. And she wanted to take matters too far. Taking off one of her wooden clogs she throws it at him hitting him on the forehead. Ross opens his eyes wide, rubs his forehead slowly but does not say anything, not a single thing. Not a sound. Nicola, who seems more shocked than anyone else, realises that the issue of male rights is at stake here.

'Tell him you're sorry ... now, I order you. You can't belittle a man like this ... a friend ... a foreigner.'

'I have to tell *him* I'm sorry?' asks Sofia in utter amazement.

'Who else?' The guttural tone of an erect phallus.

'You can't make me do it.' Sofia stands firm. I understand her. You can't force a woman to submit to a man just because he wears trousers. Women wear trousers too. 'No,' says Sofia in a hard voice. 'You can kill me. I won't do it.'

'I'll beat you to death, then,' and it's impossible not to believe him because he has already raised his hands to rain down a couple of jaw-breaking blows on her.

'Come, come, now,' says Ross jovially and he approaches to separate them. 'Come in and have a drink.'

Nicola hesitates for a few seconds. 'Why not?' he says and offers to stand the drinks. Ross stops him. We are his guests. He'll shout. As he starts off for the pub he jokingly warns Victoria and me not to bring this boozy reunion to Beniamina's attention. Sofia shuts herself up in our bathroom to wash. She does not change her stained dress. She seems to take pleasure in showing it round with that dried bloodstain on the tit. We sit in a circle, cross-legged round the coffee-table. Victoria suggests we have a friendly game of poker. The highest bid not to be more than twenty cents. Ross triumphantly begins to take the tops off the bottles.

'I wonder if he'll stay on his feet till we drain them all,' Sofia observes caustically.

'Now what's bothering you, my love?' whispers Nicola.

'Do you love me?' she asks, suddenly inspired, and gives him a little kiss on the neck.

'For heaven's sake stop it, you silly thing,' he draws back embarrassed.

'You're quite convinced now that I love you,' she insists, undaunted. It's a bit of an act for our benefit. 'You know I love you, that I'm a good girl.' She tries to explain to him and to us how much goodness and perfection is stored within her, a deep and infinite vessel for giving and receiving, how her soul makes her a perfect female, female thrice over, in fact. And so she goes on as she drinks her mixture of beer and lemonade, and the more she drinks, the more it makes us sick. A foamy gush of liquid bullshit, which defies written description. Her words flow like butter and honey. She's a real artist in laying them out, frying them up, flipping them over, doing them to a turn. Really crunchy. They go whence they come. It pains me. Just my luck that in the end I win twelve dollars.

I am sleeping. I was sleeping. What time is it? I was dreaming about Sofia's huge black mouth spewing forth sticky black worms. Beniamina is shaking me. Since I always tell the truth she demands to know who has drunk the dozen bottles of beer hidden behind the fridge. I beat around the bush. I don't want to give her the bad news. But she is not the type you can lie to. She was scrutinising me with suspicion, with malice. She kept insisting I tell her—anyway she would have found out sooner or later. I told her. She almost fainted in my arms. 'Swine,' she kept muttering, 'that swine.' When she was away that swine would organise orgies and wild parties. It was her money. It cost her blood and sweat. That ingrate, that guttersnipe, that drunk, gaily squandered it. Another shock like this one and she would lose the child. I thought I wasn't hearing right, that I was bemused by alcohol, that I had misunderstood. When I'm half asleep my reflexes are somewhat dulled, they are slow to react or they are deaf. Impossible. I just did not see her in the guise of a loving mother, but rather as a monster which devours its children. Anger swept over me. I thrust my head under the pillow, cursing my tongue which runs more swiftly than my thoughts. 'I'll teach him a lesson,' she was saying, gasping. I was thinking of the little monster growing in her womb who, poor little thing, had one chance in a hundred of seeing the light, with a parent who squeezed herself like a turnip. This rotten thing, this fetid creature standing there next to my bed, was complaining over a few dollars. If she could have done so, she would have shoved her fingers down my throat to make me bring up the libations, make me pay for my participation in the matter. Since the two of us had never been really close, it stung her even more that I could have enjoyed myself at her expense. Those desecrated, stinking dollars she wanted to keep dead and embalmed, cadavers to be resurrected in the expectation of a better life, which she would never be in a position to appreciate no matter how long she lived. 'I'll never forgive him for this, never,' I heard her scream as she slammed the door.

I fell asleep again and in my sleep I was falling, falling, screaming. This time it was Sofia speaking on the telephone who woke me up. I got up, bent on giving her the news of Beniamina's maternity. The unnaturalness of the dream still pervaded me and this fresh piece of news seemed so far from the truth. I had to have it confirmed by her amazement, by her envy, why not. Like the other women she was utterly convinced that the business-like understanding between Beniamina and Ross would not have lasted long. I came upon her silently. She had the *Sydney Morning Herald* in front of her opened out at the 'to let' page. She looked all topsy-turvy. Bruises and scratches on her arms. As she turned round she blinked a black eye. I noted with satisfaction that her big ape of a darling had run true to form this time too. During the night he had bestowed upon her the usual tender caresses as well as something extra. She ignored me in a scornful manner. I did not ask what happened to her nor did I say 'hello'. Throwing her an ironic glance, I went away as silently as I had appeared. The room had to be swept, it was my turn, the bathroom had to be cleaned, I had to make my bed. I didn't feel like it. I threw a towel and my bathing costume in a canvas bag, made a mortadella sandwich and slipped out the little door at the front.

The sun was already burning. I walked quickly to the pool and lay down on the Luna Park jetty to watch the boys fish. Flat sea. Pure flat silence. Statuesque silence as in a picture-postcard landscape. You wouldn't have said it was normal. Nor was I normal. I had a screw loose somewhere. What was I doing here? Why stay? Should I go away? Remain? I was sure of one thing. Even though I often thought of my home, my real home in the old country, of going back there to Viale Agrelli, dusty and provincial, wrapped in nostalgia and an illusion of growth, I also wanted to die here surrounded by beauty and harmony. Here or elsewhere, nothing was as beautiful as this, in a nightmare of perfection and nullity. The spires of the Opera House, white, beautiful. The little miniature islands, beautiful. Sea. Sails. Hypochondriac poetry. Lord preserve me. Pain makes chickens and poets cry out. Thus spoke that unhappy man long ago. As a young man he used to render inspired readings of the bible before his fellows. Then he lost his faith in God and made himself God. The breeze carried to me the sound of hooting from Circular Quay. Less than ten minutes and the ferry was at the jetty disgorging its few passengers. Among them the Canadian girl, Beniamina's workmate who came and bumped against me. She was high on drugs. I quickly turned my head. It irritated me to start gossiping, given the state of grace in which I found myself. At the pool I went straight to the kiosk to order a vanilla milkshake. I amused myself for a couple of hours in peace and tranquillity under the sun then went back home where I surprised Sofia surrounded by chaos in the middle of piles of cardboard boxes, dresses, packed suitcase, swearing and kicking at a broken-bottomed basket. She was leaving, then. I let out a whistle and she assailed me with her age-old litany about being down on her luck and having nothing but misfortune, and, since I had gone as red as a glowing ember, she asked me to lend her thirty dollars. Thirty dollars—she might as well have said thirty cents. I must have gone pale, because she lowered her bid down to five dollars, just to pay for the taxi, and since the pallor did not pass from my face, she hastened to reassure me with a slap on the back. 'I understand,' she said, 'you forgot to go to the bank.' Then she announced that she had broken off with Nicola. Sign that she was getting some sense back into her. 'Wrap up that coffee table in the blanket. Wrap it up well, so the legs won't show. It'll be useful in my new home,' she said. And she added that Zio was coming because she had begged him as you would pray to a saint. She still felt embarrassed and humiliated because she had to entreat him. There was no longer any satisfaction in resorting to Zio.

I set about giving her a hand. She was moving out. Shortly I too would move out, also Victoria and Beniamina. I was thinking of moving in with Lella for a couple of weeks, but her changed ways aroused nervousness and respect for her privacy. Just a hint of an idea already discarded. Nothing doing. Because, damn it, settling in is sheer torture, the first night, almost always without electricity and without dinner, worn-out incomplete acts which do not become a habit after a long line of streets you have begun to love, faces you have begun to tolerate, so-called beds, so-called chairs, broken-down fridges, defective hotplates, encrusted baths, guilt complexes which are added to the constant stream of fairies, witches, martians, lunatics dripping down out of a medicine dropper, drop by drop, dissipated to no place, dispatched to no destination. Only fate dislodges them, up down, up down, back and forth, restless. Move on, move on. Keep moving, there's room for everyone. Here you are, do you want a first, second or third class ticket? Your choice. Less than third class, thanks. As long as there are wattles, birds, celestial blue skies, butterflies pinned to the branches, a yellow curtain of determination along the road, and millimetres of dream creepers to climb on. Woe is me, how dazed and unhappy I feel. Zio's impending visit makes me even more depressed because it reminds me of Fabia's going on the skids. She wanted to die but didn't manage it. And yet I bet that if we hadn't caught them in the act they would have kept her in the group despite their reservations and griping. They had cast her out, relegated her to forgetfulness. It seemed as though a Fabia had never existed. But not for Zio. Zio did not forget, did not forgive. He had forbidden us to ring him, to bother him. He had come at a run just to throw it all in Sofia's face and he took to insulting her in a way I had rarely seen him do, and he insulted me as well. In the end he was so exhausted and emptied that he had to sit down on the bed.

'You're a parasite in this bastard society. You can't even manage to pretend. As soon as you become a little bit integrated you become bastardised and lose your common sense,' he said.

'What does it matter if someone becomes bastardised, as long as they become integrated, as long as they survive?' asked Sofia, winking at me.

I knew what she was getting at and so did Zio. Ah, Sofia, nothing upsets you. You don't care a damn. You would destroy him for the pleasure of taking him away from Fabia. Once again she's at the root of it all. Why don't you offer him your sympathies? It's no longer a secret that they're packing him off to Africa as a punishment. Too many messes. And now he stands in need of a friendly word. Don't let him leave with the regret of abandoning Fabia in a land more desolate, more sterile and more alien that the most remote and impenetrable African villages. Even though he's superficial, getting on, and little given to comprehending the feminine psyche, he's had some glimmers of understanding. He's understood that Fabia would find greater safety amid Zulus and headhunters. But you're stubborn and a rotter, you don't give in. You won't say that one little word. Your lips mutter, cowardly, coward, perjurer, insisting that she's his niece, his sister's daughter. And has he any sisters anyway? you say. Have you examined the bums? you say. The bums definitely do not match. There's no physical resemblance or blood relationship. Look at Zio's buttocks, spherical in shape, attached to high hips, hips which were once narrow like a male dancer's although now they are understandably ruined by middle age it's a natural process due to the tissue becoming flabby but despite this he can still be classified as a biped. It's a humanoid bum while to identify Fabia's you need an optical instrument used at a distance with both eyes. Whether from far off or close up, it's an arduous task to take in her buttocks all in one go. You need to compare them separately. They are two great lumps of cotton before spinning, two cathedral arches, two Pandora's boxes, two ambulances racing along with sirens at full blast throwing out patients as they swerve round corners, two big fat bulging cow's buttocks, which stop billygoats in their tracks, two gelatinous masses ready to collide, and you, Sofia, yes, you, should dust her behind and reverently append thereto two laurel wreaths, not suddenly cry scandal or tremble prudish and upset as if you had never seen a bum in your life. As if you too did not have one to offer every once in a while. Go on, make some sound waves for Zio. Don't give him that doll-like stare. Give him a little word of encouragement, lighten the melancholy that is in his heart. If I aspired to make a pact I would whisper in his ear the final words of farewell, even though, according to the rules, it's up to you more than any of the other women, scum that you are. For you, rogue and grudge-bearer that you are, he was the evergreen womb which constantly sprouted snake-skin belts, crocodile-skin bags, provisions for the four seasons, welfare and public charity. To you he was father, uncle, friend, benefactor … Who knows if the hairy calves and the underpants with the common swimmer design were really Zio's. He denies it, crossing his heart. He's never worn that junk. Prick, shithead, Sofia says to him, she looked under the door. Childish excuses. The car was his, the underpants were his. No way out of that. It was by chance that we discovered Zio's car at the end of the dark street. Chance, the rain and the flooded gutters. A light was on in Fabia's window. We did not call out to her from the street. Led by Sofia we silently climbed the stairs. And it was she, still in command, who began to spy through the keyhole which was blocked with paper. She swore, cursed, fiddled with a knitting needle, blew into it, spat into it, wanted to set fire to the door, that damned piece of newspaper which did not allow her to catch them in an obscene pose. She wanted to see them rush out without pants like fire-frightened mice. She was giving that locked door and blocked keyhole an almost vital importance, to get satisfaction in front of all the girls. Jealousy was making her jumpy. When she realised that under the door there was a good five centimetre gap where the light came through, she lay down on the floor and saw the underpants with the swimmer design and the hairy calves that she attributed there and then to Zio. It was the last straw. She let out a war cry. The light in the room suddenly went on. Afterwards Zio denied the whole thing and he keeps on doing so. Fabia denied it and we haven't seen her since. Later we learned receiving the news with sincere grief and a good laugh that she had tried to cut her veins. I hope, I love to think, that her action was inspired not so much by some idiotic whim, as was the custom with us, but rather because she was racked and prostrate with grief at Zio's imminent desertion. A sensitive soul, she had taken umbrage because of the panties and bra hoisted like flags on the aerial of Zio's car. It was Sofia's idea, of course, since she wanted to leave a visible trace of our passing. She took the underwear from the rotary hoist in the yard of the barrack-like building and hung it on the aerial. She also muddied the car windows using a small branch to apply the mud.

How hot it is. A humid slobbery heat. I drag myself from the bed to the sofa, from the sofa to the mat on the floor. We don't sleep much at night. We shoo the mosquitoes away and wipe the beads of sweat off Beniamina. Her swelling belly is a malaise which disturbs our nights. She suffers from the heat. She has become a burden. All is flat, motionless, sticky. We are forced to sleep with the windows shut for fear of poisonous spiders. Beniamina saw two on the sofa cushion and fainted. We set about hunting the two spiders and impaled one with the barbecue fork. We often touch Beniamina's belly, put our ear to it, measure it, note its growth centimetre by centimetre on our little blackboard, bet on the sex of the newborn babe. There are about six or seven months to go. Not even

Beniamina and Ross know when the event will take place. I observe that Beniamina has grown just a little bit beautiful, big enormous feet, huge ankles, fat hands, fat fingers like sausages, tired and sluggish in her short dressing gown. I go to visit Sofia and to meet Tom, that good, dear, virtuous Australian man, so different from the exploiters, from brutes like Nicola, from cry-babies like Zio. Straight away I note his dentures, his erect posture, blue eyes, big leonine head with white and yellow hair, but he's still a fine-looking man, as Australians can be when they've not been subjected to the ravages of alcohol. He apologises as he's in a hurry to go, welcomes me warmly. When we're alone I pull Sofia's leg, advising her not to kiss him in the mouth.

'Why?' she asks, eyes opening wide.

'Well, you know, the dentures could remain clamped to your lips.'

'Oh, stop it, stupid. How can you tell that he wears dentures?' she protests, blushing slightly.

'Well, I've warned you,' I insist. 'So do what you like best and be prepared. It could happen that you won't be able to force it open there and then or even for days and days, and then you've had it, what'll you do, eh? Will you tell me what you will do? You'll take it round with you when you go shopping, to the pictures, dancing it wouldn't be so bad if they were gold teeth.'

'I don't kiss him,' she yells, horrified. 'I've never kissed him. He hasn't asked me yet and he won't ask me. He's a gentleman. The first gentleman I've ever met, disinterested and understanding. He respects me.'

'Strange.'

'What's strange about it?'

'I saw him when he was pawing your arm.'

'Jesus, you make me mad. Are you envious? It goes against the grain to see that I'm sociable and full of energy. Well, he was pawing me, what's it to you? Are you spying on me? That's a laugh. You can't even take care of yourself,' she says, getting hot under the collar. 'If it was anyone else I'd throw them out.'

We are on the ground floor, in her little room at the end of the corridor, a dark cubicle with a little window set high up on the wall covered by a greyish net curtain heavy with dust and virtually falling to pieces. On top of the dresser a little amphora with artificial flowers and a few terracotta knick-knacks, left there by kind courtesy of Tom, and a duck with three ducklings. Very chic, very Greek. I don't comment on the refinement nor on the ostentation. She would take offence. A moment ago, in Tom's company, she was quiet, placid, hardly drew breath, hardly said a word but yawned and scratched herself. In that same instant I would have gone on a tour of the cosmos with my nerves on edge, I would have rocketed up to the stars and plunged down head first to shatter my cranium in the shit. That's how I would have acted. I know, for weeks, if I had bitten anyone, I would have done him in on the spot. Strike me down if I've ever understood anything about Sofia. She lives rent free in this hole, yet I wouldn't stay here even free. When he goes out Tom gives her the keys of his room so she can watch television or munch sugared almonds and lollies or dine on canned pasta and beans and other rubbish like dog food. Tom has won four thousand dollars on the horses. He didn't even give her one. Worse still he rushed out to place it all on bets right to the last cent. Sofia won't admit it but she was quite disappointed about it. That's why she is touchy and a bit nervous. I don't know what to do about it. They haven't let me get even sight or sound of that lovely pile of money. Maybe I'm overreacting. I am touched because Sofia is acting strangely and smiles at me.

'Are you hungry? I'm feeling rather peckish. Upstairs there's plenty to eat and there's the telephone.'

'Can I ring Italy?'

'Sure, America too,' she says.

When Tom has been away she has, on three occasions, rung through to the police station in her village in Sardinia to talk to her uncle and cousins who don't have the phone at home.

'What if Tom catches us while we're on the phone?' I object without much conviction.

'Should you worry? Do I worry? He says I'm a good girl, an unfortunate girl who doesn't have a place to sleep. And he hopes, keeps hoping and waiting that I find a good job so I can pay off my debt for arrears in rent. If only he knew how I am racking my brains. If anything, I'm working on a plan to clean him out. When he's not broke, when he wins, he leaves his money around. I've searched all over, looking for a hiding place. Now that you're here, let's have another look around, together listen, sleep here tonight. Tomorrow you can come with me while I look for work, at least we can pretend to. I can't get round to doing it on my own, it gets me down. I don't understand how you can manage to live with that lousy amount the government gives you. You look like a woman in chronic despair. I'd become a halfwit or I'd steal.'

'And Nicola?' I ask.

'Disappeared,' she clucks happily. 'Didn't have any backbone.'

'Hmmm, I wouldn't bet on it.'

'I'll level with you,' she says laughingly, 'I'm going out with one of Ross's friends, you know, that Irishman who came to the barbecue on the rocks. Do you remember him?'

Yes. I remember too that it wasn't her he was asking after, it wasn't her he was making sheep's eyes at as soon as he arrived, but she latched on to him making like a fresh young filly and then they disappeared into the bushes.

'Bob, you know, he's crazier than Nicola,' she says with a touch of pride. 'They came to blows over me. I should have told Bob Nicola wouldn't stop bothering me. Bob is a very decisive guy, tough. He's bought a shotgun and will shoot him if he sees him hanging around me again.'

There was one thing Robert didn't know, it wasn't Nicola who was persecuting Sofia, it was the other way round. And Sofia would have to learn some hard bitter facts about tough Irishmen who were more backward, aggressive, had more hang-ups about women than Italian and

Greek men, and who would have led her a tragic and vertiginous song and dance to the point of making her hair turn irreversibly white. But she was blinded by the man, blinded by two trapeze-artist's legs, by the attractive slimness of the alcoholic. Among other things Robert drank like a sponge, beginning at six in the morning to drown his hang-ups and homesickness. By way of recompense he had two penetrating enchanting eyes, sparkling and shiny like polished diamonds. There was no tenderness in those eyes, nor admiration for Sofia, and in fact he gave little or no thought to the idea of shacking up with her, nor did he take her to the pictures, to a restaurant, to a dance, or out and about unless his masculine vanity required it.

I call Naples. No answer. The operator asks if she should try again later. Yes, certainly. I'm not moving from here, I assure her. Sofia butters slices of bread and adds gherkins. We eat and talk, turned to face the sea. In the full light of day it's like a paradise lost round there. Now the few lampposts scattered among the trees and at the sides of the wooden stairway which leads down to the little beach and the jetty give out their light. Patches of light and patches of pitch darkness. Two women, one naked and one dressed in a petticoat, walk in a zigzag pattern, appearing and disappearing from the lit-up patches, screaming and grunting like pigs at the slaughterhouse, and they could really be having their throats cut and no one would intervene, because people here couldn't give a damn, whether you live or die, laugh or cry, eat or go hungry.

'A bonus to go with the view,' Sofia sniggers jubilantly. 'You want a thrill, there you are, examine it, write about it, these are first-hand experiences, there's nothing else, I tell you.'

The naked woman has got in among the trees and now comes back into view at the top of the stairs where she trips and threshes about, her bottom exposed to view. The other woman, wielding a brick, has almost caught up to her and is about to hit her on the head when the victim slips away from under her on all fours in an attempt to find refuge in the nearest house. The face of the woman in the petticoat is thrown into focus by the street lamp, it looks like a man's face with make-up. She makes some strange-looking grimaces as she raises her arm and hurls the brick smack into the middle of a window. A man rushes into the street like greased lightning, grabs the naked woman and hurls her to the ground again in a fury of kicks and flying fists, shouting all the while that they nearly killed the baby in its cot and every so often menacing with his fists the other woman who looks on from round the corner without intervening although she is jumping up and down throwing handfuls of dirt at him and threatening death and destruction. By this stage the man is satisfied, stops a moment to gaze at the senseless woman on the pavement and then goes back in the house. At this point the one who looks like a man goes up to her friend, shakes her, caresses her, calls her 'My dear, my dear,' and other heartbreaking crap.

'Ah,' says Sofia. 'The lesbian has copped it. They'll make like turtledoves, all the better for it, you'll see. How disgusting, I'd give them the rest of their deserts but I can't because they rent the room next to mine. Spit on their heads 'cause you'd be doing me a favour. They don't know you. You don't have anything to do with them, and you really needn't ever come round here again anyway. It's different for me as I have to mix with them, say hello because they do, ask after their health, talk about the weather and swallow the landslide of swear-words I would like to pour out against them. If I had the money I'd take a room in a hotel. I'm like you, I can't stand shouting in the night. Those two just don't know how to stay among civilised people, believe me. Why is it that they have to bash each other up every night? Don't they love, adore, worship each other, what kind of feelings have they, can you tell me? They're sick, maybe their parents were alcoholics, you couldn't explain it otherwise. Who'd go near them decrepit as they are and with all those rolls of fat on their stomach? Would you suck the tits of those dirty old women?'

The dirty old woman, supported by her companion, is painfully limping back to her lair exhausted. I thought that the curtain had come down on the performance when instead the paddy wagon and an ambulance rush up, sirens going full blast, music to Sofia's ears as she rubs her hands with glee.

'They'll arrest them,' she says.

The ambulance attendants are struggling to get the injured woman into the vehicle as she doesn't want to go without her friend. Her friend is screaming that she has to go with her as she has to look after her, she's the only one who knows how to handle her etc. The police hold her on the street together with the man against whom she has laid a complaint. The man is holding the baby tight and every now and again bumps it against the police as if in his defence arguing that it's not fair, that there's no justice in this country, the two women are a public menace, their behaviour is indecent, it's a miracle that his son didn't die, they deserve to be put away for life, or to be abandoned on a desert island. On her part the lesbian retorts that he has lamed her friend, attacked a defenceless woman, battered a gentle flower, he's the one who should be put away, savage monster, beater of women, women shouldn't be hit, it's against the law, women are queens, women should be respected …

'Like hell,' screams Sofia from the balcony.

'You numbskull, control yourself or they'll summon us as witnesses,' I whisper.

'But why don't they put the handcuffs on them? It's crazy. What are they waiting for, Jesus, I'd line them up against the wall,' she says.

'Calm down, they're taking them away.'

In fact the police were intimating that the woman should get into the wagon, then the man. Ladies first. The man hands the baby to his wife, kisses her.

'Looking for understanding,' says Sofia, gazing into the empty street.

Past midnight and Tom still has not come back. I have to wash cups, utensils, saucers. Sofia has become lazy, she has set her sights high, ever higher. She dreams about striking it lucky. Who would have thought she was a dreamer? She dreams about security, the riches which Robert will bestow upon her. We go downstairs to sleep. I have completely forgotten about the call to Naples. I go in the bathroom for a moment, there are traces of blood in the bath, blood on the tiles, on the edges of the lavatory bowl, bloody hair on the wooden floor which sticks to my bare feet. A dense tangible sticky stench of constipated faeces hangs in the air suffocating me. I react violently, vomit into the bathtub, spewing my guts out as well. To think that I am sleeping with Sofia in this stinking hole, in that narrow bed with the mattress impregnated with putrid matter and disease, between these walls which ooze wickedness and misdeeds by stinking people, a procession of stinking dregs filing past in dribs and drabs and then mysteriously disappearing. They have vanished but their stench has remained in the cracks and fissures, in the grains of dust, and that stench nips like a tarantula, that stench contaminates us. Sofia stinks. I stink.

'Are you awake?' Sofia asks.

'Yes.'

'We'll go to the pool tomorrow.'

'Didn't you want to look for a job?'

'I've changed my mind, or rather I've put it off ...' she interrupts herself, bringing her fingers to her lips. 'Ssh, I hear noises.'

Someone is working away at the lock. I get goose pimples. Sofia lifts her head off the pillow. I have the impression that the blond mass of Sofia's loose hair spreads itself over too wide a space, that her mouth dilates emitting hoarse weak sounds, too faint for that mouth now opened as wide as a cooking-pot. The door flies open with a thud. In the entrance stands Tom in pyjamas. I remember the phone call left in abeyance and give Sofia a kick in the shins.

'Tell him that they're relatives of yours,' I mutter. 'He'll give you credit, understood.'

'Leave it to me,' she replies.

Tom advances like a blind man, whispering, 'Sophia, Sophia, where are you?'

'What is it? What's happening?' she flutters, jumping out of bed. 'Turn on the light. Why do you sneak into other people's rooms without knocking? Aren't you accustomed to knocking?'

She is giving him a telling-off in an irate tone of voice which Tom does not like one little bit and he retorts, 'It's my house and I'll sneak in whenever I like.'

And Sofia replies in a tired-sounding voice, 'Sure, it's all yours. And to say so you come in like a thief frightening your tenants.'

Tom cannot and will not consider Sofia on the same plane as the common or garden tenant. Someone who doesn't pay, who doesn't meet commitments, who has no honour, who is perpetually in the red, doesn't have any rights. We can all agree on this. But how can you possibly work out why he had taken her in so enthusiastically and willingly, allowing her free access to his room, food included? Perhaps because Sofia is beautiful but poor and it was an act of homage to beauty. After all, he says, he had taken her to his heart, wanted to protect her, purify her. From what, though? Good God, I cannot see any logic to it. I have to feel out, chew over, this act of charity. I am like Saint Thomas, who doesn't even believe in Christ and holy miracles. I don't believe in anything, not even in myself, imagine if I were to believe in the drivelling charity of a decrepit kangaroo who in his haste has forgotten to button his pants ... though, looking more closely ... it's not that the buttons have been left undone, the opening has only one button and you vaguely distinguish, very vaguely, his flaccid wrinkled prick. I can't take my eyes off it. It makes me smile. And he is so furious, seeing what overseas phone calls cost, that he is half inclined to throw us out in the street at this time of night. But he won't do it this time, this time he will show what an understanding person he is and forgive us. He will give her just one more chance, just one more respite, just so long as that perfidious lazy immoral hustler changes her behaviour. Confidentially, it is the gospel truth. But who is he, anyway? How dare he! That is not the way to behave. Sure, sure, go hang himself, Sofia is trembling like a beaten dog but does not dare draw breath. I had got out of bed and now climbed back in. Sofia remains seated in the only chair in the room, there in the corner, her head hanging on her breast and her little heart in turmoil meditating that from now on she will be a good girl, a well-behaved girl. Seeing her is like seeing myself utterly devoid of will, and this gives me a painful feeling indeed.

In the morning we went to the pool. On the way there Sofia was singing under her breath. In the water Irma, accompanied by a fine delicate-looking lad, came up to us, introducing the young gentleman as her boyfriend. He was very young and Irma easily passed for his mother. On her head was a bathing cap decorated with posies bunched up like a cabbage. When she went to take the sun she took it off and tied her hair with the mauve-coloured ribbon she was wearing the first time I met her. She was wearing a very skimpy costume, layers of lard bulging out, tits spilling out, thick black down sticking out from under the tiny triangle of cloth. She hung round the North Shore because the young gentleman lived at Kirribilli. Here was a woman, mad or not, truly serene and free from worries. She told a few stories of the type which pass from one lewd mouth to another which made us split our sides with laughter. I had to hold my belly and Sofia had tears in her eyes, but as soon as the boy got distracted and didn't pay any attention to us, Irma, almost involuntarily, would demolish his demure facade with snobbish allusions. She thought she had taken up with an honest-to-goodness ladies' man, she bubbled and puffed herself up in a supreme attempt to exhibit an appearance of urbanity. She went on and on talking about him in undertones, winking furtively at his strong profile, whispering about his blond locks, the nape of his neck golden in the sunset. He was her little slave, awfully effeminate, fragile and snobbish. Mentally naked, she sensed that whenever we caught sight of her before she saw us, we would immediately race for cover among the passers-by or in a shop, thus depriving her of the satisfaction of showing off her pride in her poofterish companion. She would always bear down on us to hug and kiss us wherever there was a crowd, a thing which really grated on my nerves so much that I would have strangled her. To tell the truth I would have hated to kiss a poofter of his sort and, observing him, I asked myself how on earth he could get it up and keep it up for more than two seconds at a time, the lovely lad. Who could deny him, lovely, delicate, sophisticated, cruel lad that he was … maybe he was good at handling riding crops and imprecations, Sofia insinuated maliciously, and Irma, the scoundrel, grew in volume and understanding like a water-logged bale of wool which sprays out jets of saliva when squeezed. She complained that we were really hitting below the belt and distressed her with our old-fogey jesting. Wherever she hung round there was no need for funeral rites, nazi-comic ceremonies, mourning clothes, black masses, sadism and torture, because she would arouse violent passions even in stones.

'Hey, hey,' joked Sofia. 'And yet you have a certain Slavic charm.'

'You're a real shit, you know, and you really get my goat,' was Irma's reply.

'And what about me?' I added.

'I don't take you into consideration,' was her prompt reply, and she tried to shove back into her costume the clumps of hair which were sticking out along the sides of her thighs. 'You've such odd views and they don't coincide with mine at all.'

'Hey, want an ice-cream? Rosa's shouting. She's quite normal, I assure you, even though she doesn't give a damn. Couldn't care less about anything. She lives her life upside down and walks backwards like crabs do when you stir them, don't get her all upset because she doesn't cry like the rest of us when she's sad, you know, she sings and plays. Go on, sing, intoxicate Irma with your singing,' Sofia egged me on, in the meantime groping among my things in search of coins for the ice-cream.

'Bugger it,' Irma said violently. 'I couldn't care a damn about her singing. And, anyway, I sing too, and so does he, gracefully and tunefully.' And she pointed to the little gent who was absorbed in reading his newspaper.

'Whatever you might say about him,' Sofia objected, 'he's a wanker. Pardon me,' she sniggered, 'perhaps you prefer that I call you female wankers. Sounds more correct. You're two female wankers, always scuffling.'

'You're my type,' Irma said to Sofia. 'Let's get together, I like you. We'll really get on, the two of us. We've got a lot in common. You're refined and appreciate beautiful things. You're a genuine, sincere person, and I enjoy talking to you. I can't get on with her at all. She's full of airs. And anyway I've seen her collect cigarette butts. I'd rather ... I'd rather kill myself instead of ... instead of ...'

She was grasping round for a jibe. She'd got lost. Cheer up! The day is short. Three-quarters has already flown away. The sun is burning. There is no beach umbrella to provide shelter and I have delicate skin. Spread some lotion on my back or tonight it'll be covered in little blisters and another hundred or so freckles will flower. Yes, I have freckles on my nose. Put some lotion on my nose. Yes, I look like an eskimo with eyes turned inside out. No, I'm not frigid. Poor fool. Not even mentally frigid. You can be sure of it. And Irma started to laugh. Loud and long.

'You know that when I laugh I can't stop myself. Hit me on the head.' Her boyfriend was standing at the other end of the pool drinking a coke. 'We love each other,' she said emphatically. 'Isn't it marvellous? It's siesta time and we're used to taking our nap locked in each other's arms.' She made a sign to the lad to go to the dressing shed but he dived in and swam over to us.

Since I was overwhelmed by aimless commitments, Sofia likewise, we no longer saw each other and Tom replied monotonously on the telephone that she was out looking for work, that she had an interview with the general manager of this or that firm, often adding that she was finally headed on the straight and narrow path to finding a job. His pathetic paternal tone of voice nauseated me so I gave up the idea of tracking her down. In any case Beniamina's wedding date was fast approaching and I was mixed up in the proceedings as if I were family, writing and sending invitations, drawing up lists of expenditure and food for the wedding feast, imploring Lella, who absolutely did not want to go, to come and take the photos, engaging a band and a singer for as little money as possible, or even tracking down a band and a singer willing to perform for nothing. Despite the very considerable efforts of us all it was impossible to obtain performers who would sing and play for free. But she struck it lucky with the white wedding dress and train. A fellow worker at the electric cable factory would lend it to her complete with tiara, gloves, tulle and lace handbag, still in excellent condition, for only the cost of getting it dry-cleaned. And whether it was because of the tension or because of the emotion or because of the pregnancy causing her pain, she had to give up work before the time she had anticipated, and between one bout of vomiting and another she attended to the preparations and knitted booties and dresses which were miniature masterpieces. The expression on her face had softened, the uncertainties had been smoothed out, only her eyes flashed restless and rapacious. Our room was heavy with the sort of atmosphere which heralds partings and goodbyes, and I was ready to transport my memories and keepsakes, my few belongings, the brush and dustpan, the broom, which belonged to me, along the roads of the far western suburbs in search of a low-rent shack bathed in eternal melancholy.

One evening, when we'd just finished dinner, Tom turned up like a lightning bolt. Although Beniamina had fallen out with Sofia, she welcomed him with theatrical ceremony and, without even enquiring after the reason for his visit, immediately ordered me to uncork the bottle of Barolo I had stolen when working at the restaurant-pizzeria, and that I had planned to lay by and drink all on my lonesome on some future special occasion. In her opinion there could be no more splendid and propitious occasion than that of toasting her health, happiness and wedding in Tom's presence, since he would report to Sofia word for word and impression for impression all the luxury of that imported wine offered casually to the guest. Beniamina had heard about Tom, he was in touch with Sofia, and that sufficed to give her a reason for showing off, to put on a show of happy gratification and even generosity, as if she had changed her spots. She sent for Ross and all together we toasted Beniamina's new unit, Beniamina's huge belly, Beniamina's ever-growing finances, Beniamina's and Ross's bright rosy future.

When only the dregs were left and there was no sign that other bottles might appear, Tom began to show signs of nervousness, glancing at the door in a circumspect and bitter fashion.

'Where's Sofia?' he said.

'You come to look for her here!' Beniamina reacted as though a slap had taken her entirely by surprise.

'Are you friends or aren't you?' he hadn't expected this reaction. 'I thought ... She's been missing for four days and four nights and ...'

'My good man,' Beniamina interrupted him, 'you'd go mad if you took Sofia's disappearances seriously. Get hold of yourself. Stop upsetting yourself and stop upsetting us. It's clear that you don't know Sofia very well. If you knew her better, shall we say in depth, you'd accept her strange behaviour philosophically. Sofia is way out. She's impossible. Perhaps you find her cheerful and charming, do you? You're mistaken, believe me. Every so often a couple of lashes with a leather belt wouldn't be out of place. Sofia likes it. She's twisted and a masochist. To suffer and be beaten is like being showered with roses and flowers ...'

'I get the impression you've jumped to the wrong conclusion about why I've come here,' Tom replied calmly. 'When I came in you gave me such a warm welcome that I didn't get the chance to explain.'

'Well then what's it all about? Didn't you come to announce your engagement to Sofia? Didn't Sofia send you as an ambassador of peace?' Tom looked at her, uncomprehending, such a funny expression on his face that Victoria and I had to double up behind the sofa hysterical with laughter.

'You flatter me,' he said, recovering from his surprise. 'You were joking when you mentioned engagement, weren't you? Or maybe Sofia has been throwing hints about it?'

'No, no. I was joking,' Beniamina hastened to reassure him.

'Good, good,' he nodded, not at all convinced and with a crooked smile.

'Can you identify Sofia as Concetta? Seeing she's two women in one, or three or four in one, where has that one woman gone to?'

'I knew it,' Beniamina cries out in triumph. 'That wretched woman has stirred up more trouble. What's the matter this time?'

Tom did not answer directly. Slowly and deliberately he took out of his pocket a Commonwealth Bank passbook and before he could hand it to her Beniamina grabbed it.

'Oh, great!' she burst out, beside herself with rage after examining it at length. 'It's so incredible that I can hardly believe it. What a bastard, daughter of a bitch, brazen-faced hussy, she-devil. I'm just a beginner compared to her. If that chicken-claw signature of hers weren't here I wouldn't even believe that these deposits are real, I'd think that the stamps and the deposits were false and nonexistent just as she is false and nonexistent, liar and con-artist. And you,' she turned on me angrily, 'you should have known.'

I shrugged my shoulders.

'You two have been inseparable lately and you must have been up to some dirty deed or other. Admit she's turned to prostitution.'

'You overestimate her,' I said, grabbing the passbook out of her hands. I glanced at the number at the end of the page, nearly a thousand dollars deposited in small sums over the past year, that's why Beniamina was seething with indignation. She remembered being accused of usury at the hospital and the undeserved derision she had received for living on bread and water for two months. 'Of course you haven't asked yourself how he came into possession of Sofia's money,' I told her rudely.

'I don't want her to die,' she exclaimed. 'I can't imagine her dead, bloodsucker though she is, she's better alive than dead.'

'Women like Sofia don't die young. They never die,' I said.

'Why? What's special about her? She's not immortal, is she? You attach too much importance to her, and you delight in treating me badly, I who am pregnant and in pain. But I've understood your plan. It's clear to me. You've plotted together to frighten me and make me lose the child.

You're jealous that I'm pregnant and you're not, jealous of my happiness, that's what it is.'

'Mrs Beniamina,' old Tom protested horrified. 'I'm not, I don't …'

'Don't you dare butt in, you've got a knack of upsetting me. You should be ashamed, a man of your age going along with Sofia's dirty tricks,' she was screaming on undaunted. 'You can be really proud of yourself, you look like an intelligent person, you could be my grandfather. You should be ashamed of yourself. Acting in cahoots with Sofia to frighten me into giving birth prematurely and ruining the wedding. But you can tell her from me, you can tell her that she'll never come up with a paramour who will marry her unless it's some silly old man foreigner.'

Poor Tom from blushing pink turned yellow.

'Get hold of yourself. You're blowing it out of all proportion,' Ross reproved her gently.

'There's no reason why I should restrain myself, and anyway I have to let fly when I get the urge, the doctor said so too,' she insisted obstinately.

'Mrs … lady,' Tom stammered hesitantly. 'Please let me speak. I'm looking for Sofia, or Concetta if that's her name, because she has taken advantage of my trust to con me. She hasn't paid me the rent for her room for a month. I'm a good man but not a fool and I have suspected something for a long time. And I obtained conclusive proof when I did a thorough search of her room. I found the passbook under a pile of dirty clothes …'

'Big deal,' Beniamina cut in sarcastically.

'I had the right to,' Tom protested. 'Anyone else would have done the same.'

'Not me,' she zeroed in on her point. 'And anyway what's all this yacking about, what do you expect us to do?'

What Tom expected us to do he got out between bouts of apologies and stammering. He placed particular emphasis on swindle, fraud and moral subjugation, adding that Sofia had reduced him to such a state of subjugation as to deprive him of the power of speech in her presence. I was somewhat struck by this and didn't hear the rest. It was known for a fact that we Italians all belonged to criminal-type associations and that the bonds of friendship which existed among us made us protect each other when we got up to some piece of mischief or other, so he didn't trust us but at the same time he asked us to help him.

Now if Beniamina and I had had any patriotic feelings we would have immediately grabbed Tom, thrown him on the floor, ripped his pants off his posterior, beaten him to a pulp and even crushed his dentures underfoot. We should have given him a good beating, just like this, no more and no less. Instead Beniamina pulled me aside and advised me, seeing that I knew him, to accompany him out in the street, buy him a drink, maybe get him drunk, get him into a taxi and tell the driver to take him home. On the strength of that bond of friendship Tom had been raving about she did everything in her power to keep the passbook, offering him as security the furnishings and rags belonging to Sofia which she had left there. Tom didn't want any of that rubbish as security as it had no value and was only fit for burning.

'Listen, get him out of here,' Beniamina muttered. 'Promise him you'll follow the matter up, promise him anything. Arrange for him to meet Sofia. Reassure him that he will get the rent money, that he'll get everything back, and apologise profusely. Promise him that next time we'll invite him to lunch and you'll arrange it so he can go to bed with Sofia. I don't think he has been otherwise he wouldn't carry on like this. Tell him that she can't wait to get into bed with him either. Tell him she's run off because she's shy and she didn't mean to do him out of the rent, that you knew about the situation and will arrange matters in such a way that he'll be completely satisfied. Do it for me. This guy looks like staying here all night. I know you hate me and wouldn't inconvenience yourself in any way for me, but I'm not asking you out of selfishness. You know that if I get upset we'll have one hell of a night. Let him understand that it's an honour for you to ...'

'It would be an honour for you, who've been a pimp all your life,' I hissed through my teeth.

'If you don't sling mud around, you explode,' she retorted calmly.

'No matter what, I'm not going out with him.'

'It's not a case of going out with him, it's a case of getting him out of here. I'd send Victoria but she's an idiot and would make a mess of things. You're the only one who can pull it off,' she concluded.

I considered it useless to argue the point so, politely taking Tom's arm, I tried to drag him off, mentioning the pub at Milson's Point station where we would be sure to run into Sofia. He was reluctant to come with me, shuffled his feet saying it was a waste of time. I observed Beniamina, her eyes popping out of her head as she advanced towards the centre of the room. In shuffling about she tipped over the cane sofa, attacked him, kicking him, her joined hands supporting her belly and holding it up, shouting at the top of her voice that in deference to mother nature we'd better go and shit under the bridge otherwise she'd drop the baby a month prematurely. I tugged at Tom's arm and was amazed to note that the poor man was nearly paralysed. I shook him and he moved stupefied towards the door. He walked quickly and I had to stumble along behind him, chatting about this and that, I promised to ask Sofia for an explanation. Truth is that everyone can make promises while chatting away and I'm better at it than anyone else, but this wasn't the problem, and you didn't have to move heaven and earth to get to the bottom of it. It was a dead cert that Sofia was having a great time with Robert at Manly and she was neither dead nor in trouble. Tom walked in a murderous silence and probably didn't believe a word of any of my promises.

'Will she be there?' he asked out of the blue.

'How can I be sure of it,' I replied abruptly, but seeing that he was about to change colour and begin complaining, I altered my strategy, became cooperative and compliant to his immediate concern which was flushing out Sofia. Finding her was in his interests and in ours too. I told him that we felt her absence so keenly, loved her so and held her in such esteem that tomorrow we would place advertisements in the missing persons column of the papers. 'I'll see to it personally,' I said, and I shook his hand to sanction my promise. His handshake, I must admit, was reluctant and doubtful. I could feel his coldness towards me with such violence that I would have thrown Robert's address in his face there and then. All those expedients, all that discretion and caution strained my patience to the limit. He even found cause for complaint in the fact that I hadn't called a taxi for him and claimed that I should pay for it seeing it was up to me to call it. If it had cost me twenty cents, same as the ferry, I would have waved my arms wildly to stop one, I don't shed tears over twenty miserable cents, and if I see a twenty cent coin in the street I don't even bother to pick it up. I have magnetic eyes and the devil's own luck in spotting a dollar, two dollars, ten dollars, fifty dollars, piles of coins in the sand and in clumps of grass, even unopened pay packets with the name written on, and may they shoot me or deport me if an honest urge or a flash of Christian remorse has ever been aroused in me regarding the unfortunate losers. Rather (and I boast about it), I pray, desire, throw the evil eye at workers and employed persons so that their bankrolls may fall at my feet, whether it's Friday, Thursday or Wednesday.

'My lucky day is Friday the thirteenth, Black Friday, the day which everyone tries to avoid like the plague,' I was telling Tom, quite satisfied with myself. 'Thirteen is my lucky number, you know, and so is seventeen, you know.'

'Why don't you talk to me about Sofia?' he sighed.

'Oh, I don't know,' I replied lazily.

'I don't think she's a respectable girl.'

'She gives that impression,' I said, 'but when you get to know her she's innocence personified.'

'That's enough. She's a little scamp,' he said, and smiled despite himself.

Just look how infatuated with Sofia he has become, and at his age too! And that foolish woman, what a strange and incurable frenzy she has to belong to someone, suffer and destroy, make and break. There are some odd types of affection—it all depends on the type of cross our inner being has to bear and on the particular bewitchment which holds us in its spell. I got the urge to cut loose, run away. If we found Sofia in the company of Robert and friends I would have been the least suitable person for indulging in an exchange of bullshit on life and love. Suddenly I calmed down, remembering that Sofia could not possibly be in this pub because she was at Manly. In fact, Sofia was not there, neither in the crowded public bar, nor in the private bar, nor in the garden where enormous steaks three fingers thick and white Australian sausages were sizzling on the barbecue. Tom plumped down on a wooden bench.

'Maybe she'll come later,' I said.

'I'll stop here to eat,' he replied.

By way of farewell Beniamina said that she had never seen me cry, and that a woman who doesn't cry cuts herself off from all wisdom. That may be so. It was a torridly hot February, a cursed February, when I was starving and I decided to surrender and cried until I was in a daze. Every once in a while I allow myself a little restorative cry, but now, after what she has just told me, I am no longer certain whether I dare call those ignominious drops, which are flowing warm and salty down my cheeks, tears or corneal irritation or cold or sinusitis. And, fuck it, allow me to be so bold, a woman who is pushed to the edge of suicide and plans in earnest to ladle out her soul, and nearly does so, but then changes her mind and backs off, in my opinion, has every right to sharpen her claws and grind her teeth. I had crushed the demon which is in each of us and had opened myself out to hope and knowledge. I put cynicism, pessimism, cunning, dishonesty, to sleep and in doing so I became aware how easy it was to annihilate myself, enslave myself, destroy myself. What for? What was smoothing the way to my own death? No. I didn't kill myself. I agreed that it was too early and too convenient to die. The time hadn't come to surrender. Death, eternal sleep and oblivion could go stuff themselves. Death became a stranger to me. I saw myself riding the tiger and on the back of the tiger I climbed again. Survival, for all that survival was a paradox occurring in parallel with the funeral of my ideas and my enthusiasm for the golden land, a petty mirage in the middle of the desert where even sunlight and moonlight repudiated each other. I was born again from a hibernation which was not physical and mental lethargy but a pure and simple coma. Suspension of the 'I' for personal ends. Oh, how this makes me laugh, how apt it is. In this passage only those who have risen again can understand me. Let's hope that not many have been resurrected, because the dribbling of Lazarus troubles me to the point of annihilating my imagination and vitality. So I took root again on the golden crust and there I perched on the summit of the great human wall. Yes, certainly, superiority generates order and justice, generates love, maturity, humility, intelligence, jobs, hot meals, woollen blankets …

For years now all social strata have been pissing on me from a great height. Hey, and hey again, not to mention the stray opportunistic prick. Am I perhaps a slave bought in chains and with rings in her nose, that they think they can piss on me? By all the devils in hell and all the demons in my head, by Christ and the most Holy Madonna, by all the false saints in paradise, I invoke the rights of man and all humanity. I have stored up so much of that piss over these wretched years that I could piss down from the top of the wall for centuries on end and unleash a second flood of biblical proportions. The truth of the matter is that my piss is priceless, piss streaked with blood and cancer, piss that asks no quarter, not to run to waste because in its flight it curves like a colour-changing rainbow and paints cities, plains, mountains, rivers, lakes and seas. Gather the sparkling fluid in buckets, bins, baths, troughs. A woman who has suffered too much and has learnt to piss for want of any better consolation offers it to you as a gift.

A cloudy lead-grey day, the day Beniamina went away with the bridal dress over her arm. She was getting married the day after and I had threatened to pierce her belly with a huge pin as a wedding gift. It all ended there, our friendship, I mean, without upsets, without traumas. We made our pact as mutely as two fish. The last insults fell like stones and seals. We would never meet again, no doubt. And since I considered it an inadmissible miracle to have won out over her, I surprised myself humming religious hymns and warbling as I have never warbled before in my life, and since the room suddenly seemed a cage exclusively mine, at least for another two weeks already paid up by the bond money, so I didn't have a worry in the world, I decided to go to the pictures and on the way to look into the estate agents' windows and at the notices hanging outside the houses where they offered rooms to let. In a euphoric state, I considered it my duty to set in motion the handle of the little piano which was playing in my ribs so that the music would envelop me while I danced in front of the mirror in an attempt to stick on a pair of false eyelashes which I had found in a drawer, and to paint two vermilion spots on my cheeks. In the end I got fed up because I didn't have a wig or a hat to put on and cover my dirty hair and so I shortened my hair convict style and stuck a carnation over my ear. Now, with glassy eyes, my reflection almost looked as though it was not myself but a phantom stretching towards the cosmos. Hurray, cosmos, ferment, 'cause I'm heading for adventure, off to the pictures and to have a pizza. I'm still able to smile and to interpret the music which clogs up Falcon Street. Which road looks the most promising, the one leading straight ahead, or the one on the right?

The sky is clouded, the lamps are out. And just round the corner there's the yelling universe, the musicians, the acrobats, the country fair. If only I could get there they might welcome me in a kind and brotherly fashion, but I don't believe it. I can't believe it. I don't want to believe it. I couldn't care a damn. And all of a sudden I turned round and, all dressed up as I was, I ran as swift as a rabbit to the refuge of my niche-lair to wall myself up alive for two weeks, so that I wouldn't see the sun set nor the coming of dawn and nothing would trouble me nor anyone bother me. Obviously. And don't change your mind, daughter of a bitch, since you change according to which way the wind's blowing and turn your ideas inside out because you have a head which works like a spinning-top.

Idiot head, it's got you into such a lot of trouble that if it would be any use I'd unscrew it off its neck and hurl it in a sewer. Now, listen carefully to what I have to say, run as much and as far as you like, but once you get home, rest your bum on the steps under the pergola and slowly breathe in this sweet spring breeze, which isn't spring because it's autumn, even though it's all the same anyway. Rest your head against the creeper and sleep if you want the dawn to wake you. You love dawns and sunsets. I know. That's how it is. Only that you elaborate complicated contrasting thoughts believing that you have stumbled into a tunnel of grief which will never come to an end. But it will end, I know it will, and all this will not have happened, because what has happened and continues to happen belongs to too many people and to recognise oneself in all of this is impossible.

About the Author

Rosa Cappiello was born in Caviano, Italy, in 1942. She migrated to Australia in 1971 with no knowledge of English and no skills and worked in various manual occupations. She published her first novel, *I semi neri* [The Black Seeds], a fictional love story, in Italy in 1977.

She began writing *Oh Lucky Country* in 1978 while recovering in hospital from a car accident. This semi-autobiographical novel, originally titled *Paese fortunato*, was first published in Italy in May 1981. It was well received by critics and received the Premio Calabria literature prize, although it drew criticism from the Italian community in Australia.

In 1983, Cappiello was writer-in-residence at the University of Wollongong, where she met Italian lecturer Gaetano Rando. Rando went on to translate *Oh Lucky Country* into English in 1984. Its publication again sparked criticism such as: 'Rosa's feeling of alienation from the angrifying world around her is a great starting point for a putative novelist. One can only hope that she not only maintains her rage, but now sets about learning something—anything would do—of the novelist's craft' (*The Australian*, 12/1/85). Despite such critique, *Oh Lucky Country* went on to be awarded the New South Wales Premier's Literary Award for Ethnic Writing in 1985.

She received Australia Council grants in both 1982 and 1985 for her writing. She has published no other novels in English, although her poetry and short stories have been produced in anthologies and journals such as *Scripsi*, *Overland* and *Meanjin*. She appeared on SBS television in 1989, reading her work aloud. She died in Italy in 2008.